Praise for the Charlie Thorne series

"Stuart Gibbs's *Charlie Thorne and the Last Equation*
is fast-paced, smart, and action-packed. Gibbs knows how to
write a real page-burner. Charlie Thorne is a younger,
smarter, cooler version of Jason Bourne."
—CHRIS GRABENSTEIN, #1 *New York Times* bestselling author

"Whether she's catching big air on her snowboard or
deciphering clues hidden by Albert Einstein, Charlie Thorne
is an ideal hero for a new generation. Her pulse pounding
adventure unfolds like one of the equations she's so skilled
at solving—the final answer remains concealed
until every last variable has been uncovered."
—JAMES PONTI, Edgar Award–winning author of
the Framed! and City Spies series

"Charlie is a terrific hero—outrageously smart, courageous,
and still believable as a kid. After this explosive start, young
readers will eagerly await her next adventure."
—*Publishers Weekly*

"Gibbs deftly pens an Alex Rider–level adventure with this
series starter . . . It doesn't take a theoretical physicist to
predict that this series will be popular."
—*Booklist*

"Action-packed and thrilling."
—*School Library Connection*, recommended

"Will appeal to readers who appreciate action-oriented tales."
—*Kirkus Reviews*

Also by Stuart Gibbs

The FunJungle series
Belly Up
Poached
Big Game
Panda-monium
Lion Down
Tyrannosaurus Wrecks
Bear Bottom

The Spy School series
Spy School
Spy Camp
Evil Spy School
Spy Ski School
Spy School Secret Service
Spy School Goes South
Spy School British Invasion
Spy School Revolution
Spy School at Sea

The Moon Base Alpha series
Space Case
Spaced Out
Waste of Space

The Charlie Thorne series
Charlie Thorne and the Last Equation

Once Upon a Tim

The Last Musketeer

A CHARLIE THORNE NOVEL

CHARLIE THORNE

AND THE

LOST CITY

STUART GIBBS

Simon & Schuster Books for Young Readers

New York London Toronto Sydney New Delhi

SIMON & SCHUSTER BOOKS FOR YOUNG READERS
An imprint of Simon & Schuster Children's Publishing Division
1230 Avenue of the Americas, New York, New York 10020
This book is a work of fiction. Any references to historical events, real people, or real places are used fictitiously. Other names, characters, places, and events are products of the author's imagination, and any resemblance to actual events or places or persons, living or dead, is entirely coincidental.
Text © 2021 by Stuart Gibbs
Jacket design and illustration by Lucy Ruth Cummins © 2021 by Simon & Schuster, Inc.
All rights reserved, including the right of reproduction in whole or in part in any form.
SIMON & SCHUSTER BOOKS FOR YOUNG READERS
and related marks are trademarks of Simon & Schuster, Inc.
For information about special discounts for bulk purchases,
please contact Simon & Schuster Special Sales at 1-866-506-1949 or
business@simonandschuster.com.
The Simon & Schuster Speakers Bureau can bring authors to your live event. For more information or to book an event, contact the Simon & Schuster Speakers Bureau at
1-866-248-3049 or visit our website at www.simonspeakers.com.
Also available in a Simon & Schuster Books for Young Readers hardcover edition
Interior design by Hilary Zarycky
The text for this book was set in New Caledonia.
Manufactured in the United States of America
0122 OFF
First Simon & Schuster Books for Young Readers paperback edition March 2022
2 4 6 8 10 9 7 5 3 1
The Library of Congress has cataloged the hardcover edition as follows:
Names: Gibbs, Stuart, 1969– author.
Title: Charlie Thorne and the lost city / Stuart Gibbs.
Description: First edition. | New York : Simon & Schuster Books for Young Readers, [2021] | Series: Charlie Thorne; vol 2 | Audience: Ages 8 to 12 | Audience: Grades 4–6 | Summary: "Charlie Thorne must search for Charles Darwin's hidden treasure in South America—with plenty of enemies hot on her trail"— Provided by publisher.
Identifiers: LCCN 2020017301 (print) | LCCN 2020017302 (ebook) |
ISBN 9781534443815 (hardcover) | ISBN 9781534443822 (pbk) |
ISBN 9781534443839 (ebook)
Subjects: LCSH: Darwin, Charles, 1809–1882—Fiction. | CYAC: Genius—Fiction. | Spies—Fiction. | Adventure and adventurers—Fiction. | Buried treasure—Fiction.
Classification: LCC PZ7.G339236 Ck 2021 (print) | LCC PZ7.G339236 (ebook) |
DDC [Fic]—dc23
LC record available at https://lccn.loc.gov/2020017301
LC ebook record available at https://lccn.loc.gov/2020017302

In memory of Suzanne, my wonderful wife

We stopped looking for monsters under our bed
when we realized that they were inside us.

—CHARLES DARWIN

PROLOGUE

Guayaquil, Ecuador
August 18, 1835
12:58 a.m.

Charles Darwin was late.

He had already kept the crew of the HMS *Beagle* in South America for an extra ten months, waiting for him to return from his mysterious journey—and now he had missed their appointed meeting time by three hours.

Robert FitzRoy, the captain of the *Beagle*, was furious. He paced the rickety pier of the port like a caged animal, thinking that he should simply leave and strand that fool Darwin in South America once and for all. In fact, he should have done that nearly a year ago, when they had first returned to this dock, expecting to meet Darwin but instead finding only a local boy with a letter from the young naturalist, saying it would be another three months until his return.

That had happened twice more, and each time the

crew had wanted to abandon Darwin and continue on with their journey, but FitzRoy had fought his own instincts and refused. Charles Darwin was a member of the English upper class: His grandfather was a respected philosopher, his father was a wealthy physician, and his mother was the heiress to the Wedgwood pottery fortune. If it were discovered that FitzRoy had abandoned the son of such a family in a lawless territory like Ecuador out of spite . . . his head would roll.

And yet he was tempted to do so now.

Although Darwin had officially been brought on this voyage to help with geological surveys of South America, the true reason for his presence was to provide funding and friendship for FitzRoy, who wanted a fellow gentleman as company on the long voyage. (FitzRoy was a member of the aristocracy himself, whereas the entire crew were from the lower classes of society.) Although Darwin was only twenty-two years old at the time of departure, he had succeeded on both counts: He had plenty of money and was a very fine companion. However, the idea of doing scientific surveying had gone to his head. First he had collected so many specimens that the hold of the *Beagle* was already crammed full of them, and then he had undertaken this insane adventure to the interior of the continent: an expedition he claimed would take a month at most, but which had now dragged on for over ten times longer.

The *Beagle*'s journey had originally been planned for only two years, but they had been gone nearly twice that—and they still had half the world left to circumnavigate. The crew was on the verge of mutiny. FitzRoy himself desperately wanted to go home. He had spent most of the last year surveying the coast of Chile, which was harsh and unforgiving, but still better than Guayaquil, which sat almost directly on the equator and was surrounded by swampland. The humidity was brutal, even in the middle of the night, and the mosquitoes were relentless, hovering in thick, humming clouds. Plus, the inhabitants of Guayaquil were rogues, hucksters, and scoundrels. FitzRoy hated this place. If Darwin didn't show this time, he would weigh anchor and head for home. . . .

There was a shout in the night. FitzRoy stopped his pacing and turned toward land.

He couldn't see anything. Thick tendrils of fog had crept in from the ocean, and the feeble glow of the *Beagle*'s gas lamps barely made a dent in the gloom.

But the pier was suddenly alive with noise, its rotted planks creaking wildly, as though several people were moving along it toward the *Beagle*, and moving quickly, too.

"Hello?" FitzRoy called into the darkness.

"Robert?" came the response. The voice was familiar, and yet it had changed since the last time FitzRoy had heard it. Hearing it should have filled him with relief, but instead it gave him the sense that something was very wrong.

"Charles?" FitzRoy asked.

"Yes!" Charles Darwin raced out of the fog, looking like the devil itself was on his heels. "Wake the crew!" he ordered. "We must get the *Beagle* to sea at once!"

Despite the urgency in Darwin's voice and manner, FitzRoy didn't react right away. Instead, he stared at the young naturalist in astonishment. Darwin's brusque attitude and failure to apologize for all the trouble he'd caused were disturbing, but what really unsettled Fitz-Roy was his friend's appearance.

Darwin barely looked human anymore. His clothes were in tatters, his shirt so filthy it was more dirt than linen, his shoes bound together with twine. And as for his body . . . Darwin was almost emaciated, at least thirty pounds lighter than he had been before. His skin was baked brown as leather, and his arms, legs, and chest were covered with dozens of sores, many of which appeared to be infected. His once clean-shaven face was consumed by a ragged beard, while his eyes were wild with what looked like madness.

When Darwin had encountered the native tribes of Tierra del Fuego, he had been shocked that humans could live in such a primitive fashion, referring to them as savages and remarking that he could not believe the difference between them and civilized men. Now, he appeared even more wretched and feral than the natives he had disdained.

But while Darwin *looked* deranged, he still had his wits about him. He immediately grew annoyed at Fitz-Roy's lack of action. "Robert!" he demanded. "Did you not hear me? We must set sail immediately!"

His tone startled FitzRoy into a response. "In the middle of the night? This bay is treacherous! It's far too risky to negotiate its passage without light. . . ."

"It would be far riskier to remain here." Darwin was nervously hopping from foot to foot, like a small boy who needed to go to the bathroom. "I have made some enemies during my travels. And I now have something in my possession that they do not wish the outside world to know of."

"What?" FitzRoy asked.

"You'll see soon enough," Darwin replied. "Once we are underway."

Before FitzRoy could press for more information, two other men emerged from the fog. They looked as though they were of Incan descent, shorter than Europeans, with squat, wide bodies that belied their physical strength; FitzRoy had heard tales of Incas running a hundred miles at a stretch through the mountains along the Pacific coast.

These Incas appeared to have embraced Western culture and even wore European clothes. To FitzRoy's eyes, they looked far more civilized than Darwin now did. And yet FitzRoy still considered the natives inferior and he knew Darwin did as well. So there must have been something major at stake for Darwin to be relying on them.

The Incas carried something strange between them. It looked to FitzRoy like a large, handmade wooden chest, hacked from the trunk of a single large tree, although it was rough-hewn and unfinished.

Darwin shouted to the two men in a language FitzRoy did not understand—the language of the Incas, he presumed. The men dutifully nodded and hauled the chest up the gangplank to the *Beagle*. Darwin followed them.

FitzRoy remained rooted to the pier. "Where are the rest of my men who went with you?" he asked.

"Dead," Darwin replied.

FitzRoy gasped, then pursued him up the gangplank. "There were eleven men! How could all of them be dead?"

"Many ways," Darwin said quickly. "Disease, savages, vicious beasts. Robert, in the past months, I have seen things you could never even begin to imagine." He shouted to the Incas in their own language once again, pointing toward the entrance to the hold.

FitzRoy arrived on the deck. The *Beagle* was not a

particularly large vessel, only ninety feet from stem to stern and thirty feet at the widest. Living space was in such short supply that the seventy-four crew members rotated hammocks and slept in shifts. And yet the boat was finely built and sturdy and had well weathered the turbulent seas and vicious storms it had encountered.

The crewmen on the night shift had gathered around. FitzRoy knew they were angry to have been kept waiting for so many months and had expected them to greet the naturalist with taunts and jeers, if not outright derision. But Darwin's wild looks and strange behavior had grabbed their attention. They watched his arrival with shock, rather than scorn.

Angry voices echoed in the distance, carrying across the water from shore.

FitzRoy turned that way and saw torches through the haze of fog. It seemed a mob might be coming their way.

Darwin wheeled on FitzRoy. "Robert! They're coming for us! We need to leave now!"

FitzRoy shouted orders to his men, who quickly leapt into action, coiling the mooring lines and unfurling the sails.

While the ship came alive around him, FitzRoy approached Darwin, who was attending to the rough-hewn chest. It was so large, it would need to be lowered into the hold with a winch, but there was no time for that, so Darwin was having the Incas lash it tightly to the rail. "Where are the rest of your specimens?"

"This is it," Darwin replied curtly.

"But you were gone nearly a year! You collected a hundred times this much in mere weeks in the Pampas."

"This is what's important." Darwin knelt to help the Incas with the chest.

"But if you saw such incredible things, things I couldn't even imagine, as you said . . ."

"I collected them. But I had to leave them behind . . . for *this*." Darwin reverently ran a hand across the wooden chest.

FitzRoy felt his eyes drawn to it, wondering what could possibly be inside. Darwin cared more for his specimens than any naturalist FitzRoy had ever known. He was an expert at collecting, gathering, and preparing them. He had commissioned the construction of dozens of curio cabinets to hold them, and nearly filled them all. If Darwin had abandoned everything he had discovered on his adventure for this single item, then it must have been something incredible.

"Please," he said. "I must know what's in the chest."

"Once we are underway," Darwin repeated, and ran to retrieve a rifle from the small armory on deck.

"Charles!" FitzRoy shouted after him. "I am the captain of this ship and I have a right to know what is on board! I am ordering you to open this chest at once!"

Even as FitzRoy spoke, the *Beagle* was sliding away from the pier. After nearly four years at sea, his crew was quick and accomplished. The ship was already prepared for sea, the sails furled and the lines stowed.

The angry mob was now racing down the long pier from land, their torches glowing brighter as they came closer—and their voices growing more agitated as they realized the *Beagle* was getting away.

Darwin shouldered his rifle and stared down the barrel at the mob. He had grown up hunting for sport in the English countryside and was one of the finest shots FitzRoy had ever encountered. Now he took several moments to assess the threat on the pier—and ultimately decided the *Beagle* was well enough underway to be safe. He lowered the rifle and returned his attention to Fitz-Roy. "Very well, Robert. I'd be happy to oblige you." His manner had changed dramatically. But it wasn't merely the relief at having escaped the mob. He seemed to be brimming with excitement, as well. Now that they were out of danger, he was eager to share his discovery.

"I saw many incredible things on my journey," he said, striding confidently across the deck. "But they all paled compared to this. Everything I have ever encountered in my life pales compared to this."

On the pier behind them, the mob arrived in full.

FitzRoy couldn't see them through the fog and the night, save for their torches, but he could certainly hear them. They shouted in rage, using a language he did not know. Some threw their torches in desperation, as if hoping to set the *Beagle* ablaze, but they fell far short and harmlessly fizzled out in the bay.

With each second of distance between them and the dock, Darwin seemed to grow less panicked and more enthusiastic. The wild stare from his eyes was replaced by the thrill of discovery FitzRoy had seen many times before.

"Prepare yourself for the incredible," he announced, and then shoved the lid of the chest aside. It thudded to the deck, revealing what Darwin had found.

FitzRoy gasped.

"Incredible, isn't it?" Darwin asked.

FitzRoy nodded agreement, but he didn't reply. He couldn't bring himself to do so, as he wanted to conceal his true response. While he strained to show Darwin a facade of excitement, deep down, he was horrified. What lay within the chest was an affront to God.

Robert FitzRoy knew he must get rid of it—and then destroy any evidence that it had ever existed at all.

PART ONE
THE EDGE OF THE EARTH

Nothing can be more improving to a young
naturalist than a journey in distant countries.
—CHARLES DARWIN,
Voyage of the *Beagle*

ONE

Puerto Villamil
Isla Isabela
The Galápagos Islands, Ecuador
Present day

A hammerhead shark slid through the water beneath Charlie Thorne.

Charlie watched it glide below her feet as her surfboard bobbed in the ocean. It was a big shark, about nine feet long, capable of doing some serious damage. But Charlie's reaction upon seeing it was excitement, rather than fear. Charlie had seen plenty of hammerheads while surfing in Puerto Villamil. Despite their threatening appearance, statistically, she had little reason for alarm as long as she didn't do anything stupid around them—and Charlie Thorne was as far from stupid as you could get.

Even though she was only twelve, Charlie had an IQ that rivaled that of anyone who had ever lived. In a situation like this, she couldn't help but analyze the numbers. She knew that out of the billions of people on earth, fewer than twenty died each year from shark attacks; far more humans were killed annually by falling coconuts. But then, few people actively went surfing in shark-infested waters, where the chances of getting attacked were much greater. Most shark attacks were thought to be mistakes; from underneath, a human on a surfboard had a silhouette similar to that of a sea lion, the preferred food of many sharks. So Charlie was always careful; she didn't surf while she was bleeding, or wear shiny jewelry that a shark might mistake for the flash of fish scales, or thrash around in the water like a wounded animal. Now, watching the hammerhead, she stayed calm and still.

The shark didn't seem to care about her at all. It certainly knew she was there, but it continued onward as though the thought of consuming her had never even entered its mind. It was paralleling the coastline of Isla Isabela, heading toward a rocky outcropping where the sea lion rookeries were. Why sharks would pass up an easy meal like a human in favor of harder-to-catch prey like a sea lion was unexplained, but most scientists presumed that sharks simply thought humans didn't taste very good.

Another hammerhead passed beneath Charlie, and another after that. They were both smaller than the first, but not by much.

This didn't surprise Charlie: Hammerheads often swam in schools, sometimes numbering up to a hundred.

She turned on her board to look behind her. Sure enough, more sharks were coming, their large dorsal fins poking above the surface.

Charlie figured it was time to get out of the water. The odds of an accidental attack were rising by the second.

Fortunately, a good-size wave was coming her way, a bulge in the ocean building as it approached the shore. Charlie watched it—and the numbers came to her.

They simply appeared in her mind, as usual: instant calculations of the speed of the wave, the most likely cresting point, and how fast she would need to paddle to put herself there. Puerto Villamil wasn't home to many other surfers—or many other people, period—but Charlie had already become legendary among the few who lived there. Even surfers with decades of experience mistimed a wave on occasion, but Charlie never did. Somehow, she was always exactly where she needed to be.

Whenever anyone tried to talk to Charlie about how she read the waves so well, she dodged the question. *"Tuve suerte"* was all she would say. "I was lucky."

The others surfers knew that no one could be *that* lucky, but Charlie wouldn't say anything else. Charlie had barely spoken to anyone in Puerto Villamil since arriving four weeks earlier. No one knew where she was from or why she had come to such a far-flung place—and they certainly didn't know her age. Since Charlie looked and behaved much older than her years, everyone assumed she was at least eighteen. The only information she had volunteered was that her name was "Mariposa Espina," which wasn't true.

Charlie could pass herself off as a native of almost any place on earth, because ethnically, she was a mix of different races—although she didn't look like one more than any other. Plus, she spoke over a dozen languages and could understand many more. In a single day, while en route to the Galápagos, she had told different people that she was Thai, Greek, Kenyan, Guatemalan, *and* aboriginal Australian, and no one had questioned her at all.

Fewer than two thousand people lived in Puerto Villamil, so the arrival of one more was of interest to the locals. There were many rumors as to who Charlie really was and why she had ended up there. Many of them were bizarre and outlandish. Although none were anywhere near as bizarre and outlandish as the truth.

Now Charlie lay flat on the board and paddled with her arms, taking care to do so with smooth, strong strokes that wouldn't startle the hammerheads below her. She headed directly to the spot where she had calculated the wave would break. Sure enough, the swell rose behind her, exactly as she had predicted, and grew into a ten-foot wall of water. Charlie quickly leapt to her feet upon the board, caught the front slope of the wave, and expertly rode down it. As the wave broke, she surfed right through the curl. She stayed upright all the way to shore, even as the wave collapsed upon itself behind her, then slid into the shallow water and calmly stepped off the board and onto the beach as casually as though she were stepping off a bus onto the curb.

The locals gathered on the shore watched with amazement. Charlie had been a novice surfer when she had arrived in Puerto Villamil. Even though she had been able to spot where the waves would break, she hadn't been able to ride them. But within a few weeks, using her natural athleticism and her unnatural skill at reading the waves, she was surfing better than most people could after years of practice. The people watching her now shook their heads and uttered the name they all called her behind her back. *"Perfecta."*

It was warm on the beach, as usual. Since Isla Isabela sat directly on the equator, the temperature didn't vary much. Charlie peeled off the neoprene suit she had used to stay warm in the water, revealing the bathing suit she wore underneath, then picked up her board and started home barefoot through town.

There wasn't much to Puerto Villamil, which made sense, given that it was one of the most remote towns on earth. It sat on the southern fringe of Isla Isabela in the Galápagos Islands, which were well off the coast of mainland South America. Isla Isabela was actually the largest of the Galápagos, but most of it was uninhabitable, as it was quite volcanic and almost devoid of fresh water. The Sierra Negra volcano constituted much of the island; its crater was the second largest on earth, after Ngorongoro in Africa.

Therefore Puerto Villamil, set at the base of Sierra Negra, was about as far from civilization as one could get. Should a riptide have snapped Charlie away from shore, it was nearly nine thousand miles until she'd see land again. For this reason, it sometimes felt as though the little town was on the very edge of the earth.

That was one of the reasons that Charlie had chosen to come here. She wanted isolation. She wanted to be as far from other people as possible. It was safer that way.

There were more marine iguanas in Puerto Villamil than people. The lizards were quite large, growing up to five feet long, and they were everywhere: lazing on the beach, walking along the dusty streets, lounging on porches, and wandering into the stores. They were just as fearless of humans as they had been back when Charles Darwin had arrived, as was the case with most of the wildlife in the Galápagos. Animals often needed a long time to evolve a healthy fear of humans—and here, there hadn't been enough. As Charlie headed through town, two sea lions were sleeping directly in the middle of the street, while three penguins waddled toward the small marina. Many people were surprised to learn there were penguins in the Galápagos, as opposed to Antarctica, but this species was endemic to the islands. It was endangered, with only 1,500 left, although they were relatively common on Isla Isabela. One of the things that Charlie liked the best about the Galápagos, in addition to its remoteness, was that it was the only place on earth where you could snorkel with an iguana, a sea lion, and a penguin all at once.

The roar of outboard motors suddenly cut through the town. They were loud enough to startle the penguins, which scurried away frantically, although the sea lions continued snoring loudly. Charlie paused in the street and looked back toward the dock at the eastern edge of Puerto Villamil.

A speedboat had rounded the southern tip of the island and was headed toward town. It was big for a speedboat, with two enormous engines attached to the stern, and it skimmed across the water like a skipped stone.

In the four weeks that Charlie had been in Puerto Villamil, she had never seen a boat like this. Every day, a few boats bringing ecotourists would arrive, but those were all small cruise ships, built for comfort rather than speed. Some of the local fishermen had boats as well, but those were all old, battered, and weather-beaten. This boat was very different; It was expensive and built to go at very high speeds, the sort of craft you'd see millionaires racing along the coast in Miami or the Côte D'Azur in France.

That didn't necessarily mean anything was wrong, but Charlie was always on the lookout for things that were out of the ordinary. When you lived your life on the run, you had to stay attuned to your surroundings at all times.

Charlie resumed walking toward her home. She didn't run, because that would draw attention. But she did pick up her pace, striding briskly through the town.

The house Charlie rented was small and ramshackle—there really wasn't anything big or well built in Puerto Villamil—but she didn't need much. It sat beside the marsh that marked the western boundary of town. Just behind the house, a path snaked through the wetlands to the Tupiza Tortoise Breeding Center, where Charlie volunteered her time, helping to keep the celebrated Galápagos tortoises from going extinct.

A woman she had never met before was on her porch.

Charlie noticed her from two blocks away. It wasn't hard, as the woman apparently wanted to be seen. She was sitting in the rocking chair on the porch, reading a book.

She wasn't from Puerto Villamil. Charlie could recognize every one of the town's residents. The woman had unusually slim features: her face, nose, and lips were all narrow lines, although her eyes were wide and round.

She reminded Charlie of a Modigliani sculpture. She was dressed in the same outfit that the volunteers at Tupiza wore: khaki shirt and shorts, although instead of dusty, thick-soled work boots, she wore running shoes. Despite the workmanlike clothing, she was strikingly beautiful.

A visitor was also an unusual occurrence; Charlie had never had one since arriving in Puerto Villamil. None of her friends or family knew she was here—and ideally, her enemies didn't either. Combined with the arrival of the speedboat, the visitor's presence set Charlie's brain humming, analyzing the probabilities of all that was happening. She didn't like what she came up with.

Still, Charlie didn't run. She had nowhere to run *to*. And the woman didn't seem to be a threat. Threatening people tended to ambush you. They didn't sit on your front porch in broad daylight.

As Charlie got closer, she noticed that the woman was wearing makeup. Not much, just a bit of eyeshadow and lipstick, but most people around here didn't bother with makeup at all. The woman had also spent time doing her hair, and her clothes were spotless and expertly pressed. All of it indicated that this was a woman who cared about how she presented herself.

She looked up as Charlie approached, dog-eared a page of her book, and smiled pleasantly. "Hello, Mariposa. My name is Esmerelda Castle." There was a slight accent to her words, as if English was not her first language.

Charlie's immediate response was to pretend as though she couldn't speak English at all. Any time a tourist had approached her over the past few weeks, she had quickly said *"No hablo inglés"* and walked away. But Esmerelda seemed very well aware that Charlie understood English, so Charlie figured there was no point in acting like she didn't. "Hi," she said, propping her surfboard against the wall of her house.

"I work at the Darwin Research Station on Isla Santa Cruz," Esmerelda said. "We've found something of great interest there, and my friends at Tupiza suggested you might be able to help us with it."

"Who at Tupiza?" Charlie asked suspiciously.

Esmerelda smiled again, as though she found Charlie's suspicions amusing. "Everyone, really. Raoul Cabazon. Stacy Devillers. Arturo and Fred and Johnny. They all say that you have a gift for codes and puzzles and that sort of thing."

Charlie nodded. There didn't seem to be any point in denying this. The names Esmerelda had mentioned were all people who worked at Tupiza, and Charlie often solved puzzles during her breaks there. Crosswords, cryptics, acrostics, and that sort of thing. She was addicted to them. And what Esmerelda was talking about struck her as strange but intriguing. "You found a puzzle at the research station?"

"Yes. A code of some sort, we believe. It was etched into the shell of a tortoise."

Charlie's eyes widened in surprise. "Who would etch a code into the shell of a tortoise?"

"That's where this gets *really* interesting," Esmerelda replied. "It appears the code was left by Charles Darwin himself. And we could use your help figuring it out."

TWO

Langley, Virginia

CIA Director Jamilla Carter was in a bad mood.

A cold front had slammed into northern Virginia, and she was outside in the middle of it. It was early April, and it should have been spring, but instead the temperature had plummeted into the single digits. The snow was coming down in sheets. And yet Carter was trudging around in it in a park along the Potomac, looking for a stupid dead drop.

A dead drop was a covert location where agents could leave information for one another without having to meet. It was common to use one in the intelligence game . . . if you were a field agent. The director of the CIA wasn't supposed to use dead drops, though. She was supposed to order *other people* to use them. She was supposed to sit in her nice, warm office and wait for her agents to bring information to her. But Agent Dante Garcia didn't trust anyone at CIA headquarters besides Jamilla Carter, and Carter had to admit, there was good reason for that. Garcia's last mission had gone sideways because of a traitorous CIA agent, so now he was exercising extreme caution.

And Carter was willing to put up with that, willing to come out here and stomp around in the freezing cold on her own, because Pandora was at stake. Pandora was an equation that Einstein himself had discovered, a corollary to his famous $E = MC^2$. While $E = MC^2$ explained that there was a tremendous amount of energy locked away inside every single atom in the universe, Pandora revealed how to *access* that energy. In the right hands, it could solve the world's energy problems. But in the wrong hands, it was incredibly dangerous. It would allow governments—or even small groups of zealots—to build weapons of mass destruction. That was why the US government wanted it—and more importantly, they wanted to make sure no one else had it.

However, Einstein had also realized how dangerous Pandora could be, so he had hidden it. With his great wisdom, he had made it extremely hard to find. Over the next few decades, the CIA had failed to locate the equation—as had every other intelligence agency on earth—until Garcia, a young and innovative agent, had suggested a radical idea: If you wanted to find something Einstein had hidden, then maybe you needed someone as smart as Einstein to do it. And the closest person to Einstein, at least intellectually, was Charlie Thorne.

Thorne was a wild card, but she had come through—in a way. She had successfully tracked down Pandora, but she hadn't turned it over to the CIA. During a final battle between the CIA and their enemies, a fire had broken out, and Charlie appeared to have been killed in it—at first. Afterward, Agent Garcia had discovered that she had actually committed the equation to memory, destroyed the original, and escaped. So now the only remaining copy of Pandora in existence was inside Charlie's mind.

Therefore, finding Charlie Thorne was of paramount importance to the CIA. And they needed to find her before anyone else did. Because there were lots of dangerous people out there who would do whatever it took to get Charlie to cough up the equation. Carter had assigned Garcia to the operation, but because they knew the CIA had been compromised, the mission was off the books. The only people who knew what Garcia was tasked with—or that Charlie Thorne was alive at all—were Carter, Garcia himself, and Garcia's fellow agent Milana Moon.

As a further security measure, Garcia refused to use any direct electronic correspondence with Carter, even with encryption. He didn't trust it. So there were no emails or phone calls. There was only the dead drop. Like it was 1950 and they were fighting the Cold War.

Carter had no idea where on earth Garcia and Moon even were. That was secret too.

The way the dead drop worked was, Garcia had a friend he trusted in Virginia. Carter didn't know who, but chances were, they weren't even in intelligence. It might have been Garcia's best friend from grade school, or his neighbor, or his podiatrist. Garcia would mail his friend an encrypted message in a specially sealed envelope that they wouldn't open. Instead, they would deliver it to the dead drop at the park near CIA headquarters. Once it was in place, they would let Garcia know, and then Garcia would send Carter an innocuous message from a fake email account. Every time Carter got spam from World-Wide Travel, it was a signal that there was something in the dead drop for her. Today, just before noon, she had received a message from WorldWide Travel offering her incredibly low deals on a weekend in Vegas.

So Carter had canceled her lunch and headed out into the cold.

There *was* one advantage of the crummy weather; no one else was in the park. On a nice spring day, there would have been hikers or picnickers or families out with their kids. But today there hadn't been a single other car in the parking lot when Carter arrived.

Since the storm had come late in the year, many of the trees had already sprouted spring leaves, and the snow weighed heavily on the branches. Carter picked her way along a trail through the snow-shrouded forest until she came to a medium-size oak tree, then turned off through the underbrush until she came to a small brook. The brook carved a narrow gully, and when Carter clambered down into it, it was deep enough to hide her from the sight of anyone on the trail—not that anyone else was dumb enough to be out in this weather. Twenty paces upstream, there was an ancient tree stump with a hollow underneath it. The dead drop.

Carter reached into the hollow and found an envelope wrapped in a plastic baggie to protect it from the elements. She broke the seal on the envelope and removed the small piece of paper inside.

As if it weren't enough to have all this other secrecy, the message was encoded, using a cipher that Carter and Garcia had worked out beforehand. Carter sat on the stump in the snow and decrypted the message, too eager now to even return to the warmth of her car. She quickly came up with the translation:

Tracked down the item you were looking for. Hoping to procure it for you soon.

Despite the cold and the snow, Director Carter's mood instantly lifted and a smile spread across her face.

Dante Garcia had found Charlie Thorne.

THREE

harlie wanted to hear all about the code on the tortoise, but she also desperately wanted to take a shower. Her body was sticky and briny from the ocean, and she considered the speedboat a bad omen. There was a good chance that she would soon have to be on the move, and she wanted to at least be clean when that happened.

So she decided to multitask. She got right in the shower and had Esmerelda explain everything at the same time.

The house Charlie was renting was only three rooms: tiny bedroom, even tinier bathroom, and a combination living room/kitchen/dining room. It was small enough, and the walls were thin enough, that Esmerelda could sit at the dining table and easily converse with Charlie in the bathroom, even with the water running. The shower wasn't loud because there was no water pressure; only a meager stream of water trickled from the showerhead.

The house had come furnished. The only personal effects Charlie had were books, most of which she had gotten from tourists; when people finished reading something on vacation, they often didn't feel like lugging it back home again. There were quite a few books of puzzles as well, which Charlie had bummed off visitors who couldn't solve the hardest ones. The books were piled everywhere: on the bed, the kitchen counters, the floor. Esmerelda had to remove a stack from the single chair at the dining table before she could sit down.

She said, "The tortoise died a few days ago, and it was only when we brought it in to autopsy it that we found the words carved into its plastron."

In her time volunteering at the breeding facility, Charlie had learned all the parts of a tortoise. The plastron was the lower part of the shell, the flat piece that covered the animal's belly. "And how do you know it was Darwin who carved them?"

"Because he signed his name. And though carving isn't exactly the same as handwriting, there are some similarities. We know what Darwin's writing looked like. This seems to be a match."

Charlie furiously shampooed the salt water from her

hair. "Darwin visited these islands in 1835. You think this tortoise was almost two hundred years old?"

"It's certainly possible. Our estimates for how old these animals can get are really just guesses. Although we've known about them for two centuries, we've only been studying them scientifically for a few decades. Some of our researchers think they could live as long as four hundred or five hundred years. We really won't know for sure until we can observe one for its entire life—which would require several generations of scientists to document."

"I guess that makes sense." Charlie knew there were other species of animal that lived exceptionally long lives. Recently, a Greenland shark had been determined to be at least four hundred by carbon-dating the lenses of its eyes. "And in all those years, no one ever noticed there was something written on this tortoise's plastron?"

"Well, it's not really our policy to go around flipping all the tortoises over. And it's not easy to do. The big tortoises can weigh nearly half a ton. Plus, the plastron is usually flat on the ground, and the tortoises are often wallowing in mud or half-submerged in ponds, so the carving was hidden from view. If we hadn't done the autopsy, no one might have ever seen it."

"Why *did* you autopsy it?"

"We autopsy *all* the tortoises when they die. It helps

us estimate how old they were—and may give us clues to the secrets of their longevity. If we can learn why a creature like a Galápagos tortoise lives so long, that might have ramifications for helping humans live longer too."

Charlie finished rinsing herself, turned off the water, and grabbed a towel. "So what did Darwin carve into this shell?"

"It's probably better if I show you," Esmerelda said. "I brought some photographs of what he wrote."

"Cool. Give me a few moments." Charlie toweled herself off—although, it was so humid, she didn't feel much drier. She quickly pulled on shorts, a T-shirt, and sneakers and emerged from the bedroom to find Esmerelda scrolling through photos on a laptop computer.

The first photos Charlie saw were of the dead tortoise in what looked like a laboratory. It lay on the floor, with four people standing around it. The tortoise was enormous, about the size of a bumper car. Its carapace—the upper shell—was big enough that several small children could have hidden under it.

Charlie had known, even before coming to the Galápagos, that tortoises on different islands had evolved radically different shells. Some carapaces were domed, while others were shaped more like saddles; some had large openings behind the neck, while others had smaller ones. And of course, the tortoises themselves varied greatly in size. According to history, this was one of the things that had intrigued Darwin upon visiting the Galápagos; he had wondered why each island had a completely different type of tortoise living on it.

While questions like this had led Darwin to develop his theory of evolution, scientists who visited the islands later had determined that the ecology of each island had driven the evolutionary change in the shells. For example, on some islands, the tortoises grazed on grass, while on others they ate taller plants. A taller-plant-eating tortoise would evolve a carapace with a larger opening around the neck, which would allow the tortoise to lift its head higher, while a tortoise that ate grass had a lower opening behind the neck, since the tortoise was always looking down.

Since her arrival, Charlie had learned to differentiate the species of tortoise by island. The one in the photos had a domed shell with a lower space for the neck. She asked, "That's a tortoise from Santa Cruz island?"

"Yes. From the highlands above where the research station is located."

Charlie nodded acceptance, although something struck her as odd about this. Darwin had visited four of the Galápagos islands: San Cristóbal, Floreana, Santiago, and Isabela—the island on which they now stood. But Darwin *hadn't* visited Santa Cruz. So how had a tortoise that lived there wound up with his name scratched into its shell?

Charlie didn't bring this up, however, because Esmerelda had moved on to the next photos, the ones with the carving in question.

In the photos, both pieces of the shell—the carapace and the plastron—had been removed from the tortoise. Esmerelda clicked past a few that showed some researchers holding the plastron to give an idea of how big it was. It was twice the size of a manhole cover.

Esmerelda was one of the people in the photos. Charlie noted, once again, that she had taken care with her appearance and was smiling brightly for the camera, while the others were somewhat unkempt, while trying to present themselves as stoic and serious.

The next photos showed the carving more closely. The letters were messy and ragged, as one might have expected, given that they had been etched into the shell of a living animal. The tortoise would have been much smaller in 1835, Charlie figured, so perhaps Darwin wouldn't have had much trouble flipping it over, but it still wouldn't have been an easy surface to carve on—and the tortoise probably wouldn't have been happy about it. A considerable amount of time and energy must have been spent on the effort: The carvings were deep enough to last for the next nearly two hundred years. The letters had grown as the shell had, the same way that letters carved into a tree would grow larger as the tree expanded, but they had also been worn down over the decades of being dragged across the ground, so that they were quite faint now.

The message was in two parts. One set of words curved around the perimeter of the plastron:

The Greatest Treasure in Human History.

The others were a block of text in the center of the plastron:

If in death, Eros
and evil shall rest on earth.
Minds quit obeying.
—C. Darwin

"You can see why we think it's a coded message," Esmerelda said. "It doesn't make any sense."

"Gotcha," Charlie said. "But what's more intriguing to me is the part that's *not* coded. What's all this about a treasure?"

Esmerelda shrugged. "At this point, you know as much about it as I do. Given those words, it seems that Darwin must have discovered one. And we're assuming that the next part is the clue to finding it."

"The Greatest Treasure in Human History," Charlie read aloud. As she did, she caught a glimpse of something beyond the computer screen, in the distance through the windows of her house.

A man was walking down the main street of Puerto Villamil. He looked like the locals, with dark hair and skin bronzed by the sun, and he was dressed in shorts, a short-sleeved button-down shirt, sunglasses, and a well-worn baseball cap. But he wasn't a local. Charlie assumed he was one of the people who had arrived on the speedboat.

The man was chatting amiably with Russell and Benita, who were fellow surfers. They were still in their wet suits, looking like they had bailed after seeing the hammerheads arrive. As Charlie watched, the man showed Russell and Benita what might have been a photograph. Russell and Benita both nodded, then pointed toward Charlie's house.

The strange man smiled pleasantly, like they had just done him a favor.

Meanwhile, Esmerelda was still fixated on the photo of the tortoise plastron, zooming in with her laptop to show the etching better. "I *do* have some theories about this treasure . . . ," she was saying.

"Why don't you explain them to me on the plane?" Charlie asked.

Esmerelda looked at her, surprised. "What plane?"

"The one you came here on," Charlie explained

calmly. "You didn't come by boat. I've been surfing near the marina all morning. And you can't drive anywhere from Puerto Villamil. There aren't any roads. But there *is* an old seaplane float dock on the far side of the rescue station." It surprised Charlie that she had missed the arrival of a plane, as planes were loud and Puerto Villamil was very quiet. But there were times when the surf had been noisy and distracting, and a plane that had come in from the north would have its approach mostly hidden by the volcano.

Out in the street, two blocks away, the strange man whistled in the way you did to get the attention of other people. In response, two other men who looked kind of like him appeared from around the corner and joined him in heading toward Charlie's house.

A large male marine iguana lazed in the middle of the street in their path. The first man could have easily gone around it, but instead he kicked it roughly, then laughed as it scuttled away.

"I *do* have a plane at that dock," Esmerelda was saying. "But . . ."

"To decrypt this code, I need to see the actual plastron," Charlie told her. "It's possible there are additional clues that I can't see in this photo. Can we go there now?"

"Well . . . sure," Esmerelda replied, slightly thrown. "How long will it take you to pack?"

"Already done." A large backpack sat by the bedroom door, stuffed with everything Charlie needed to leave in a hurry. Because Charlie was always ready to go, just in case trouble showed up. Which seemed to be happening now.

Out in the street, the three men were two blocks away from Charlie's house. Not running, because that would have grabbed attention. But walking with purpose.

Charlie grabbed the backpack, then opened a cabinet under the kitchen sink and turned a valve on something hidden there. Esmerelda didn't notice what that was, because the next thing Charlie did was head to her bedroom window, which faced the opposite side of the house from the men in the street. She opened the window, tossed the backpack out, then started through after it.

"Why are you going out the window?" Esmerelda asked.

"It's faster to get to the plane this way," Charlie said casually, then jumped out onto the sandy ground behind the house.

Esmerelda had heard rumors that the girl from Puerto Villamil was a bit strange. Brilliant, but strange. Like her brain was functioning on a level that other people couldn't quite grasp. Therefore, Esmerelda had expected some eccentricities. And she desperately wanted any help the girl could give. So she quickly closed her computer, stuffed it into her backpack, and followed Charlie out the window.

Charlie was already heading down the path that led through the marsh, walking briskly in the direction of the floating dock where the plane would have been, casually stepping over the marine iguanas that were lying in her way.

Esmerelda hurried after her. "It's only about a ten-minute flight to Santa Cruz."

"Cool," Charlie said, although the truth was, she didn't really care about Santa Cruz at all. Everything she had said about needing to see the plastron was a lie. Charlie had already cracked Darwin's code.

She just needed an excuse to get out of Puerto Villamil fast.

FOUR

van Spetz was Russian, but even his closest friends didn't know that.

He had been working for his country's external intelligence service, the SVR, in Central and South America for more than twenty-four years now, advancing the Russian agenda in the region. He had been one of the top agents in his class, intelligent and capable, but the real reason he'd been assigned to the Americas was his appearance: He was from the southernmost portion of Russia, a small town on the border of Azerbaijan, close to the Middle East, and with his dark-brown skin and thick black hair, he looked far more Hispanic than most of his fellow agents. All of them were from farther north, with pale complexions and blue eyes, which would have made them stick out in South America like polar bears in the desert.

Ivan had never complained. He *liked* working in the Americas—while he had hated Moscow, especially in the winter, where the temperatures were often below zero, the streets were piled with snow, and the sun was out for only a few hours a day. Meanwhile, the Americas were almost always sunny and warm, the food was delicious, the beaches were lovely, and the people were kind and friendly. So Ivan had done the best job he could and thus had never been reassigned.

But after spending more than half of his life pretending to be something he wasn't, he often felt more like a South American than a Russian. Even though he had never heard a word of Spanish until he was eighteen, he now *thought* in Spanish, rather than in his native tongue. (He was also fluent in Portuguese, as that was the main language of Brazil.) He almost never thought of himself as Ivan, but instead as Juan or Pablo or Enrique, or whomever he was pretending to be at the time. He had a current girlfriend—and a dozen ex-girlfriends—who didn't have the slightest idea he was Russian; every single thing he had told them about his background was a lie, but he could say it all with ease, as though he had actually lived that life.

During his time in the Americas, Ivan had been assigned a wide variety of missions. He had helped topple governments that weren't friendly to Russia and helped establish governments that were; he had supported the illegal drug trade, because Russian oligarchs made money off it; he had sabotaged oil fields so that more people would buy petroleum from Russia. But the mission he was on now was the strangest he could remember.

All he had been asked to do was kidnap a girl.

His handlers at the SVR had made it clear that this girl wasn't a normal girl, that she was possibly smarter than anyone else on earth. And yet . . . she wasn't even thirteen yet. A girl so young might have book smarts, but she wouldn't know anything about how the world worked. Ivan had taken down enemy agents with decades of training; capturing a girl should have been no trouble at all.

He'd had plenty of questions about *why* this girl was so important. His handlers had answered some of them and pretended they didn't know the answers to the others, which was standard procedure at the SVR.

The basic story was that the girl knew something important. She had information that the SVR wanted, information that could help cement Russia's status as a superpower, information that no one else on earth knew. Ivan's handlers called it Pandora. Russia wasn't the only country after this asset; two months before, there had been some heated activity in Israel involving the girl, the CIA, the Mossad, and a sect of radical terrorists. The SVR had learned about it all via a mole in the Mossad.

After that, the girl had disappeared. The official story was that she had died in a fire in California, but the SVR suspected that was only a cover story. An operative in California had failed to locate her but found evidence that she might have gone south. The girl had done an impressive job of covering her tracks, but still, there was a faint trail leading to South America.

So Ivan had been put on the job. The SVR had said it was highest priority, so he was working day and night, pursuing every lead he could find, no matter how slight. It wasn't easy, finding someone smart who wanted to stay hidden. But people noticed young girls on their own.

After two months of dead ends, Ivan had gotten a bite in the Galápagos, of all places.

He knew someone who knew someone who worked at the Charles Darwin Research Station on Isla Santa Cruz. A day before, the researchers there had found some sort of code carved into the shell of a tortoise and been stumped by it. So they had got to talking about how to best crack the code, and someone had mentioned there was a girl at another one of the tortoise facilities, this time out on Isla Isabela, who was crazy smart and good at puzzles. The girl was rumored to be a bit strange, a loner who kept to herself, spending most of her time surfing or reading. It was believed that the girl was in her late teens, possibly early twenties, but Ivan figured that made sense because a twelve-year-old girl who wanted to stay hidden certainly wouldn't advertise her real age. Even in Ecuador, the authorities still weren't going to let a twelve-year-old live on her own like that.

At first Ivan had found it perplexing that the girl he was hunting would be off in the Galápagos, but then he consulted a map of the islands. On second consideration, it began to make sense. If the girl was looking to hide from civilization, there were few places farther away from it than Puerto Villamil. The town was as small as towns got, thousands of miles from just about everything.

So Ivan Spetz decided to check things out for himself. It took him nearly twenty-four hours to make the trip, as he'd been in Nicaragua when he'd gotten the tip, and it wasn't easy to get to Puerto Villamil from there. Frankly, it wasn't easy to get to Puerto Villamil from *anywhere*. Ivan had needed three flights and had to spend one night sleeping in the airport in Panama City to make it all work.

In all the time that Ivan had been working in the Americas, his job had never taken him to the Galápagos. Which made sense. The Galápagos were just some far-flung islands. They might have been important to science and tourism, but they had no bearing on politics. The only reason anyone usually visited them was to see the wild animals there, and Ivan didn't care much for wild animals.

The main airport in the Galápagos was a refurbished air force base on a sun-blasted speck of rock named Isla Baltra. From there, Ivan had to take a boat to Puerto Ayora, the biggest town in the Galápagos, which the Darwin Research Station sat on the outskirts of. Ivan always carried plenty of false identification, and in Puerto Ayora, he pretended to be a police officer from Guayaquil on the mainland, looking for a young girl wanted for drug smuggling. He had rounded up two local policemen to help him. They were the ones who had suggested a speedboat would be the fastest way to get to Isla Isabela, possibly because the Puerto Ayora police department didn't have a plane of its own.

So that was how Ivan had finally arrived in Puerto Villamil, which was about the worst excuse for a town he'd ever encountered. The streets were dirt, the houses were falling apart, and the place was crawling with marine iguanas, which might have been the most butt-ugly animals imaginable. They looked like something straight out of a nightmare, and yet everyone was letting the disgusting things hang out on their porches and sidewalks.

But Ivan seemed to be on the right track.

The only photo Ivan had of the girl was a grainy copy of a video grab from a Mossad camera. And yet the moment he'd showed it to the two surfers walking down the street, they had immediately recognized her.

"That's Mariposa," one had said. "Did she do something wrong?"

Ivan had assured the guy that it wasn't anything major, he only needed to talk to the girl, and the guy had dutifully pointed out her house, a run-down shack at the end of the town, right on the edge of what looked like a swamp. Ivan had called to the police officers and they had headed that way, nice and casual, not wanting to cause a commotion, keeping their guns out of sight, tucked under their shirts. Then they came up the front steps and knocked on the door.

There was no answer. The front door was locked, but the jamb was so old and weather-beaten, it broke apart when Ivan yanked hard on the knob. The door swung open and Ivan stepped inside.

He could hear water dripping in the shower and went to check it. The shower floor was still wet and a damp towel dangled on a hook. The girl had used it recently.

The policemen were searching the main room. Ivan could hear them rooting roughly through the cabinets. Ivan stepped out of the bathroom just as one of the policemen was checking under the kitchen sink. As the man yanked open the cabinet door, Ivan saw something spark.

Ivan had been in the spy game long enough to know what he was seeing. The girl had rigged a booby trap, the kind of thing a professional would do.

"Get down!" Ivan yelled, while he flung himself into the bathroom.

The policeman was too close and too surprised to react. He had never encountered anything like this before.

The trap was simple enough. Charlie Thorne had fixed a piece of metal to the door and a flint rock to the jamb. When the metal scraped the flint, it sparked.

Which ignited the gas from the small propane tank that Charlie had opened under the sink, right before fleeing out the bedroom window.

The resulting explosion blew the policeman off his feet, throwing him across the tiny kitchen. The cabinets all burst open, spilling glasses and plates, which shattered on the floor, while the building trembled enough to topple all the stacks of books.

Ivan waited in the bathroom for a few seconds, then emerged into the kitchen to assess the aftermath of the explosion. The scorched propane tank lay in what remained of the cabinet, a small jet of flame still flickering from the open valve. Ivan noticed something was written on it in black Sharpie:

DON'T MESS WITH MY STUFF.

The policeman who'd been thrown by the blast staggered to his feet. He was startled and the eyebrows had been scorched off his face, but he was otherwise all right.

Ivan was still staring at the propane tank. It was quite large. "That blast should have been much bigger," he said in Spanish. The fire flickering from the open valve indicated gas was still venting out of it. He walked across the kitchen, the broken plates crunching under his feet, shut off the valve, then lifted the tank. It was heavy, with plenty of propane still sloshing around inside. "Most of the gas is still in here," he observed, then realized what that meant. "This wasn't open long. She must have just left."

The second policeman shook his head dumbly. "We would have seen her leaving."

"Only if she came through the door, you idiot." Ivan ran into the bedroom. The rear window was open. In the dirt on the ground outside were two sets of footprints, leading to a path through the swamp.

"This way!" Ivan yelled, then scrambled out the window. He was much bigger than either Charlie or Esmerelda, so it was a tight squeeze. He managed to get through and ran down the path.

Other people with less on their minds might have found the marsh quite beautiful. Hundreds of birds, including a small flock of flamingos, waded in the still pools, surrounded by thickets of mangrove trees. But Ivan Spetz did not have an eye for beauty.

It was quiet in the marsh, so he could easily hear the roar of the airplane engine starting in the distance. Ivan cursed under his breath in Russian. Times like this, when he was really angry, were the only occasions where his facade slipped and he used his native tongue.

He charged onward down the trail, knowing he would be too late, but not willing to give up, either. The trail ended by a squat cement facility in the woods, surrounded by a dozen outdoor pens, each filled with tortoises of varying sizes. A breeding facility. Beyond that was a rocky beach with a floating dock extending out into the ocean.

A seaplane was skimming along the water. As Ivan arrived, it lifted into the air, whisking Charlie Thorne away from him.

Ivan was so angry, he wanted to take out his gun and open fire on the plane. It was far off, but Ivan was a crack shot. He could possibly hit the fuselage and bring the plane down.

But Ivan's orders weren't to kill the girl. Russia wanted her alive.

So Ivan willed himself to stay calm and focus. He stared after the plane and memorized the registration numbers on the tail. NC7821. It wouldn't take long for him to call those in and figure out where the plane was heading. Once he knew that, he could find Charlie Thorne and bring her in.

He wouldn't underestimate the girl again.

FIVE

In the passenger seat of the seaplane, Charlie Thorne observed the man on the beach, the man who had come looking for her. She couldn't tell much about him from this distance, but the way he moved indicated he was upset.

Her gaze then shifted to the tortoise breeding facility, the marsh, the tiny town of Puerto Villamil, the sweep of the beach and the crystal water beyond it. Sadness crept over her. She had liked this place, but it appeared she wouldn't be returning to it anytime soon. Maybe never again.

Someone had found her.

She had known that would happen eventually. That was why she had always kept a packed backpack and booby-trapped her home. Although she had hoped it would take far longer than this. Now she would have to move on and find another place, to try to cover her tracks even better this time. She had made a mistake by choosing to volunteer at the breeding facility. She had feared that might be the case, but the place was doing important work, helping species back from the brink of extinction, and Charlie wanted to do something important. But in working there, she had allowed people to know about her. That was how Esmerelda had found her, which meant that was probably how this stranger had tracked her down too. So the next place she went, she would have to keep her contact with other humans to a bare minimum.

The thought didn't appeal to her. Charlie missed having friends. She missed being able to tell people the truth about herself. To her surprise, at times she even missed her half brother, Dante. Even though their relationship had been prickly, she often found herself thinking that it would have been nice to get to know him better. Unfortunately, being alone seemed to be the only way to protect Pandora. And protecting Pandora was Charlie's burden to bear. No one else could be trusted with it.

The town disappeared behind the bulk of the volcano, and Charlie found herself staring down into the gaping crater, several miles of blistered igneous rock that still smoked in spots, surrounded by a green fringe of tropical forest. Beyond it, Charlie could already see Isla Santa Cruz in the distance; none of the Galápagos Islands were very far from one another.

"Mariposa, is something wrong?" Esmerelda asked.

The seaplane was old and loud. Both of them had to wear headsets to block out the roar of the engines; the headsets were fitted with radio-microphones so they could talk to each other.

Charlie turned from the window. "You can call me Charlie."

"Charlie? But I thought . . ."

"I like Charlie better than Mariposa," Charlie said, then quickly changed the subject. "You said you had theories about this treasure of Darwin's?"

"Yes. Though maybe I misspoke. They're not really *my* theories. There's a story you hear about Darwin when you work at the research station. More of a myth, actually." Esmerelda stared straight ahead as she spoke, angling the plane over the crater toward Isla Santa Cruz. "For the past two centuries, there have been rumors that Darwin discovered a treasure on his travels in South America. But there hadn't been any direct evidence for that . . . until now."

"What kind of treasure?" Charlie asked.

"No one knows. But most people assume that it's gold. There have always been tales of a lost golden city built by the Incas, or a cache of gold hidden somewhere in the jungle."

Charlie nodded. She had heard the stories of lost

golden cities herself. South American lore was full of them. But she had never heard anything about Darwin finding a treasure. "So why would people think Darwin had found something like this?"

"There are some strange things about the voyage of the *Beagle* that have never been fully explained. To begin with, it was supposed to only be a two-year journey, but it took nearly five years. . . ."

"Four of which were spent in South America," Charlie finished.

Esmerelda turned to Charlie, seeming surprised that she knew this.

"I've read *The Voyage of the Beagle*," Charlie explained. "And pretty much everything else Darwin wrote."

"Really?"

"You hang out in these islands, Darwin gets mentioned about a hundred times a day, so I figured I should read his stuff. Plus, half the tourists who come here are reading his books, so they're not hard to get. Darwin never mentions a treasure in any of them."

"The prevailing theory is he wanted to keep it a secret. So he altered his journals to hide any mention of it—or the expedition he took to find it. He was traveling for nearly a year after leaving South America. He would have had plenty of time to rewrite his journals during that time."

"There were almost eighty other people aboard the *Beagle*," Charlie said. "None of them mentioned a treasure either."

"That was my concern about the story too," Esmerelda admitted. "But there are other strange things that point to a possible cover-up. Darwin and the captain of the *Beagle*, Robert FitzRoy, had a serious falling-out after the voyage. They started out as friends and ended up not talking to each other. . . ."

"I'm sure five years on a cramped ship could test anyone's friendship. And FitzRoy could be a real jerk to the crew."

"But they could also have had arguments over the treasure. And then Darwin mysteriously cut fifty pages from one of his own notebooks and never explained why. . . ."

"Maybe he spilled wine on it."

"I know none of this is concrete evidence," Esmerelda said. "That's why most people have regarded the stories as rumors. But then, you could argue that the rumors themselves are a sort of evidence. After all, maybe the rumors started because people from the *Beagle did* talk about the treasure."

"I suppose that makes sense."

"Still, I was as dismissive of them as you . . . until we found that carved shell. Which seems to indicate that the rumors are true after all."

They were already closing in on Isla Santa Cruz. As Esmerelda had said, the flight wasn't long. Isla Isabela had fallen behind them, while Isla Santiago, another place Darwin had visited, was to their left.

The islands all looked dramatically different from the air. The geology of each had shaped its ecology, which had led to the great differentiation of species in the Galápagos. Isla Santa Cruz had a good-size mountain in the center, a dormant volcano that caught the clouds, which led to lots of rain at the higher elevations, so it was lush and green. Meanwhile, Santiago was flat and dry. Isabela, with its multiple volcanoes, had dozens of different ecosystems, some with species so rare they were found nowhere else on earth.

Charlie could also see Puerto Ayora on Santa Cruz ahead of them. The town was much bigger than Puerto Villamil, far bigger than she had expected to find on an island chain that was supposed to be a nature preserve. It had surprised her when she'd first seen it. The country of Ecuador, it seemed, was having trouble corralling development in Puerto Ayora, and there were many new roads and hotels and homes. To Charlie, it all looked like a scar on the landscape.

To the east of Puerto Ayora was the Charles Darwin Research Center, which Charlie had visited upon arriving in the islands. There was a dock nearby with other seaplanes. Their destination. The town also had a large marina, where dozens of boats were moored: tourist boats and scuba charters and fishing boats and a few speedboats like the one that had brought the man who was looking for her to Puerto Villamil.

Charlie figured the man had rented the boat in Puerto Ayora. There was no other place in the islands to get something like that. So he was probably heading back this way. They were moving much faster than he could, but still, the speedboat was quick enough to make the trip in less than an hour.

Of additional concern was that the seaplane had its registration number clearly marked on its tail. Charlie had noticed it when she climbed aboard. That was standard for all private planes, like license plates were for cars. It wouldn't be hard to determine that the plane belonged to the research station. The strange man had likely done so already. Which meant it wouldn't be long before he showed up at the research station looking for her.

"Is there anything important you need in Puerto Ayora?" Charlie asked suddenly.

Esmerelda pulled her attention from piloting the seaplane toward the town. "The plastron is there. . . ."

"I mean for you. Would you be okay if we left the Galápagos right now? Or do you need any medication or anything like that?"

"No."

"Then forget about Puerto Ayora. Let's go right to the airport."

Esmerelda gave her a confused look. "I thought you wanted to see the plastron."

"I don't. I've already figured out the code."

Esmerelda's eyes went wide in surprise. "Just now?"

"No. The moment I saw it, actually. It wasn't that complicated."

In the brief period Esmerelda had known Charlie, she had been caught off guard many times, but now she was so flabbergasted she didn't quite know what to say. A dozen ideas were tumbling through her mind all at once. "But . . . How did you . . . ? When . . . ?" She had to take a moment to collect her thoughts. "Why didn't you tell me earlier?"

"I'd just met you. I needed to talk to you a bit . . ."

". . . to see if you could trust me," Esmerelda concluded, understanding. "So what does it say?"

"It says we need to be heading toward the airport."

"All right." Esmerelda quickly twisted the steering column, and the plane banked away from Puerto Ayora, heading north.

The most direct route to the airport on Isla Baltra took them straight over Isla Santa Cruz. Below them, Charlie could see the sprawl of Puerto Ayora give way to farmland on the lush green slopes of the island's dormant volcano.

She asked, "It won't be a problem, taking this plane to the airport?"

"No," Esmerelda replied. "There's a dock near the runway for seaplanes, so landing there isn't an issue."

"I meant, will it be a problem taking this plane, since it belongs to the Darwin Institute?"

"Oh." Esmerelda thought a beat, and then shook her head. "No. I'll let them know what's going on once we land. The airport isn't really that far from the station. If they need the plane, they'll be able to come get it."

Charlie nodded, watching the landscape beneath her. As the small plane banked around the volcano, it was low enough that Charlie could see individual tortoises below, roaming freely across the farms and ranches. The giant reptiles looked like stones strewn across the emerald-green grass. "The tortoise you found lived up here?" she asked.

"Yes."

Charlie briefly wondered why Charles Darwin would have gone through so much trouble to conceal a treasure he had found but then leave a clue on a tortoise shell. But she didn't mention that. There were other things to discuss.

She reached into her backpack, dug out a notebook and a pen, and quickly jotted down what had been carved into the plastron of the tortoise from memory, making a few extra marks. When she was done, she held up the page so that Esmerelda could read it.

If in death, Eros
and evil shall rest on earth.
Minds quit obeying.
—C. Darwin

Esmerelda read only what Charlie had underlined with amazement. "Find the devil's stone in Quito." Then she looked to Charlie and smiled. "Apparently, I came to the right person. You figured that out immediately when an entire team of scientists couldn't do it in two days!"

"Maybe it helps to speak English as your primary language," Charlie said humbly.

"I suppose so." Esmerelda's smile suddenly became a frown as something occurred to her. "In Quito," she repeated. "But Darwin was never in Quito. Or any part of mainland Ecuador."

"If he could fudge his journals to hide the existence of a huge treasure, he could certainly hide the fact that he'd been to Quito."

They passed through a curtain of clouds, and the small island to the north where the airport was came into view.

Esmerelda nodded agreement at what Charlie had

said, but the frown stayed on her face. "What on earth is a devil's stone? And how are we supposed to find one in a city as big as Quito?"

"Leave that to me," Charlie said confidently. "I think I know where it is."

SIX

Charles Darwin Research Station
Isla Santa Cruz, Ecuador

The Darwin Research Station at Puerto Ayora was much nicer than the Tupiza Tortoise Breeding Center in Puerto Villamil. The breeding facility at Darwin was state-of-the-art, and part of a larger complex of modern buildings that included a museum, a public library, and several research facilities, all surrounded by well-tended landscaping and sited along a beautiful stretch of beach.

A young docent named Luis was giving a tour of the grounds to a group of American tourists when Ivan Spetz arrived. "If it weren't for our breeding programs, the famous tortoises of these islands would have gone extinct," Luis was saying. "Their populations were already being decimated by the time Darwin visited here. Sailors were devouring them by the thousands."

A few younger children made faces of disgust at the thought of eating a tortoise.

"They might not look tasty to you," Luis said. "But imagine you had been at sea for weeks with only weevil-infested hardtack to eat. And then you get here and suddenly there's fresh meat everywhere. Plus, these tortoises can live for months without food or water, so sailors would fill their holds with hundreds of them and continue to eat them over the course of their travels. Darwin ate plenty of them himself, as well as some of the iguanas."

While the tourists considered the idea of eating a marine iguana, Ivan pushed through the crowd, grabbed Luis by the arm, and dragged him away. "Your guide will be right back," he informed the crowd pleasantly. "There's a small problem he needs to deal with."

"What problem?" Luis asked, wondering who this man was.

"I need to know where your seaplane is going." While Ivan spoke in a casual, almost friendly tone, there was still an air of menace to it. He continued gripping Luis's arm firmly as he dragged the young docent along.

Luis sensed this man was dangerous and looked back toward the tourists, like he was thinking about calling for help.

"Cause me any trouble and I'll break your arm," Ivan said. "All I want is the destination of the plane."

"I . . . I don't know," Luis stammered. "I swear. I don't have anything to do with the plane."

"Then you'd better find someone who does." Ivan tightened his grip on Luis's arm, making the young man wince in pain.

Ivan was in a foul mood. As Charlie had suspected, it hadn't taken him long to use the plane's registration number and discover it belonged to the Darwin Research Station. So he had returned to Puerto Ayora as quickly as possible, racing over choppy seas that had made him heave his breakfast over the side; there were still flecks of vomit on his shirt. But when he had finally arrived at the research station, the seaplane wasn't docked there.

Ivan had ditched the police he'd been working with so he could handle things his own way, thinking that might be frowned upon by law enforcement.

Luis didn't know exactly where the plane was heading, but he *did* know who had taken it—and why. Once the code on the tortoise shell had been discovered, the news had traveled quickly through the station. Luis had spent quite a bit of time staring at the shell himself, trying to crack the code. So he had heard that Esmerelda Castle had gone to find a girl who could maybe help decipher Darwin's message. Esmerelda had always been nice to Luis, so he didn't want to cause her any trouble— but Ivan was hurting him and seemed like he wouldn't hesitate to cause more pain. So he obediently led the SVR agent across the property to the tortoise research laboratory, a single-story white stucco and stone building.

There was a sign out front saying EMPLOYEES ONLY, but the doors weren't locked. Ivan and Luis walked right through the small entry foyer and directly into one of the labs, where a scientist was hunched over a table, dissecting a marine iguana.

She was visibly upset by the intrusion. "You can't come in here!" she shouted in Spanish. "This is a restricted area."

"I'm sorry, Dr. Salinas," Luis said. "This man wants to know where Esmerelda is going with the plane."

Dr. Salinas registered the fear in Luis's voice and grew concerned herself. However, she remained calm and directed her attention to Ivan. "Ms. Castle is on a scientific mission to one of the other islands."

Ivan could recognize a lie when he heard one. His patience was already wearing thin. In one swift movement, he spun Luis around, wrenching the young man's arm behind his back so that he cried out in pain. "The truth, please," he told Dr. Salinas calmly. "What is Ms. Castle really doing?"

Dr. Salinas hesitated a moment, as if wondering whether Ivan was bluffing or not. Her eyes nervously flicked toward something across the room.

Ivan looked that way. The shell from an enormous tortoise sat in the corner. There were two parts to it: the rounded part that covered the back of the tortoise, which sat on the floor, and the flat part that covered the belly, which was propped against the wall. At first glance, the shell didn't seem important, but then Ivan noticed the words carved into the flat piece, which seemed unusual.

He headed closer to the shell, shoving Luis in front of him, keeping the man's arm twisted behind his back.

Once he was close enough, Ivan read the inscription. His English wasn't nearly as good as his Spanish, but he could understand it well enough to know that the part about the treasure made sense, but the three lines in the center of the shell were gibberish. It seemed to him like some sort of code, and it appeared that the scientists at the research station thought so too, because a nearby whiteboard was covered with efforts to parse some meaning from the words. Attempts had been made to anagram the letters, to assign numeric values to them, and a few other things that Ivan couldn't understand.

Ivan knew a much faster way to decipher codes. There was an entire division of the SVR devoted to doing it. So he roughly shoved Luis aside, warned him not to try anything stupid, then snapped a photo of the shell with his phone and sent it as an encrypted message to the coding team marked PRIORITY.

Then he turned back to Luis and Dr. Salinas and calmly withdrew the gun from his holster. He didn't aim it at either of them. He simply let them know that he had it. Then he said, "Tell me about this treasure."

Luis and Dr. Salinas immediately told him everything. The decades-old rumors about Darwin and the treasure. The discovery of the code on the dead tortoise. How they had tried to crack it and failed and how it had been decided that Esmerelda Castle should go seek out the help of the unusual girl in Puerto Villamil.

They were frightened and spoke quickly, volunteering all they could. It took only a few minutes before Dr. Salinas was insisting, "That's all we know. I swear."

"Do you have a photo of Esmerelda Castle?" Ivan asked.

Luis pointed to the wall, where there was a framed photograph of the research station staff. "She's in the front row, at the far left."

Ivan smashed the glass with the butt of his gun, then removed the photograph and studied it. Esmerelda Castle was a beautiful woman with striking features. Ivan probably would have easily recognized her if he saw her again, but he pocketed the photograph anyhow, just to be safe.

His phone buzzed with an email. The cryptography team had already cracked the code.

Find the devil's stone in Quito.

Ivan put the phone away, then stuck the gun back in

his holster. "Thanks for your time," he told Luis and Dr. Salinas, nice and friendly, like he had just borrowed a cup of sugar, rather than threatened their lives. Then he walked out of the lab and quickly left the research station, thinking about the words that were etched in the tortoise shell:

The Greatest Treasure in Human History.

He could bring in the girl for the SVR and get rich in the process. This assignment might have started off badly, but it was beginning to sound a whole lot better.

SEVEN

Iglesia de San Francisco
Quito, Ecuador

Quito was the second-highest capital city on earth, nestled on a high plateau in the Andes Mountains, nearly two miles above sea level. It had been founded by Spanish conquistadores in the 1500s and was surrounded by snow-capped volcanoes and steep, treacherous ravines.

Since Charlie had spent the last two months at sea level, the change in altitude hit her hard. When she had first climbed out of the cab from the airport, she had nearly passed out from the lack of oxygen. She had managed to stay conscious, but she still had a nagging headache and her stomach was queasy from altitude sickness. However, she was soldiering on, driven by the excitement of tracking down the Devil's Stone.

Esmerelda was having even more trouble, struggling to get a breath in the thin air. "Charlie, please," she gasped as they cut through the Plaza Grande in the heart of the city. "I need to go slower."

Charlie stopped in front of the Carondelet Palace, where the president of Ecuador lived, and looked back at Esmerelda with obvious frustration. "The church is closing soon."

"I'm doing the best that I can." Ever since meeting Charlie Thorne, Esmerelda had been struggling to keep up with the girl, physically and mentally. Charlie had surprised her so many times, it already seemed routine. There had been their abrupt departure from the house in Puerto Villamil, her equally abrupt decision to head directly to the airport, the revelation that she had solved Darwin's code almost instantly. Then, despite the meager life she had been living in Puerto Villamil, Charlie had turned out to be rich. At the airport in the Galápagos, she had been able to purchase two tickets on the next flight to Quito on the spur of the moment, at a hefty cost. And upon arriving in the city, she had insisted on paying for rooms for both of them at a pricey hotel. Esmerelda had told Charlie she would be happy to get a room with twin beds to save money—or even sleep on a couch—but Charlie had replied, "It isn't an issue," and handed over enough cash to cover the night.

But perhaps most surprising of all was Charlie's encyclopedic range of knowledge. She appeared to know about almost everything.

The legend of the Devil's Stone, for instance. Charlie had come across it in a history of Quito, which she had decided to read upon visiting the city en route to the Galápagos. She was recounting it now for Esmerelda as they wound their way through the city, using a tourist map from their hotel as a guide.

"The church of San Francisco was built shortly after the founding of Quito," Charlie said. "And as you can see, it was a major construction job for a remote Spanish outpost in the 1500s." She pointed down the narrow street they had just turned on. At the end of it, Esmerelda saw the church, a great stone and white stucco edifice at the edge of another large plaza.

Charlie continued. "The legend is that the head priest asked a man named Cantuña to help build it. Cantuña agreed, but realized he would need help. So he called upon God. Only, God didn't answer. So Cantuña asked for the help of the devil instead.

"The devil answered instantly, but being the devil, he was kind of a jerk. He made a deal with Cantuña: He would build the church in only a day, but he wanted Cantuña's soul in return. Cantuña accepted the deal—with one condition. If the church wasn't one hundred percent completed by sunrise, down to the very last stone, the deal would be canceled."

They emerged into the plaza, and Esmerelda stopped

again, not because she was out of breath, but because she was amazed by the spectacle before her. The plaza had been gaily decorated with lanterns and strings of lights, and everywhere around her, people were in costumes. Some wore the traditional native dress of the Incas, some wore biblical robes and tunics, some were dressed as colonial Spaniards, and quite a few were elaborately costumed as angels and devils.

"It's Holy Week," Charlie told Esmerelda. "Today is Jueves Santo—Maundy Thursday."

"Of course," Esmerelda said, feeling a bit foolish. The next day would be Good Friday and Sunday would be Easter. "I'd forgotten. In the Galápagos, every day feels almost the same, so sometimes you lose track of where you are on the calendar."

"There's a huge parade here for Good Friday," Charlie said. "But I guess they're already celebrating." She noticed Esmerelda staring at a group of devils in the plaza and explained, "They're dressed as the *diabolitos* who helped the devil build the church. Kind of like the devil's subcontractors, I guess."

Hundreds of people were gathered around the church doors, working their way inside. Charlie and Esmerelda fell in with the crowd. "So what happened to Cantuña?" Esmerelda asked.

"He found a way to get out of the contract," Charlie

said. "While the devil and the *diabolitos* were slaving away to build the church, Cantuña secretly removed a stone from a place where the mortar wasn't dry and hid it under his robes. The devil finished the church by sunrise—or so he thought. He came to Cantuña, all proud of himself, and said, 'You owe me your soul'—and then Cantuña said, 'Not so fast, pal. You missed a spot.' He pointed to the gap where the stone was supposed to be. The devil flipped out and threw a huge fit, but he knew he was beaten. So in the end, he just slinked away, vowing revenge—and Cantuña became a hero."

"But that's only a folktale," Esmerelda said. "So the Devil's Stone isn't real."

"Maybe not," Charlie agreed. "But there's still a gap in the masonry somewhere in this church—and there's a stone that fits into it. The legend says that someday the devil will return through that gap to exact his revenge, and when he does, they can plug the hole with the stone and trap him inside."

They finally managed to work their way into the church, and once again Esmerelda froze in amazement. While the exterior of the church had been quite plain, the interior was lavishly decorated. No matter where she looked, there was art. Every last inch of the walls was bedecked with beautiful paintings, intricate mosaics, or delicate carvings. A great dome soared above the altar, painted iridescent blue and studded with golden stars to look like a twilight sky.

The church also extended farther than Esmerelda had expected. The central chapel was quite large, while an open archway to their right led to an atrium the size of a city block. That, in turn, was ringed by what appeared to be a monastery.

"This place is enormous," Esmerelda said, sounding daunted. "Do you have any idea where the Devil's Stone is supposed to be in here?"

"No," Charlie admitted. "So let's find someone who might."

Most of the other church visitors were filing into the atrium, where monks were ladling out bowls of fanesca, a traditional soup served during Holy Week, for the masses. Charlie went that way.

With hundreds of people filing out to the atrium or back into the church, there was a tight squeeze to pass through the doorway. One of the other pilgrims jostled Esmerelda roughly as she entered the atrium, knocking her down. She landed hard on the stone pathway and winced in pain.

Charlie rushed to her side to help her. "Are you all right?"

"I'm fine," Esmerelda said, getting back to her feet.

Charlie noticed there was a great deal of blood on

Esmerelda's hand—although Esmerelda herself seemed completely unaware of this.

"You're sure you're okay?" Charlie asked.

"Yes," Esmerelda said, like she really meant it—and then she noticed the blood herself. She turned her hand over, and both of them saw there was a shard of glass sticking out of her palm. It appeared that a drinking glass had been broken earlier but this fragment had failed to have been cleaned up—and now Esmerelda had put her hand right on it. The shard was small and it hadn't gone in deep, but it had cut a good-size slash across her palm. "Oh," Esmerelda said, like she was as surprised to see this as Charlie. "I better get this cleaned up." She made a beeline for one of the soup tables and grabbed some napkins to stanch the flow of blood.

"I didn't realize you were Italian," Charlie said.

Esmerelda looked to her, surprised once again. "How did you . . . ?" she began, and then understanding dawned on her. "You know about that, too?"

"I know there's an unusual family from Italy whose members feel pain differently from other people." Charlie carefully plucked the shard of glass from Esmerelda's palm. "They *feel* it when it happens, but then it instantly fades instead of lingering, like it does in other people. So they're sort of impervious to it. I've also heard there's a family in Pakistan with the same genetic trait, but you look much more Italian than Pakistani."

Esmerelda shook her head in amazement. "My last name is really Castello. How do you know so much at such a young age?"

"I read a lot."

"And apparently never forget anything."

That was true, although Charlie wasn't going to admit to it. She didn't exactly have a photographic memory, but hers was as close to that as memories got.

One of the monks on duty in the atrium rushed over, having noticed Esmerelda's bleeding. He was a young man, not much beyond his teens, with a tonsured haircut and wearing a dark-brown robe. "Are you all right?" he asked in Spanish.

"I could use some disinfectant," Esmerelda replied. "And perhaps a bandage."

"We have a first aid kit," the young monk replied. "Follow me." He led them away from the crowds and across the atrium.

Charlie was now able to get a better look at her surroundings. A large ornate fountain dominated the center of the atrium, while several cages full of Amazonian parrots and macaws were arrayed around the gardens. Many monks were showing the birds to excited young visitors.

"Do you know where the Devil's Stone is in this church?" Charlie asked.

The young monk's features clouded, and for a moment Charlie thought she had offended him, but when he spoke she realized it wasn't her that he was upset with. "It is no longer here," he said sourly. "It was taken from us."

"When?" Charlie asked, upset to hear this herself. "And by who?"

"Decades ago." The monk led them up a flight of stairs in the dormitory building, which ringed the atrium. "By our own country. To build the Basilica of the National Vow."

"What's that?" Esmerelda asked.

"Another church. One that the government seemed to feel was more important than this one," the monk said, entering a small infirmary on the second floor. In contrast to the ancient building around them, it was extremely modern. "The country helped fund the construction of it, and then they demanded that every other church donate something precious to signify that the Basilica would be the most precious of all. The church elders at the time didn't want to give up any precious artworks, so they gave them the stone." The monk opened a medicine cabinet and took out gauze and rubbing alcohol.

"Is this church far away?" Esmerelda asked.

"Not at all. It's right there." The monk pointed out the window.

A few blocks from where they stood, an enormous Gothic church perched atop a steep hill. There were two great bell towers at one end and a massive spire at the other. It appeared to have been designed to be imposing, to loom over every other church in Quito.

"And the Devil's Stone is somewhere inside there?" Charlie asked.

"In the spire," the monk said, uncapping the rubbing alcohol. "At the very top."

He splashed some alcohol on the gash in Esmerelda's hand. Esmerelda winced the moment it touched her, but then the pain seemed to pass almost instantaneously.

Charlie noticed this, but her attention was drawn to the spire in the distance. It emerged from the top of the cathedral roof, stabbing high into the sky. It was ornately decorated and looked to be at least three hundred and fifty feet tall.

Esmerelda looked to her and spoke in English, presuming that the monk wouldn't understand them. "Maybe we should check the place in this church where the stone used to be first."

"Darwin's message said to find the stone itself," Charlie reminded her.

Esmerelda considered the spire of the cathedral with trepidation. "That's awfully tall and exposed. Do you really think we can find the stone up there?"

"Of course," Charlie replied confidently. "But we need to get some sporting goods first."

EIGHT

Basilica of the National Vow
Quito, Ecuador
Good Friday

The sun had barely poked above the horizon when Charlie and Esmerelda approached the Basilica the next morning.

To be on the safe side, the night before, they had visited the spot at the Iglesia de San Francisco where the Devil's Stone had once been kept but found nothing of interest. So now they were on their way to climb the Basilica's spire and locate the stone itself.

Throughout Quito, Good Friday celebrations had already begun. The highlight of the day was the great processional that ran through the city. Thousands of penitents would participate, while an even greater number of people would watch. The procession began early, and so celebrants were already lining up along the route. They were gathered so thickly on the sidewalks that Charlie and Esmerelda could hardly squeeze through.

Furthermore, services were already underway at the Basilica, and churchgoers in their finest clothes were crowded around the doors.

Many of those people might have been suspicious of two women carrying large coils of climbing ropes into the Basilica. So Charlie and Esmerelda had come in disguise.

An unusual aspect of the Good Friday procession in Quito were the cucuruchos, penitents who walked the route in bright-purple robes. The robes looked disturbingly like those worn by members of the Ku Klux Klan in America, with the same pointed conical cowls, but in Quito, they had a very different significance. The cones symbolized humility, hiding the faces of the wearers except for the eyes, while the purple color represented repentance. Until recently, women had not been allowed to wear them. But times had changed. Esmerelda had purchased two the night before, at Charlie's suggestion, while Charlie had been buying climbing ropes, harnesses, and other sporting goods.

Charlie had paid for everything once again. She had explained to Esmerelda that she could easily afford it because her parents were rich and that she had a huge trust fund.

This was a lie.

Charlie had earned the money herself—in a way. Technically, she had stolen it from the Lightning Corporation, one of the biggest tech firms in the world. Although, in Charlie's defense, the Lightning Corporation had stolen something from her first: a security program she had created that was worth millions. Charlie felt she was simply taking back what was rightfully hers; however, the Lightning Corporation—and the CIA—considered it theft. Which was how the CIA had blackmailed Charlie into helping them look for Einstein's equation in the first place.

Charlie didn't feel like explaining all that to Esmerelda, though. And besides, being a trust fund kid sounded much more believable than the truth.

Charlie hadn't gone to an ATM to get the money, because ATM visits could easily be traced. She'd already had the cash; inside her backpack from Puerto Villamil was a money belt containing $20,000 in hundred-dollar bills. (The money was in American dollars because no matter where they were, black markets always accepted US currency.) The pack also held clean clothes, a first aid kit, snacks, a lighter, and a fake passport that Charlie had paid a forger $15,000 for. It was expensive, but necessary, as she needed it to be top-quality.

Charlie was wearing the money belt now, concealed beneath her shirt. She had winnowed down her few belongings even further. Along with her remaining cash, she had crammed in the passport, a spare set of underwear, and the lighter, which had been a gift from her grandfather.

The cucurucho robe wasn't made for comfort. The fabric was coarse and itchy and it was stifling inside, even at that early hour. Charlie pitied the people who would be walking miles in such robes in the equatorial heat—even though she knew some of the point of the procession was suffering. Of course, it didn't help that she was lugging twenty-five pounds of climbing rope under her robe, along with an assortment of carabiners, nylon slings, and belay devices. She had acclimatized to the high altitude over the night, but climbing the steep hill to the cathedral with all the gear and the heavy robe still wasn't easy. Her thighs were screaming by the time she reached her destination.

The robe served its purpose well, however. No one gave Charlie or Esmerelda a second glance as they entered the Basilica. The cathedral was built in a Gothic style, designed to look like one of the great churches of Europe. It was enormous, as long as one and a half football fields, with a sanctuary tall enough to fit a ten-story building inside. The interior walls were lined with statues of religious figures and stained-glass windows.

But Charlie and Esmerelda didn't enter the sanctuary. There was a large foyer at the entrance of the Basilica, flanked by the two great bell towers, much like those at Notre Dame in Paris. Charlie and Esmerelda slipped through the crowd of celebrants and headed up the stairs of the closest bell tower.

The stairs led upward several stories to a landing that was even with the roof of the sanctuary. No one else was there, so Charlie and Esmerelda quickly peeled off their cucurucho robes. In the middle of the landing was a doorway marked CERRADO. NO HAY ENTRADA. CLOSED. NO ADMITTANCE.

Charlie brushed it aside and picked the lock on the door.

This led to a walkway that crossed over the very peak of the sanctuary. For structural reasons, the roof of the cathedral was much higher than the roof of the sanctuary, creating a large attic space that was almost completely empty. Charlie had done some research on the Basilica the night before and learned that on most days, this route was open to tourists who wanted to visit the spire, but since today was one of the holiest days of the year, it was closed to the public. Which made it the perfect time to access the spire; no one else was there.

And yet the building was alive with the sound of people. The music of the organ in the sanctuary and the chorus of voices singing was so loud, it made the roof vibrate as Charlie and Esmerelda walked across it.

At the far end of the attic space, another stairway rose.

This one was far more narrow and rickety than the one in the bell tower, and Charlie and Esmerelda struggled to lug their ropes and gear up it.

At the top, there was another door, although this one wasn't locked. Charlie and Esmerelda passed through it and found themselves out on the cathedral roof at the base of the spire.

The spire didn't have walls; it was merely a framework of ornately designed steel, completely open to the elements. It rose high into the sky from the dead center of the roof, which sloped away precipitously on both sides. A dozen iron flights of stairs circled upward around the spire, with only a thin railing to keep climbers from tumbling to their deaths. Charlie imagined that the spire would be a nightmare for anyone with a healthy fear of heights. There was no other way to get to the Devil's Stone, however, so she and Esmerelda kept on climbing.

It was a cloudless, sunny day and the spire was the highest point for miles; as Charlie climbed it, she could see all of Quito spread out around her. At the base of the hill below the Basilica was the Iglesia de San Francisco, where the Good Friday procession would end; the plaza in front of it was already thronged with spectators. Beyond that, Charlie could see the glassy skyscrapers where rich people lived and the tumbledown homes of the poor. And beyond those, green mountains circled one side of the city, while steep ravines spilled down from the other.

Eventually, Charlie and Esmerelda arrived at a small octagonal platform. This was as high as tourists were allowed to go, although the spire itself continued even higher. An ornate conical cap rose another three stories into the sky. It reminded Charlie of the conical top of the cucurucho costumes, having almost the exact same proportions.

There was no sign of the Devil's Stone anywhere around the platform. Which Charlie had assumed would be the case. Nothing was ever that easy. Which was why they'd brought the climbing gear.

"Guess I'm going up," Charlie said.

Esmerelda had balked at the idea of this when Charlie had first suggested it the day before. "It's too dangerous," she had said. "I can't ask you to do it."

But Charlie had insisted she could, pointing out that she was an adept rock climber. Back when she had been in college at the University of Colorado, she had spent more time scaling the pinnacles around Boulder than she had in class. (Although, in truth, Charlie had spent almost no time in class at all.)

Meanwhile, Esmerelda didn't know the first thing about rock climbing. Once they had acquired the proper gear, Charlie had to give her a primer. Charlie might have been a daredevil, but she wasn't stupid. She never climbed without a partner who could safely belay her. The idea was, both of them would be harnessed to a climbing rope. While Charlie climbed, she would occasionally attach a metal ring called a carabiner to the spire and pass the rope through it, while Esmerelda anchored the other end down below. If Charlie fell, Esmerelda would keep the rope from playing out—and thus prevent Charlie from falling to her death. So Charlie had to literally show Esmerelda the ropes.

Working the belay wasn't complicated, but a single mistake could have grave consequences, so Charlie had made Esmerelda practice for well over an hour the night before, until they were confident in her abilities. Now, on the platform, they strapped on their climbing harnesses, linked themselves to the rope, and did several safety checks to make sure that everything had been set up properly.

Then Charlie began to climb.

The moment she left the small platform behind and found herself clinging to the spire, Charlie was struck by a sense of vertigo, the feeling that she was way too high above the ground for comfort. But while most people would have felt fear, Charlie felt exhilarated. Partly, this was because she had run the numbers in her mind; she knew that with the combination of her skills and a proper belay, she was in less danger than she would have been in a car in rush-hour traffic. And partly because she was caught up in the thrill of discovery, hoping that her instincts were correct and that she would find what Darwin had left behind.

Like the great churches of Europe, the entire Basilica—including the spire—was decorated with grotesques, ornate carvings of human and animal figures. (People commonly referred to these as gargoyles, but in fact a gargoyle was a grotesque that was specifically designed to be used as a water spout; the word "gargoyle" came from the French word for "throat," as they were often designed so that the rainwater spewed from their mouths.) However, the grotesques on the Basilica differed from the European ones in that they only represented animals native to Ecuador, like monkeys, armadillos, marine iguanas, and Galápagos tortoises. Fortunately for Charlie, all the statues provided plenty of good hand- and footholds as she climbed. In addition, a metal cable ran down the spire to direct lightning strikes to the ground. It was easy to slip the carabiners around, allowing Charlie to readily secure the rope time and again. Thus her climb was far easier than many others she had done, as simple as climbing a jungle gym, the only concern being the height.

After just a few minutes, Charlie reached the narrow peak of the spire's conical cap. A perfect orb of stone perched there, with an iron cross rising above it.

Charlie affixed a final carabiner around the cross, and then clipped her rope into it, securing herself so that she could use both her hands to examine the orb. She had originally assumed the Devil's Stone would be square, as one might find in the walls of a church, but now it occurred to her that an orb made sense. Throughout history, orbs had been ascribed mystical powers and were often made part of important Christian art.

The orb she faced now was much larger than it had appeared from down at street level, nearly as big as a basketball. It was completely smooth, a sphere perfectly sculpted from stone.

And then she touched it.

The orb spun on its axis, revealing its other side. A jumble of numbers had been etched there, carved deep into the stone:

21343131345244231533113534422451542

15114344214234321334131121344244153314115443

45334424314423155211441542444542343
44341231343414

442315332124331444231544421515
124524314431242515

2524332243133431311522151323113511531

They didn't make any sense at all.

But then, this was exactly what Charlie had expected. It appeared to be a kind of code. She had been *hoping* to find some sort of indication that she was on the right track to find Darwin's treasure, and this certainly looked like one.

Charlie fished her phone out of her pocket and took some pictures, as a long stream of random numbers like this was incredibly hard to memorize. Still, she did her best to commit it to memory as well, just in case something went wrong.

In Charlie's experience, things went wrong far more than they went right.

Charlie scrutinized her photos, making sure that they were in focus and she could see all the numbers clearly, then carefully pocketed her phone again and started climbing back down. Even though she trusted herself to be safe, the less time she stayed up there, the better. With all the people in the streets below, sooner or later, someone would notice her.

The spire's conical cap flared out beneath her, blocking Esmerelda—and the entire platform she had started climbing from—from her view. When she looked down, she could only see the long drop to the steeply slanted roof of the Basilica. If she were to fall, she would tumble off the roof and splatter on the pavement far below.

So she climbed down quickly, using the animal grotesques as hand- and footholds again. The trickiest part was getting past the base of the cone. Since it was wider than the platform below, Charlie couldn't see where she was going. She grabbed a pair of stone marine iguanas and lowered herself over the edge, so that she was dangling in thin air.

At that point, she had intended to swing herself forward and drop onto the safety of the small platform where she had left Esmerelda. It was a relatively easy move, even at a height like this.

Only, once Charlie was hanging by her fingertips, she discovered there was a complication to her plan.

Esmerelda was aiming a gun at her.

NINE

I want whatever you found up there," Esmerelda said. "Now." Any trace of friendliness she had shown Charlie over the past day was gone. Instead, there was only a cold, determined gaze in her eyes.

Despite her precarious position, dangling high above the ground, Charlie still kept her wits about her. "I didn't find *anything*," she said earnestly. "The stone isn't up there."

"Don't lie to me!" Esmerelda yelled, loud enough to startle some pigeons that had been roosting in the spire into flight. "Tell me what you found . . . or else!"

"Or else what?" Charlie asked. "You'll shoot me? If you kill me, I won't be able to tell you anything."

"I don't have to shoot to kill," Esmerelda said. "I can just wound you. If I shoot you in the knee right now, it will hurt so badly, you'll *wish* I'd killed you."

"Oh," Charlie said. "I hadn't thought of that."

This was a lie. In truth, Charlie wasn't surprised that Esmerelda had double-crossed her. The woman had done several things to arouse Charlie's suspicions over the past day. For example, she hadn't been concerned about taking the Darwin Institute's plane to the airport until Charlie had asked her about it, which indicated that she was far more interested in Darwin's treasure than she was in the Institute. And she hadn't been forthcoming about her background—which, as Charlie knew from personal experience, was often the behavior of someone who had something to hide. Therefore, Charlie had prepared for betrayal. Now that it had actually happened, her response wasn't shock; it was disappointment that her suspicions were correct and that yet another person had turned out to be a jerk.

Even so, Charlie hadn't expected Esmerelda to ambush her *here*. She had expected it might happen later, when they were safely down on the street. But she had to admit, this was an excellent place for it. Esmerelda definitely had her in a bad spot. So while she was doing her best to act as though Esmerelda had caught her by surprise, in truth, her mind was racing, analyzing everything around her, working on an escape plan. She noticed that Esmerelda had already unclipped the climbing rope from her own harness, so if Charlie fell, they wouldn't be tied together. That had been a clever move on Esmerelda's part—although Charlie realized it gave her an option that Esmerelda would never have considered.

The rope ran from Charlie's harness up to the top of the spire fifty feet above, then snaked back through the carabiners Charlie had linked to the lightning rod. The remaining hundred feet of rope was coiled on the floor of the platform in front of Esmerelda.

"So," Charlie said. "I guess you're not a tortoise researcher after all. You're some kind of treasure hunter instead?"

Esmerelda wasn't interested in small talk. "What did you find up there?"

"Another code. But it was too complicated for me to memorize. So I had to take a picture of it on my phone."

"Then give it to me."

"Oh sure," Charlie said sarcastically. "I'll just let go of this ledge here, then magically hover in midair while I hand it over. If you want it, you either have to let me drop down onto the platform—or you'll have to get it out of my pocket yourself."

Esmerelda took a moment to consider her options.

"I don't have a whole lot of time for you to make a decision here," Charlie said. "My fingers are starting to slip."

This was the truth. Hanging from the spire wasn't

easy. Charlie's fingers were sweating and losing strength.

"I'll get it myself," Esmerelda announced. She took a step forward, over the coil of rope, keeping her gun trained squarely on Charlie's chest. "Don't try anything stupid," she warned, reaching for Charlie's pocket.

"I'm a genius," Charlie said. "Nothing I do is ever stupid."

And then she let go of the roof.

In most circumstances, this would have been a terrible idea. But Charlie had worked out the math.

Since the climbing rope was still tied to her harness, she didn't plummet, which was good—as plummeting from that height would have been deadly. Instead, the friction on the rope as it passed up through the carabiners and ran back down through the grotesques slowed her slightly. Instead of free-falling, she merely descended very fast, as though she were on a high-speed elevator.

At the same time, due to her weight, the other end of the rope snapped taut, cracking Esmerelda in the face. It scorched her cheek with a rope burn and knocked her backward. She stumbled over her own feet and dropped her gun. By the time she recovered her balance, Charlie had dropped out of view and the rope was quickly unspooling.

Esmerelda cursed and ran to the railing of the platform.

Eighty feet below her, Charlie alighted on the peak of the cathedral roof. The friction on the rope had slowed her just enough to make her landing bearable—although it wasn't pretty. The moment her feet touched down, her knees buckled and she fell backward onto her rear end. She nearly tumbled down the steeply slanted roof, but she managed to grab the railing for the stairs at the last second.

Charlie heaved a quick sigh of relief, thrilled that she wasn't dead, then snapped to her feet and ran back through the doorway into the attic space above the sanctuary, untying the rope from her harness as she ran.

High above, on the platform in the spire, Esmerelda recovered her gun, but Charlie had already disappeared into the safety of the church. Cursing again, she raced back down the rickety stairs as fast as she could, snapping her own phone out of her pocket as she did.

Thanks to the trick with the rope, Charlie had an extremely big head start on her. Too big to catch the girl herself.

It was a good thing she hadn't come alone.

"Paolo! Gianni!" she shouted in Italian. "She got the jump on me! Don't let her get away!"

Charlie raced through the attic space of the church, carabiners clanking on her climbing harness, then emerged into the large landing at the far end. From there, both bell towers had staircases that led back to the ground floor. Charlie opted for the one that she hadn't used before, because most people would have retraced their steps, and Charlie didn't like to act like most people. That was what your enemies would expect you to do, and Charlie now had enemies. Again.

Sure enough, when she exited the bell tower into the crowded foyer of the Basilica, she immediately noticed two men barging through the entrance near the other set of stairs. The men looked a great deal like Esmerelda, with similar narrow features. They were tall and menacing and had the same dark look in their eyes that Esmerelda had revealed while holding the gun. Charlie assumed they were her brothers.

One of them had a mop of dark hair, while the other's head was closely shaved. Baldy seemed to be the smarter of the two, as he was taking his time to scan the crowd, while Moptop simply barreled toward the stairs. Baldy immediately spotted her—he knew exactly who to look for—and yelled to his brother.

Charlie bolted for the closest exit. There were hundreds of people in her way—but there were even more people between her and the Castello brothers, which gave her an advantage. Plus, Charlie was thin and lithe and quick on her feet, allowing her to slip through the masses, while the thugs had to bulldoze their way through the crowd.

Esmerelda was far behind, only making her way through the attic space; it hadn't been easy to come down the rickety stairs from the spire in a hurry.

Charlie made it out the door of the Basilica and into the streets of Quito, though she had little faith that she would be able to outrun the Castellos. Luckily, she had made additional plans in case things went wrong.

On her visit to the sporting goods store the night before, Charlie had bought something besides climbing gear, something she had decided not to tell Esmerelda about: a mountain bike. It was secondhand and a bit banged up, but in good enough shape for her purposes. She had ridden it up here late the night before and locked it to a drainpipe in an alley across the street. It had been an ordeal to pedal up the steep hill—but going down it would be easy.

Many more people now lined the sidewalks in antici-pation of the procession; they already stood two and three deep. Charlie squeezed through them to get to the alley, unlocked the bike, put on the helmet she had left with it, then squeezed back through the crowds to the street again.

The brothers were out the door of the church and racing toward her—but now Charlie knew she would have no problem getting away. She gave them a taunting wave goodbye, took a moment to enjoy the stunned looks on their faces, then hopped on the bike and raced downhill, leaving her enemies far behind.

Or so she thought.

She had gone only a block when she noticed the black sedan racing up the hill, coming toward her and the Basilica. There were three men inside the car, but it was the one at the wheel who grabbed Charlie's attention.

It was the same man who had come to Puerto Villamil by speedboat the day before, looking for her.

He noticed her, too. He swerved across the street, trying to block her escape.

Charlie pedaled hard, slipping past the car at the last second. Its bumper kissed her rear tire, almost sending her flying, but she steadied herself and continued onward.

The black sedan pulled a quick U-turn, jumping the curb and making the spectators gathered on the sidewalk scatter. Then it came after her.

Charlie had expected that things might go wrong—but not *this* wrong. She had only planned to escape people on foot, not people in a car.

This wasn't going to be easy.

TEN

Charlie raced through the streets of downtown Quito, pedaling furiously while Ivan Spetz bore down on her.

Ivan hadn't been able to get on a plane out of the Galápagos until late the night before. By the time he arrived at the Iglesia de San Francisco, it was closed. So he had gotten a good night's sleep at a hotel and come back first thing in the morning, only to learn that the Devil's Stone was now in the spire at the Basilica. He had immediately headed that way, hoping to get there before Charlie—only to see his young adversary racing away from the cathedral like someone who had just made off with something very important. Now he floored the gas pedal and sped after Charlie through the city.

The streets were old and paved with stones, which rattled Charlie as she hurtled down them. Even worse, in preparation for the procession, they were empty of other cars. Barriers had been erected to keep out vehicles, but Ivan had simply ignored them in his haste to get to the Basilica. On the open streets, he was gaining on Charlie quickly.

So Charlie changed the game. When she reached the Plaza Grande in the center of town, she veered up onto the sidewalk.

The Plaza was thronged with people: Food vendors were selling fresh fruit and steaming bowls of fanesca; salesmen hawked leather goods and souvenirs; cucuruchos and other celebrants in costume headed to the start of the processional; and hundreds of locals and tourists were vying for a good spot to watch.

Charlie swerved through them all on her bicycle. She had to slow down considerably to avoid running into anyone—although she still clipped a few people and knocked one unfortunate tourist into the central fountain.

Ivan Spetz couldn't follow her though the crowds with his car. He had to go all the way around the plaza, while Charlie could cut right across it.

Charlie slalomed through a pack of tourists and emerged onto the far side of the plaza with a big lead on her pursuer . . . only to find another car barreling toward her. A silver sedan.

It appeared that whoever was after her had brought backup.

Charlie shot across the street, tucking into an alleyway as the silver sedan skidded past her. Then she pedaled with all her might.

Escaping one car on a bicycle would have been tricky, but *two* was going to be almost impossible.

Charlie had chosen a bicycle to escape for one main reason: She wasn't old enough to have a driver's license. There were some advantages to a bike; it was light and maneuverable and it could go places cars couldn't. But there was also a huge disadvantage: Charlie had to power it herself. Right now it was helpful that she had started high in a city that was built on a mountain, so she could head downhill, but she still had to pedal to do that, and after her adventure on the spire, her strength was already flagging.

She shot through a series of alleys, trying to pick routes too narrow for the cars to follow, but both drivers understood which way she was going. They were speeding down the streets on either side of her, keeping her boxed in. And they were gaining ground. Charlie caught glimpses of them every time she crossed a street.

So she changed her tactics again. The next time she entered an alley, she hit the brakes, skidding to a stop, then spun around, returned to the street she had just crossed, and cut down it, heading toward the street the black sedan was on. It took more energy to get the bike moving again, and her muscles screamed, but hopefully the sedans would keep going, not realizing she had changed course, and she would be able to escape.

Unfortunately, Ivan Spetz was onto her. He hit the brakes too and pulled a U-turn. The street was so narrow, he took out a fire hydrant, shearing it off the sidewalk. A geyser of water erupted in its place, but Ivan paid no attention.

When Charlie cut across the street he was on, she found him racing right back up it toward her.

Charlie gasped in surprise and forced herself onward. The black sedan fishtailed wildly around the corner and dropped in behind her, closing the gap between them quickly.

A park appeared up ahead, a plain of grass studded with palm trees. There were more tourists and cucuruchos crossing it, heading toward the procession.

Charlie leapt the curb and cut across the grass.

Ivan Spetz did the same.

But the park wasn't as crowded as the Central Plaza had been. The people in it saw the sedan bearing down on them and scrambled out of the way. Charlie had been hoping to gain ground on Ivan there, but she was actually losing it. The black sedan churned after her, flattening any obstacles in its path. It plowed through some decorative landscaping and sent a fruit cart flying, splattering mangos and melons.

Charlie was cruising on fumes now, her energy almost depleted.

She had one last trick up her sleeve, and it was going to be extremely risky.

The other side of the park was bordered by a major road, much bigger than the city streets she had been racing along, three lanes of traffic on each side, the cars moving at a good clip. Charlie watched them closely as she approached, assessing how fast they were moving, focusing on the gaps between them.

The numbers came to her.

She altered her direction slightly and pedaled with everything she had left.

The black sedan was almost on top of her.

Charlie fired across the sidewalk directly into traffic.

She had timed things to avoid the cars perfectly, entering just behind one set and shooting across before the next wave came.

Ivan Spetz had no such luck. His sedan was far too big to make it through the traffic. He punched the brakes as hard as he could, swerving wildly, and even then he still clipped two cars and sent them skidding. More cars crashed into those, and a traffic jam blossomed instantly.

Charlie cut across the next three lanes of traffic. On the far side of the road was one of the steep canyons that surrounded the city. It almost seemed to be from another time period, with a dirt trail running downhill between ramshackle huts, many of which had goats grazing in their yards. Charlie dropped onto the path and raced downward.

Behind her, Ivan's car was damaged but still drivable. Ivan hit the gas, leaving the traffic jam he had created behind, then sped onward. He watched Charlie drop into the ravine and veered onto the road that wound along the side of it.

Still, the course through the ravine was the much faster route out of the city. The road had to snake back and forth to descend the mountain, whereas the canyon path followed the slope directly. Charlie jounced down it, flying past homes and gardens and animal pens, dropping more than a thousand feet down from the city before she saw another road.

The ravine continued on the other side of it. Charlie was racing for it when she saw the silver sedan speeding down the road, heading right toward her.

She was so distracted by it, she didn't see the chicken until it was too late.

The bird dumbly wandered out of someone's front gate, right in front of her. Rather than plow over it, Charlie tried to avoid it, but her tires skidded in a patch of loose gravel. She caught her front tire on a root and upended, crashing down and tumbling through the dirt to the shoulder of the road.

The silver sedan braked directly beside her.

Charlie was badly banged up and exhausted and her bike had been mangled in the wreck. The frame was bent and the front tire had blown out. There was no way she was riding away and she was too wiped out to run.

All she could do was grimace and accept her fate.

And then she finally caught a glimpse of who was in the car.

It wasn't Ivan Spetz's men after all.

Dante Garcia was at the wheel, and Agent Milana Moon sat beside him.

Dante rolled down the window and shouted, "If you want to live through the next five minutes, then get in the car."

Charlie wasn't thrilled to see the CIA, but she was smart enough to understand the odds of survival.

She climbed into the back seat.

ELEVEN

lthough Esmerelda Castello had lied to Charlie
Thorne about many things, she had been honest
about working at the Darwin Research Station. She
had started there as a volunteer six years before,
although her real motivation, even then, was to track down
the mysterious treasure Charles Darwin had discovered.

The treasure was a Castello family obsession. Esmerelda had a distant ancestor who had been on the *Beagle*
with Darwin. After the voyage, the crew had been ordered
to never speak of certain things, but her ancestor had
hinted to his family that something incredible had been
found. Esmerelda knew that the story had probably been
twisted and embellished as it was passed down through
the generations, but it was evident that Darwin had found
something of great value in South America—and that the
discovery had been hushed up.

Esmerelda's father had devoted his life to unraveling the truth, a task that had consumed him. He had majored in anthropology, specializing in the cultures of South America, and that had given him access to many restricted texts. He had spent years poring over everything of Darwin's he could find, as well as the writings and journals of Captain FitzRoy and everyone else on the *Beagle* who had ever put a pen to paper. For the most part, he had come up empty, finding nothing but rumors that couldn't be verified. In the process, he had squandered his money, ruined his academic reputation, and destroyed his marriage.

But his children still loved him. Esmerelda fondly recalled how her father would tuck her into bed at night, telling her tales of the great treasure Darwin had found and how one day, he too would track it down. Not only would he find riches beyond her wildest dreams—but he would become famous as well, earning his place in the pantheon of great explorers. If Hiram Bingham had gained fame for simply stumbling across a remote outpost like Machu Picchu, imagine what would happen if he found a great city of gold!

When Esmerelda and her brothers grew older, her father had shown them the cache of information he had gathered: photocopies of Darwin's writings, notebooks filled with potential clues, even a few pages he had illegally torn from journals of sailors on the *Beagle*. Esmerelda's mother had angrily dismissed all of it as useless garbage amassed by an obsessive lunatic, but Esmerelda and her brothers were hooked.

Ultimately, her father's fascination had cost him his life. He was so busy trying to find Darwin's clues that he neglected his own health until it was too late. By the time he learned of his cancer, it was too far along, not that it would have mattered. He had no money to pay for treatment. He ended up decrepit and destitute, with nothing to show for all of his work . . .

Until the very end.

In the last days of his life, Esmerelda's father received a package. For years he had been trying to connect with other descendants of the crew of the *Beagle*, and he had come across a family in rural England who still had the letters that their great-great-great-grandfather had sent back home from the trip. Esmerelda's father had struck up a friendship over email, presenting himself as a historian interested in the untold tales of the crew on such a great voyage. The family had agreed to copy the letters for him, although with one thing or another they had kept forgetting about it, forcing Esmerelda's father to repeatedly send reminders. Finally, perhaps because they had realized how sick he was, they had forwarded them.

Esmerelda's father had spent his final days poring

over the communications, desperately searching for something of importance. And then, at the bottom of the pile, he had found it.

The last letter was merely a scrap. A remnant that had been damaged in a fire. The family apologized for the condition, thinking some ancestor or another had been careless with it, but when Esmerelda's father read the bit that remained, his conclusions were very different.

The letter began in midsentence, as though a previous page had been lost:

. . . *Master Darwin's discovery, of which I have written to you before. Darwin remains incensed at Captain FitzRoy as to how he handled it, and his behavior has been intolerable. He has blasphemed the captain and crew often and spent days at a time sulking in his cabin. Bos'n Jeffords says Darwin behaved even more strangely onshore in the Galápagos, repeatedly throwing lizards into the sea and etching nonsense into the shell of a live tortoise. But then, we have all been on edge since our hurried departure from Guayaquil. Captain FitzRoy's moods have also been erratic. He is friendly one day and monstrous the next. If he knew I was writing to you of all this, he'd give me the lash for sure. So I beg you to destroy . . .*

The rest of the letter was gone, charred to ash.

Esmerelda's father had called to her, demanding that she come to his bedside at once, then triumphantly displayed the letter when she arrived. "At long last!" he had crowed. "Proof!"

Esmerelda had spent enough time listening to her father and studying the voyage of the *Beagle* that she immediately knew what her father was responding to. There were three pieces of information in the scrap of paper that, as far as she knew, had only been speculation up until then:

First there was the reference to Darwin's discovery. Although Darwin had certainly made great discoveries on his voyage—discoveries that had altered the course of science—no one on the voyage itself had been aware of that at the time. Even Darwin himself hadn't realized what he had discovered for years afterward. For example, the Galápagos finches he had become renowned for noticing the differences between. Darwin hadn't even realized they were different varieties of finch, thinking them all to be entirely different species of bird, until he had returned to London and an ornithologist had shown him his error.

But this letter referred to a discovery of some sort— one that Captain FitzRoy had handled in a way that had greatly upset Darwin. It was well known to historians that FitzRoy and Darwin had not gotten along after their return to England, but no one was sure of the exact reason. If FitzRoy had forced Darwin to keep a great discovery a secret, that certainly would have explained the bad blood between them.

Next, there was the reference to the departure from Guayaquil. Until that point, there had been no documented evidence that the *Beagle* had ever visited mainland Ecuador at all.

And finally, there was the reference to Darwin's strange behavior on the Galápagos Islands. Darwin's throwing lizards into the sea was well documented. The world's only marine iguanas lived on the islands, and they had seen so few humans that they had no fear of them. (In fact, this remained the case in the modern day as well.) Darwin had famously thrown one into the sea, watched it swim right back to him, and had then thrown it in again several more times, fascinated by the behavior. He had also performed other odd experiments to show how docile the island's wildlife was, such as riding on a giant tortoise or shoving a hawk off the branch of a tree with the barrel of his gun.

But no one had ever mentioned him etching nonsense into the shell of a tortoise.

"I'll bet you it wasn't nonsense!" Esmerelda's father had exclaimed. "It was something about the treasure!"

"We don't know that for sure," Esmerelda had cautioned.

"What else could it be? Darwin was angry, not crazy! And he was brilliant! Perhaps this Jeffords only thought it was nonsense, but it was something else entirely! Something he couldn't understand!"

Esmerelda had many other questions, but her father had answers to all of them: Darwin had carved the clue in the tortoise because he was upset at FitzRoy for hiding his discovery and wanted others to find it. The letter had probably been burned on purpose to hide the evidence; the crewman who had written it had even left instructions to destroy it. People had always wondered why Darwin had spent so much of the final year of the *Beagle*'s voyage in his cabin, presuming it was seasickness, but being in a foul mood and angry at the captain and crew would have also explained it.

And as for the big question—What had Darwin found?—her father was emphatic. "Treasure! The Spaniards looted tons of gold from South America. More than any Europeans had ever seen in history! But no explorer could ever find the source of it. The natives wouldn't share that information. Darwin must have discovered it."

"But why would the sailors keep it a secret?" Esmerelda asked.

"So they could return and collect it for themselves.

The *Beagle* was a government ship. Anything they brought back on it would have been the property of the British government. And it was too small to haul a load of gold. The excess weight would have sunk it the moment they hit a storm."

"Then why didn't they go back?"

"Because Darwin and FitzRoy had a falling-out. Darwin was the only one who knew where the gold was. If he refused to go, then no one else could find it."

Although there was logic to her father's argument, Esmerelda had her doubts about it. But she believed Darwin had discovered *something* of great value, and her father's passion for finding it had kindled her own. She wanted to unravel the mystery herself—and garnering fame and fortune would be nice side benefits.

As they spoke, her father had suddenly begun gasping for breath, as if this burst of excitement had been too much for him. Esmerelda put her hand on his to calm him and felt his pulse racing like a rabbit's. "Father!" she had cried. "Are you all right?"

"I'm fine," he had insisted, and he'd meant it. Even though his body was failing, his final discovery had made him delirious with joy. "After all this time, here's proof that I wasn't crazy. Now you and your brothers can continue my work."

"You mean, go to the Galápagos?"

"Yes! Find what Darwin left on the tortoise! And then follow that to find what he discovered!"

Although Esmerelda was excited about the new clues, she considered telling her father that he was asking a tremendous favor from her. The Galápagos Islands were on the other side of the world. And for all she knew, the clue on the tortoise shell might not exist anymore. Or perhaps it had never existed at all.

But then her father clasped her hand. "Promise me," he gasped. "Promise me you will go."

Esmerelda could see in his eyes that the life was quickly fading from him. She couldn't deny the last wish of a dying man. "I promise," she said.

Her father managed a smile, which was the last thing he ever did.

So Esmerelda had headed to the Galápagos, motivated by the promise she had made, the desire to finish what her father had started, and the lure of fame and fortune.

Even so, she had never intended to stay as long as she had. She had expected to spend only a few weeks in the islands, perhaps a few months at most. But finding the tortoise shell Darwin had carved a message into had proved far more difficult than she had expected. And yet her father's passion for the hunt burned deep within her, too. With every day, she grew more determined to find Darwin's treasure, no matter the cost. She also became obsessed with it, reading everything she could about Darwin's life, poring over her father's notes time and again, chasing down every lead she could find in the islands.

She hid all this from everyone else at the Darwin Research Station, of course. Instead, she presented herself as an enthusiastic worker with no hidden agenda and quickly parlayed her volunteer position into a full-time job doing community outreach. But with each day, she grew more determined to find what Darwin was looking for, no matter what.

Meanwhile, her brothers had joined her in the islands. Paolo captained a scuba boat, while Gianni worked on a farm. Both helped Esmerelda with the family quest, although they knew she was the smart one and relied on her to find all the leads. They were only the muscle.

The difference, Esmerelda realized, was that they were happy with their lives in the Galápagos, while she was not.

She hated it there, out on the edge of the earth, so far from the things she loved, like art and culture and good food and wine. She missed the beauty of the Tuscan countryside, where she had grown up, and found the mostly barren volcanic landscapes of the islands to be ugly and depressing. She longed for concerts and soccer games. She found marine iguanas to be repulsive.

But she still couldn't bring herself to leave. She felt as though she had invested too much time to turn back, even though with all her searching she had come up empty. So she stuck it out, grinding out the days, pretending to be cheerful and happy at work when in reality she hated everything about the islands and couldn't wait for the day when she could leave it all behind.

And then, three days earlier, the clue she had sought for all those years had presented itself. A farmer had called the research station to report that an enormous tortoise on his property had died, and when the team brought it in for an autopsy, Darwin's engraving was discovered.

It had never occurred to Esmerelda to search the shells of tortoises that were living. Until that point, she had never realized that one Darwin had touched might still be alive. She had been searching for the shell of a dead tortoise.

Still, she was thrilled by the discovery—and then frustrated when she couldn't translate Darwin's code.

However, by that time she had learned of the girl on Isla Isabela who had a gift for codes. Esmerelda didn't want to waste another day in the islands, trying to crack a code when there was someone who could do it for her. So she had talked her boss into letting her borrow the research station's seaplane, then flown over to meet the girl. It had paid off better than she could have ever imagined.

Until the girl had dropped off the spire at the Basilica.

The most upsetting thing of all wasn't that the girl had

figured out a way to escape. It was that she hadn't seemed particularly surprised to find Esmerelda holding a gun on her. She'd even had a mountain bike at the ready to flee the scene—as if, somehow, she had been expecting all of this to happen.

Now she was gone, having left Paolo and Gianni in her dust. Which was certainly a problem.

But not an insurmountable one. Despite her escape, the girl had still done what Esmerelda had hoped she would do: She had found the next clue Darwin had left behind.

Another thing that Esmerelda had lied to the girl about was her rock-climbing ability. In truth, Esmerelda was an adept climber; it was one of the few passions she had that she could indulge in the Galápagos. She had simply felt she should let the girl take the risk of climbing the spire; plus, that had allowed Esmerelda the opportunity to ambush her.

So after the girl had escaped, Esmerelda had returned to the Basilica with Paolo, who belayed her while she climbed the spire and found what was etched in the Devil's Stone. Her first reaction was excitement to see that *something* was there, followed by dismay as she realized it was encoded, and using a far different code than the first clue she had encountered. But as she stared at the numbers that Darwin had etched into the stone so long ago, she was overcome by a new emotion: excitement.

Esmerelda knew how to crack this code. Her father had taught it to her when she was a little girl. He had been fascinated with codes and ciphers, always thinking that his quest for Darwin's treasure might eventually require knowing them. Therefore, Esmerelda could figure out where Darwin would be sending her next.

Of course, she wasn't going to crack the code right *then*. Not while she was clinging to a spire high above the rest of the city, where she was at risk of tumbling to her death.

She took out her phone and snapped dozens of pictures of the Devil's Stone, making sure that she had covered it from every angle, then climbed back down and quickly left the Basilica.

By now the Good Friday processional was underway, and downtown Quito was overrun with people. Esmerelda and her brothers had to shove their way through the crowds for a few blocks until they found a café quiet enough for them to examine the photos and think.

But first Esmerelda went to the bathroom to examine herself in the mirror. When Charlie had dropped off the spire, the climbing rope had hit Esmerelda in the face. The friction had left a burn mark across her cheek, which infuriated Esmerelda. She had no regrets about her vanity; she knew she was beautiful and that her beauty was an asset. Men and women often did things for her that they wouldn't do for someone less attractive. And now there was a blemish on her otherwise gorgeous face. It would heal, but it might take a week or two, drawing people's attention. Esmerelda hated the look of it and swore that if she ever ran into Charlie Thorne again, she wouldn't give the girl a chance to get the jump on her.

She then rejoined her brothers.

It took Esmerelda a little while to work the code out, but as she did, her excitement grew and grew. After all these years, she was finally making progress. She had the next step to finding Darwin's great treasure.

Although she worried that Charlie had also cracked the code. Given her gifts, it was a distinct possibility. But she was only a girl. A girl on her own. Even if she *did* know where Darwin said to go next, it wouldn't be easy for her to get there. Whereas Esmerelda could handle it. She didn't have tons of money, but she and her brothers had lived frugally during their years in the Galápagos and had amassed some savings. In addition, they weren't above breaking the law now and then if it furthered their interests.

Esmerelda checked her translation of Darwin's work several more times. She wasn't quite sure what it all meant, but she was sure she had it correct. And the first few lines made perfect sense, giving her explicit directions about how to begin her quest.

"Let's go," she told her brothers. "We need to find a plane."

TWELVE

Latitude 0

Just outside Quito, Ecuador

see you've gotten yourself into trouble again," Dante
Garcia told Charlie. "You're lucky we were here to
bail you out."

"I would have gotten away from them all just
fine if you hadn't come along and screwed up my escape
route," Charlie said petulantly. "I thought you were one
of them. How'd you even find me?"

She was standing directly on the equator. They were
a few miles outside Quito, at a roadside attraction, where
there were several busloads of tourists to blend in with.
The attraction was one of many in the area set on the
equator; an entire tourist industry in Ecuador was based
on standing on the exact line where the northern and
southern hemispheres met. Here, there was a wide stone
plaza with a thick red line that represented the equator
running straight through it. A thirty-foot-tall cylinder

marked 0 DEGREES LATITUDE stood in the direct center of the plaza. The tourists were from all over the world, and every single one of them was taking selfies with the cylinder in the background.

There were also three flea-bitten llamas for people to take selfies with.

Agent Milana Moon sat at the side of the plaza, keeping an eye on the entry for any sign of trouble, letting Dante and Charlie hash things out. In Charlie's experience, Milana rarely spoke unless she had to.

On the other hand, Dante often wouldn't shut up.

Charlie had an unusual relationship with Dante. Even though he was her half brother, he was sixteen years older than her and they had grown up on opposite ends of the country. They had met only four times in their lives, most recently when Dante had blackmailed her into helping him track down Pandora. Dante's leverage was that he knew Charlie had stolen more than forty million dollars from the Lightning Corporation. Charlie had argued that she never would have stolen the money if Lightning hadn't stolen something from her first, but Dante didn't see things that way. Dante tended to see things in black or white, good or bad, whereas Charlie felt that pretty much everything was gray.

For example, Dante had thought he was doing the right thing, blackmailing Charlie into helping the CIA find the equation. Charlie could respect that Dante's intentions might have been virtuous but thought that the way he had handled everything left a lot to be desired.

"Technically, I didn't find you," Dante admitted. "Ivan Spetz did. We were monitoring him."

"Who's Ivan Spetz?" Charlie asked.

Dante gave Charlie an incredulous look. "Ivan's the guy who was trying to turn you into roadkill back in Quito. You didn't know who he was?"

"All I knew was that he was after me. But in my hurry to get away from him, I didn't have time to ask for his ID."

"Ivan's SVR. And he wants Pandora."

"Oh. Just like you."

"No," Dante said, looking offended. "Ivan's not like me at all. If he gets his hands on you, he'll happily cause you a world of pain to get you to cough up Pandora. And once Russia has that information, they're not going to play nice with it. They're going to build weapons."

"That's funny," Charlie said. "As I recall, the USA was going to use Pandora to build weapons too."

"To keep the world safe!" Dante snapped.

"You want to keep the world safe?" Charlie asked. "There's only one way to do that. Keep Pandora locked away nice and tight. That's what Einstein did with it. Because he knew humans couldn't be trusted to do the right thing."

"That's what you were doing in the Galápagos? Keeping the world safe?" Dante asked sarcastically. "You weren't just surfing all day and squandering your potential again?"

Charlie stared bullets at him. "You think I *want* to live on the edge of the earth for the rest of my life? You think I *want* to be the only person alive who knows the most dangerous equation in human history? I was trying to stay away from the Ivan Spetzes of the world. Unfortunately, that seems to be impossible."

"I can help you protect it."

"How? By getting me to share it with the CIA? You might as well tweet it to the entire world. The more people who know about Pandora, the better the chance that it ends up in the wrong hands. People make mistakes. Or they do bad things on purpose."

"Not always."

"The agent who was assigned to find Pandora before you switched sides! And he was one of the best the CIA had! If he couldn't be trusted, then who can?"

Dante held his tongue, steaming mad. Although Charlie suspected he wasn't just mad at her; he was mad because he knew she was right. Or at least, she wasn't completely wrong.

"I hate to interrupt," Milana Moon said. She had approached so stealthily from where she had been sitting that Charlie hadn't even noticed her coming. "While this is definitely an important issue, there are more urgent things we need to discuss." She fixed her piercing gaze on Charlie. "What were you doing on the Basilica in Quito?"

Charlie wondered how long Dante and Milana had been watching her that day. "That was personal business."

"I'll give you a choice," Dante warned. "You can either tell us here—or in a detention cell at CIA headquarters. Which will it be?"

Charlie sighed heavily. "I was taking an architectural tour designed for adrenaline junkies. After this, we were going to hang glide over the Iglesia de San Francisco. . . ."

"Cuff her," Dante told Milana. "Let's see how funny she thinks all this is then."

Milana snapped a pair of handcuffs from her belt.

"Okay!" Charlie said quickly. "No more jokes. It turns out, Einstein wasn't the only great scientist who discovered something and kept it secret."

Dante and Milana exchanged a curious look.

It seemed to Charlie that neither was as surprised by this information as she would have expected.

"Who else did?" Dante asked. "And what did they find?"

"Charles Darwin discovered a treasure of some sort

in South America. I don't know much more than that. The information I have about it is pretty limited."

Dante said, "And how did you find out about it?"

Charlie explained everything: Esmerelda, the legend of Darwin's discovery, the first clue on the tortoise shell, escaping Ivan in Puerto Villamil, the Devil's Stone, Esmerelda's betrayal at the Basilica. Dante repeatedly tried to interrupt, but Charlie cut him off each time. Finally, she got to the part where Ivan had ambushed her and concluded, "I guess you know the rest."

By this point, Dante had so many questions, he wasn't sure where to start. The first thing that jumped to his mind was "You had a bicycle standing by just in case this Esmerelda turned on you?"

"Yes."

"How did you know that you couldn't trust her?"

"That's easy," Charlie said. "I don't trust *anybody*."

Dante frowned at that, like it was a personal affront.

Milana said, "Can we see your photos of the code Darwin left on the Devil's Stone?"

Charlie took her phone from her pocket. The glass had cracked at some point while she was fleeing from her various enemies, probably when she had wiped out to avoid the chicken. She brought up the best photo and handed the phone over so the others could see it:

21343131345244231533113534422451154 2

15114344214234321334131121344244153314115443

45334424314423155211441542444542334 3
44341231343414

44231533212433144423154442151 5
124524314431242515

25243322431334313115221513231135153 1

Milana pondered it for a few seconds, then said, "It's a box code."

Charlie looked to her, impressed. "You know about those?"

"We're in the CIA," Dante said. "Codes come up pretty often."

"And yet you all got stymied by Einstein's cipher."

"This is different," Dante said gruffly. "We know about box codes. This message only uses five digits, and the only way you can use the same five digits to encode the entire alphabet is to use a box."

That wasn't quite right, but Charlie didn't bother to contradict her brother. "Pretty much."

Dante had a pen and a scrap of paper on him. He

found a place to sit and drew a five-by-five grid with the numbers one through five along each side. Then he placed the letters A through Z in the boxes, skipping J, because there were only twenty-five boxes and twenty-six letters, and J was usually the one that was skipped in codes like this. J had been the last letter added to the alphabet, in 1524; up until that point, it had been interchangeable with the letter I, which had been used for both sounds.

	1	2	3	4	5
1	A	B	C	D	E
2	F	G	H	I	K
3	L	M	N	O	P
4	Q	R	S	T	U
5	V	W	X	Y	Z

With that, it was relatively easy to see which number combination stood for each letter: 11 was A, while 12 was B, and so on.

Dante began meticulously transcribing the code, looking back and forth from the photos to the grid he had drawn, but wrote only a few letters before he stopped and turned to Charlie. "You already know what this says, don't you?"

"Yes. I translated it in the car."

Dante narrowed his eyes. "Why didn't you tell us that?"

"I thought you wanted to impress Milana with your code-cracking skills."

Dante reddened from embarrassment, the way he always did when Charlie brought up his attraction to Milana. Then he quickly changed the subject. "So what does it say?"

To translate the code, Charlie had merely imagined the grid that Dante had drawn. In her mind, the solved code looked something like this:

```
F  O  L  L  O  W  T  H  E  N  A  P  O  R  I  V  E  R
21 34 31 31 34 52 44 23 15 33 11 35 34 42 24 51 15 42

   E  A  S  T  F  R  O  M  C  O  C  A  F  O  R
   15 11 43 44 21 42 34 32 13 34 13 11 21 34 42
            T  E  N  D  A  Y  S
            44 15 33 14 11 54 43


U  N  T  I  L  T  H  E  W  A  T  E  R  T  U  R  N  S
45 33 44 24 31 44 23 15 52 11 44 15 42 44 45 42 33 43
```

```
    T O B L O O D
44 34 12 31 34 34 14


T H E N F I N D T H E T R E E
44 23 15 33 21 24 33 14 44 23 15 44 42 15 15
    B U I L T L I K E
    12 45 24 31 44 31 24 25 15


K I N G S C O L L E G E C H A P E L
25 24 33 22 43 13 34 31 31 15 22 15 13 23 11 35 15 31
```

Charlie told them what it said.

Dante frowned in response. "Water that turns to blood?" he asked, confused. "And a tree that looks like King's College Chapel? What on earth does that even mean?"

"I don't know," Charlie answered, even though she had a very good idea what Darwin meant. "But the part of the clue that tells us where to start is pretty straightforward. Maybe we'll figure out what the rest means en route."

"En route?" Dante repeated. "You think we're going after this thing?"

"You don't want to?" Charlie asked. "It's another discovery made by a really smart guy. I'm sure all your buddies at the CIA would love for you to track it down and see if we can make a weapon out of it."

"I highly doubt that Darwin discovered a weapon," Dante said dismissively.

"Well, he still discovered *something*," Charlie replied. "And we know where the starting point to search for it is. The Napo River is a tributary of the Amazon that begins not too far from here. The three of us could go find this treasure."

Dante scratched his chin, mulling this over.

"C'mon," Charlie teased. "It'll be just like old times. The three of us will have an adventure, solve some clues, find a treasure. Maybe some bad guys will even try to kill us again."

In truth, Charlie wasn't thrilled about bringing the CIA into the hunt for Darwin's discovery, but she had done the math. She had a far better chance of locating it with Dante and Milana than she did without them.

First of all, it would be a difficult solo voyage. Charlie had enough money and intelligence to get by in civilization, but whatever Darwin had found was out in the Amazon, one of the last great stretches of wilderness left on earth. Money wouldn't mean anything out there, and her intelligence told her it would be suicidal to attempt a trip that dangerous on her own.

Then, there were other people in the mix. She had ditched Esmerelda, but that didn't mean Esmerelda was out of the game. The Devil's Stone was still atop the

Basilica. Esmerelda could translate it and pick up the trail again. Charlie wasn't completely sure what Darwin's treasure was, but she suspected that if Esmerelda—or anyone else—found it first, that would be a bad thing.

Plus, Ivan Spetz was after her. If the Russian agent had the smarts to track her down in Isla Isabela and again in Quito, he might be able to track her into the Amazon as well.

Finally, Charlie was a girl. Though she hated to admit it, in most of the world, women got treated far worse than men did. Having Dante along would make things easier.

Charlie wanted to find what Darwin had discovered. She had been bored much of her time in Puerto Villamil. Her mind had barely been challenged. She had stayed offline to protect herself, so she'd had almost no contact with the outside world. And her only mental stimulation had been the books and puzzles she had scrounged. Now she felt alive again, intrigued by the thrill of matching wits with another great thinker and uncovering his secret. She had sequestered herself at the edge of civilization in an attempt to keep Pandora safe. Since that had failed, she might as well embrace life again.

She knew Dante wanted to go after the treasure too, even though he was acting like he didn't. She wasn't quite sure how to read Milana yet, but she had the sense that Milana was at least intrigued by the prospect.

Luckily, Charlie knew how to put them over the edge.

"Do this with me," she said, "and I'll give you Pandora."

An enormous grin spread across Dante's face. "Sounds good to me," he said. "Let's go to the Amazon."

THIRTEEN

Ivan Spetz knew how to track people.

He had found the wreckage of the mountain bike near the road where it crossed the ravine, but Charlie was gone. Footprints led through the dirt to the shoulder, the right print slightly lighter than the left, as if the girl had gotten banged up and was favoring one leg. Then they vanished. Which meant she had gotten into a car. Ivan would have bet several million dollars it was the silver car that had also been chasing her through the city.

There was no sign of a struggle. The girl had gotten in of her own free will.

So she had friends.

The car had a good head start on Ivan. Two or three minutes would have been more than enough. He wasn't going to catch up to them.

But there were other ways to figure out where they had gone.

He returned to Quito. The Good Friday procession had begun, so the streets were impassable, meaning he had to park on the outskirts of town and walk back to the Basilica, where he knew the Devil's Stone was now located.

In Ivan's experience, people rarely looked up. They kept their heads down, looking at the road in front of them. Or even more often, they were looking at their phones. They barely noticed what was going on directly around them, let alone high above their heads.

That was the case now. Though there were tens of thousands of people in the streets, they were all watching the procession, or talking to their friends, or getting food from vendors. No one but him seemed to notice that there was a woman perched on the spire of the Basilica.

Ivan always carried a small pair of binoculars. Now he studied the woman through them. He instantly recognized her as the woman from the Darwin Research Station, the one whose photo he had stolen: Esmerelda Castle, who, he had learned with a little bit of research, was really Esmerelda Castello from Siena, Italy. She was roped to the spire, and another person who looked enough like her to be her brother was belaying her from below.

As Ivan watched, Esmerelda began rappelling down the spire. She had a satisfied look on her face, as though she was pleased with how things were going.

Ivan went to the doors of the church and blended into the crowd until he saw Esmerelda come out. She and her brother joined a third person, obviously yet another brother, and worked their way through the crowds, heading across the city to a café.

The Castello family were not professional spies. They were amateurs. None of them noticed Ivan following them, even though he wasn't bothering to stay hidden. It didn't seem to occur to any of them that someone might want to be following them at all.

Similarly, they didn't take any notice of Ivan when he sat down in the café two tables away from them, well within earshot. By now they were focused on what they had found atop the Basilica. Another of Darwin's clues.

They spoke in Italian. Ivan wasn't fluent in Italian, but it was a romance language, like Spanish and Portuguese, so he could follow most of what they were saying. He overheard them express excitement about the first part of the clue, how they were supposed to start down the Napo River from Coca, and confusion about the second part, finding a river that turned to blood and a tree that looked like King's College Chapel.

Ivan had no idea what that meant either.

Once they had figured out the clue, the Castellos quickly paid their check, preparing to leave.

Ivan considered his options.

It wouldn't be hard to follow them out of the café, wait until they got away from the crowds, and kill them all. Even though the Castello boys were big and tough and Esmerelda looked like she could handle herself in a fight, they would be no match for Ivan, who had been trained to kill people in a variety of ways.

But killing people was always messy. You either had to get rid of the bodies, which was time-consuming, or you had to leave them, which would attract the notice of the police.

Plus, even though Ivan didn't want anyone getting to the treasure before him, he wasn't concerned about rivals. Not at this point in the game. Sometimes you could get your rivals to do your work for you, the way he had just let the Castellos take all the risk to find the Devil's Stone and do all the work of translating it.

So, as the Castellos got up from their table, Ivan got up too. When Paolo went to the bathroom, Ivan "accidentally" bumped into him, swiping his mobile phone. Then he acted like he was on his way to the bathroom as well, but he graciously allowed Paolo to use the restroom first. While the idiot was in there, Ivan popped the back off the phone, slipped a tracking device inside, and then reassembled it. The entire process took thirty-two seconds.

Paolo took three minutes in the bathroom, so Ivan had to stand around, twiddling his thumbs, until he came back out. When he did, Ivan deftly slipped the phone back into his pocket.

He didn't bother following the Castellos after that. He already knew where they were going, and thanks to the tracker, he would know if they changed their plans.

In the meantime, he had his own travel arrangements to make.

Over his many years in South America, Ivan had spent a good amount of time in the Amazon. While he was excited by the thought of tracking down this treasure and finding Charlie Thorne again, he wasn't thrilled to be heading back into the wilderness. The Amazon could be a nasty, miserable, and dangerous place. There were a million ways to die in it. He needed to be prepared.

If there really was something hidden in the Amazon, it wasn't going to be easy to find. But Ivan Spetz was determined to beat the competition and find it.

And then he'd deliver Charlie Thorne to the SVR.

PART TWO
THE END OF THE AMAZON

Among the scenes which are deeply impressed on
my mind, none exceed in sublimity the primeval
forests undefaced by the hand of man.
—CHARLES DARWIN,
Voyage of the *Beagle*

FOURTEEN

The Amazon rain forest is the most diverse ecosystem on earth.

Three square acres of it could contain more than seven hundred and fifty types of tree—which was more types than existed in all of North America. A single Amazonian pond had been found to harbor more species of fish than lived in all of Europe, a single forest preserve in Peru had more species of birds than there were in all of the United States, and a single tree had been found to host more species of ants alone than lived in all the British Isles. Scientists hadn't even come close to cataloging all the varieties of life. It was said that if you picked a tree in the Amazon at random and examined all the insects living in it, at least one would be new to science.

The reason for this incredible array of diversity was the Amazon River itself. While it was slightly shorter than the Nile, it was by far the biggest and widest river on earth. At the point where it reached the ocean, it could be two hundred to three hundred miles wide, depending on the season, and even a thousand miles upstream, it was seven miles across. It had eleven hundred tributaries, seventeen of which were over a thousand miles long. Nearly two-thirds of all the liquid fresh water on earth at a given time was in the Amazon.

This, in turn, was due to the unique geography of South America. Unlike other continents, South America's mountains were clustered on one side, clinging to the western shore. The Andes created what was known as a rain shadow, catching the clouds that blew west across South America, so that almost all the rain fell on their eastern slopes. (The Pacific side of the Andes was so dry that there were some places where it had never rained in recorded history.) Thus, a staggering amount of water funneled into the Amazon basin—and then took its time getting to the ocean, because in addition to being incredibly large, the basin was also incredibly flat.

From the Peruvian border to the Atlantic Ocean, the Amazon descended only two hundred and fifty feet, which was less than the height of a good-size tree. Instead of flowing quickly downstream, all the water spread out across the basin, nurturing the ecosystem and giving rise to the extremely abundant array of life. The level of water fluctuated greatly throughout the year, with massive sections of the forest flooding for a few months, then slowly drying out, then flooding again.

Normally, April would have been the tail end of the floods, but there had been an unusually rainy wet season, and as Charlie, Dante, and Milana headed along the Napo tributary, the river was as high as anyone could remember. In the town of Coca, where they had flown from Quito, the river had burst its banks and the streets were filled with so much water that residents were using motorboats to navigate them, rather than cars.

It was more than twenty-three hundred miles to get from where Charlie was to the mouth of the Amazon, and yet the river here was so wide—even in a non-flood year—that it was more than a mile across. It was big enough that both Ecuador and Peru maintained navies on it.

Not surprisingly, the standard way to travel through the Amazon basin was by boat. A great swath of the rain forest didn't have a single road; from Coca, the locals traveled along the Napo in water buses, old cargo boats that had been crudely refurbished for passengers. They were slow, aging tubs that belched diesel smoke. The operators did not appear to be paying much attention to safety; Charlie thought that many boats appeared to be dangerously overloaded with passengers, who sat on every available space, including the roofs.

The tourists, being wealthier, were traveling along the Napo in slightly better style: long motorboats with several rows of seats and green canopies to block the sun or rain. Dozens of these were ferrying people up and down the Napo River, to camps or lodges located deeper in the rain forest.

But Charlie and her team felt that even these were too slow for their purposes. Dante wanted to conduct the mission as quickly as possible, so he had tracked down the fastest boat he could find, a relatively new motorboat that had been impounded from drug runners by the local police. It had dual 750-horsepower outboard motors and a small cabin for sleeping and cooking. The CIA had a long history in South America—for better *and* worse— and Dante was able to work some connections to get the police to rent it to him for a reasonable price. Meanwhile, Charlie and Milana had visited an adventure outfitter and stocked up on food and survival gear.

While doing this, Charlie had tried to strike up a conversation with Milana. "So," she'd asked, "what have you been up to since betraying my trust a few months ago?"

Milana had given her a cold stare that said she didn't think this was funny. "Our official CIA activity is classified."

"What about your unofficial activities, then? Has Dante worked up the nerve to ask you out yet?"

Milana gave Charlie another cold stare, but this time Charlie detected a hint of amusement in it. "That's also classified," Milana said.

That was all Charlie could get out of her. Milana remained stoic throughout the rest of the shopping excursion, save for detailing things like how many mangos they should buy.

Milana stayed silent for most of the trip down the Napo too. While Dante drove the boat, Milana sat at the bow, vigilantly scoping out their surroundings. She reminded Charlie somewhat of a watchdog on the alert at the front window of its house.

It had not been hard for Charlie to deduce that her half brother had a crush on Milana. And she understood why: Milana was smart and capable and beautiful. A Native American, she had grown up on the Blackfoot Reservation in Montana, earned a full scholarship to college, then had been recruited to the CIA and had excelled there. Charlie was less sure how Milana felt about Dante. She figured most women would consider Dante a good catch, as he was intelligent, accomplished, and handsome. But she presumed that Dante would never act on his crush, as his loyalty was to his job first, and dating your fellow agent probably wasn't allowed in the CIA.

Still, like most younger sisters, Charlie loved teasing her older brother about his love life. In truth, Charlie loved teasing Dante about everything she could.

He was so earnest and dutiful, it was easy to get under his skin.

Charlie sat down beside him on the pilot deck. They were half an hour downriver from Coca, and there were only a few clouds in the bright-blue sky above them. The river was the color of hot cocoa, due to all the sediment in it, and the forest was a fringe of green along each bank. It was warm and humid, but due to their speed, there was a nice breeze.

Dante was dressed for maximum protection against the blazing sun, wearing pants, a long-sleeved button-down shirt, and a hat with a wide, floppy brim. Everything was the exact same color of khaki. He was also slathering sunscreen on the few bits of skin that were still exposed. He had so much on, his face had a pale white sheen.

Meanwhile, Charlie was only wearing shorts, a T-shirt, and a baseball cap, enjoying the feel of the sun and the breeze on her skin.

"You don't have to put on quite so much sunblock," Charlie told him. "There are vampires who are less concerned about sunburn than you."

"There's no such thing as being too cautious with your health," Dante replied. "You ought to be covering yourself more."

"I want to get a little sun."

"It's not just sun that you should be concerned about here. Do you know what the most dangerous animal in the Amazon is?"

"Of course. The mosquito. Which is technically the most dangerous animal on earth."

"Right. At least a million people a year die from their bites, mostly in the tropics, which is where we are right now."

"I've had all my shots."

"That's not enough."

"I'll cover myself more once we're out of the breeze and in the rain forest," Charlie said. "Although the people in town said mosquitoes aren't much of a problem right now. They breed when the water is low and stagnant, not when it's high. The locals said the much bigger concern is anacondas."

Dante gave her a sideways glance. "Anacondas?"

"They're good swimmers. So when the water gets high, they expand their hunting grounds in a big way. They've been swimming through the streets of Coca, snatching dogs and chickens."

"But not people," Dante said, sounding slightly worried, like he was trying to convince himself of this.

"Not yet," Charlie said ominously. "Although there are rumors of some enormous ones deeper in the Amazon that have eaten humans. And of course, there's also piranhas. They've been known to reduce an entire adult man to nothing but bones within seconds."

Dante had heard this before and was pretty sure that Charlie was only saying it to unnerve him. "I think that's an exaggeration."

Charlie shrugged. "It's still probably best to stay out of the water. The candiru fish are probably worse than the piranhas anyhow."

"Candiru fish?"

"It's this really tiny relative of the catfish that can swim up your urethra, lodge itself there, and then devour you from the inside."

Dante reflexively put a protective hand over his crotch. "That's not a real thing."

"Yes it is. You've never heard of it? I thought the CIA gave you survival training."

"I trained for the desert. Because I was stationed in the Middle East. And I trained for the tundra in Russia. But I've never had any training for the rain forest." Dante had his phone out now, trying to look up the candiru fish, although the coverage was already getting spotty as they left civilization behind.

"So you don't know about bullet ants, either?"

Dante looked up from his phone, concerned. "No."

"Oh. You should. They're about an inch long and they have the most painful sting of any insect. They got their name because getting stung by one feels like being hit with a bullet. Supposedly, you're almost crippled by pain for twenty-four hours."

"You're making this up," Dante said.

"She's not," Milana said from the front of the boat.

"She's not?" Dante echoed, now sounding extremely worried.

"One of the people I trained with got stung by a bullet ant on a mission," Milana reported. "He said it was *worse* than being shot. It was the most painful thing he'd ever experienced in his life."

Dante looked as though he might have gone slightly pale with fear, although Charlie couldn't quite tell because of all the sunblock on his face. He said, "So there are ants out here with the most painful sting imaginable and giant snakes and man-eating piranhas and tiny fish that can swim into your private parts and consume you from the inside. Is there anything else completely horrifying that I should know about?"

"Brazilian wandering spiders," Charlie said. "Electric eels. Giant centipedes. Jaguars. Assassin bugs. There's also a couple dozen venomous snakes. . . ."

"And caimans," Milana added.

"Oh right!" Charlie exclaimed. "I totally forgot about those."

"What are caimans?" Dante asked.

"Relatives of crocodiles," Charlie explained. "Also known to attack humans on occasion."

Dante grimaced and noticed Charlie laugh in response. "This mission just keeps sounding better and better," he grumbled.

Charlie's laughter suddenly faded as she noticed something on the bank of the river. "To be honest," she said somberly, "all these things aren't nearly as dangerous to us as we are to them."

Dante and Milana followed Charlie's gaze.

An oil refinery sat on the river's edge. A great swath of vegetation had been scraped away around it, leaving only barren dirt. Its four oil derricks were pumping furiously, and thick, black smoke belched from its stacks. A steel dock extended into the Napo, where oil trucks rolled onto wide, flat barges for delivery downriver. Garbage lined the bank and bobbed in the water by the refinery: rusted sheets of metal, truck tires, bits of plywood, and hundreds of empty plastic soda bottles.

Given how big the Amazon basin was, Charlie had been shocked to see how far humans had encroached into it. All around Coca, the forests had been leveled and replaced with palm oil plantations and cattle fields, and ever since they had left the city, construction projects had dotted the banks of the river. In addition, they had passed dozens of barges hauling construction supplies, dump trucks, bulldozers, cranes, and other heavy machinery.

Charlie had heard that an area the size of Connecticut was being destroyed every year in the Amazon basin. Now she was seeing it with her own eyes. She couldn't help but feel that she was witnessing the end of the Amazon . . . that someday soon none of it would be left.

Milana nodded toward the refinery. "Considering that, we might have an issue with our treasure hunt here. Darwin told us to find a tree that looks like King's College Chapel . . ."

"Whatever that means," Dante interjected.

". . . but he wrote this clue well over a hundred and fifty years ago," Milana continued. "What's the chance that this tree hasn't been cut down?"

Charlie had already thought of this. "I don't know," she conceded.

"For that matter," Milana added, "it could have fallen over. Or caught fire. Or just died of old age."

"If it's the kind of tree that I think it is," Charlie answered, "then there's a very good chance it's still around."

Dante looked to her curiously. "You know what Darwin's talking about here?"

"I have a pretty good idea."

"Why don't you share that with us?"

Before Charlie could respond, she heard the sound of an airplane approaching. She looked back over her shoulder in the direction they had come from. A seaplane was heading their way.

Charlie had seen only a few planes since they had started down the river, but those had been much higher up. This one was staying quite low over the river, maybe five hundred feet tops.

"That plane's coming in awfully low," she observed. "Planes usually fly higher because it's more fuel efficient."

"Maybe they're tourists," Dante said, although he was watching the plane cautiously now as well. "If they're sightseeing, the view is better if you're low."

"Maybe they're looking for *us*," Charlie said. "I don't know if your buddy Ivan Spetz knows how to fly a plane, but Esmerelda does."

Milana climbed up onto the pilot deck from the bow, keeping her eyes locked on the plane as well.

The plane dipped downward.

"They're coming toward us," Charlie observed, concern in her voice.

"They might just be coming in for a landing," Milana said.

"On the exact stretch of river where we are?" Charlie asked doubtfully. "Right now?"

"Coincidences occur all the time," Dante said.

"There's no such thing as coincidence," Charlie replied.

Dante yanked on the steering wheel, making the boat veer suddenly.

Which turned out to be a shrewd move, because in the very next second, someone in the plane started shooting at them.

FIFTEEN

Esmerelda knew there were disadvantages to having a plane in the Amazon. It wasn't nearly as versatile as a boat. A small enough boat could go almost anywhere in the Amazon basin during the flood season, whereas a plane could only go where it could land. There were very few airstrips in the basin, and a seaplane had to land on a long, open stretch of water. Plus, a plane could carry far less weight than a boat, which meant fewer supplies and provisions—especially when two of your three passengers were big, hulking men like her brothers.

But a plane was much faster than a boat. And Esmerelda knew the others were ahead of her, which meant she had to make up time.

Also, a plane had the upper hand in battle. Especially when the other side wasn't expecting to be attacked.

There weren't very many seaplanes with artillery to

begin with, and Esmerelda hadn't expected to find one in a small outpost like Coca, so she had been forced to improvise. In a town on the edge of wilderness, it was never that hard to find weapons. Paolo and Gianni had tracked down a low-rent arms dealer who had a surprising array of weaponry, thanks to the continuous drug wars waging in South America. They had picked up two submachine guns, plenty of ammunition—and a few sticks of dynamite.

Esmerelda had taken a picture of Charlie with her phone, and it didn't take much asking around before she learned that the girl had arrived with two other people and acquired a speedboat. It also hadn't been hard to find her boat on the river, as it was the fastest-moving craft out there.

Esmerelda had hoped to attack with the element of surprise, but figured that was a distant hope at best. Charlie was unusually intelligent, and there wasn't any way to keep her approach in an airplane a secret. Still, she had given it a shot.

The old seaplane was made for low-altitude travel, so the windows could be opened. If you really wanted to take a chance, you could even open the doors in flight and step out onto the pontoons. But for the time being, Paolo and Gianni had simply aimed the semiautomatics out the windows while Esmerelda came in low with the sun behind her, just like the kamikazes did in World War II.

But her target veered away from her at the last instant. Her brothers' bullets only hit the water. Gianni got caught up in the excitement and lobbed a stick of dynamite as well. If the boat had stayed on track, he would have blown it to bits, but it swerved once again and his toss went wide, resulting in a blast that kicked up a geyser of water.

Esmerelda flew past the boat, then hooked around to come in for another attack. She might not have caught them by surprise, but she still had the advantage. There was no cover for them out on the big, wide river.

They were sitting ducks.

"That was a freaking stick of dynamite!" Charlie exclaimed.

The blast had been close enough that she, Dante, and Milana had been soaked by the plume of water. Some very stunned fish were flopping around on the deck of their boat.

"Nice friends you have there." Dante veered toward the nearest bank of the river. "They're coming back. Our only hope is to get to shore and seek cover."

Charlie gauged the distance to shore and calculated it would still take nearly a minute to get there. "It's too far! And they'll still be able to drop dynamite on us!"

"You have a better plan?" Dante demanded.

Charlie quickly took in her surroundings. They were badly exposed, way out in the open on the big, wide river. However, not far ahead of them was a barge carrying two oil tanker trucks.

"In fact, I do," Charlie said. "Get me to that barge!"

Dante saw where she was looking. "No way. If they hit any of those trucks, we'll be incinerated in seconds!"

The seaplane was coming back.

"I don't have time to explain everything!" Charlie yelled over the speedboat's motors. "Just get to the barge!"

"It's too dangerous," Dante told her.

Charlie screamed in frustration, exasperated by her half brother. She knew he was never going to listen to her—so she took matters into her own hands. As the seaplane swooped around for another pass, she ran across the pilot deck and dove into the Amazon.

"The girl just went into the river!" Gianni announced. He was keeping an eye on the boat while Esmerelda focused on the controls.

She came around, seeing the river laid out ahead of her. Sure enough, there were only two people standing on the pilot deck of the speedboat now. "Where is she?"

Gianni squinted at the water. He couldn't see anything in the dark-brown murk, and now they were flying toward the sun, so the reflection off the surface was blinding. "I don't know! But she dove off to the right!"

Esmerelda didn't have much time to weigh her options. In the single day she had known Charlie, she had learned that the girl was smarter than just about anyone she had ever met, perhaps smarter than *everyone*. So it was possible that she had a plan of some sort.

Then again, Charlie was still young. Maybe she had simply panicked. Or maybe she had decided to abandon the speedboat before someone dropped a stick of dynamite directly on it.

Esmerelda didn't know who the people on the boat with Charlie were, but she suspected that they needed Charlie to find Darwin's treasure. Therefore, taking out Charlie was still the priority.

But at the moment, she had no idea where Charlie *was*. So she decided to focus on the boat. If they destroyed it, Charlie would be stranded. Then they could take their time to track her down. Or they could just abandon her here. Or who knows, maybe the girl would get eaten by a caiman.

So Esmerelda aimed toward the speedboat and directed her brothers, "Blow that thing out of the water."

Despite all the dangerous animals that Charlie had told her brother about, she wasn't particularly concerned about any of them. It would certainly be bad to run into a full-grown caiman or a school of piranhas while swimming in the river, but as far as she knew, the chances of that were extremely slim—and even then she probably wouldn't be attacked. Animals rarely killed humans. *Humans* killed other humans. In fact, this was the second time today someone had tried to kill her.

The murky water hid her from the airplane, but on the other hand, she couldn't see a darn thing. Just below the surface, she could barely see her hand in front of her face; three feet down, everything was black. But she didn't want to surface, because then the Castellos might spot her, so she held her breath as long as she could and swam in the direction of the barge.

Although she couldn't see anything, she could still hear what was happening. Sound carried far better through water than it did through air. So she could pick up the slow rumbling of the barge's motor in the distance, the loud whir of the speedboat's motors closer by, and the thrum of the seaplane's propellers as it came closer.

Something skipped through the water close to Charlie. A bullet, she figured. A shot that had come dangerously close.

And then there was a loud, concussive blast, followed by a shock wave that rippled past her. That was followed by more motion, a large school of fish that had been startled and fled.

They had dropped another stick of dynamite.

Charlie risked surfacing again. She desperately needed air—and she wanted to see what had happened.

The plane was racing away, having made another pass, and the speedboat was still all in one piece.

But Esmerelda and her brothers probably had more dynamite, and it was only a matter of time before they hit their mark.

Charlie had been swimming along the perfect vector, though. The barge was bearing down on her.

While the plane was still going the other way, Charlie swam as hard as she could across the surface of the river, hoping she was right and that her plan would work.

Dante was doing everything he could to keep from getting killed, weaving back and forth across the river in an unpredictable serpentine pattern, while trying to keep an eye out for Charlie, too. His plan to head for shore had been dashed when his bullheaded sister had impetuously jumped off the boat. He didn't want to leave her behind—but he didn't want to run over her and slice her up with the outboard motors, either.

Beside him, Milana had her gun out, ready to fire on the approaching plane, but she wasn't firing, because they couldn't afford to waste ammunition. They had only packed a few clips and there weren't going to be gun stores in the Amazon. They had expected they might encounter trouble—but not an aerial assault. So Milana kept her eyes locked on the plane as it approached, waiting for her best shot.

It wasn't going to be easy to hit her target, given that the boat was skimming along the river and Dante was changing direction every few seconds and the plane now had the sun behind it again. Still, Milana was as good a shot as there was in the CIA, and part of being a good shot meant being patient and waiting for the right moment.

The plane came in low. One man hung out the door, one foot on the pontoon, firing with his submachine gun. A line of bullets stitched across the water, just missing them as Dante juked the boat to the right.

Milana saw her opportunity and seized it, squeezing off a few quick shots.

Not all of them hit, but one struck the engine housing, one webbed the windshield, and one caught the guy on the pontoon in the arm, making him drop the machine gun, which plunked into the river.

The engine coughed smoke, but the plane kept flying. And the other guy, the one still inside the plane, dropped a stick of dynamite as they zoomed overhead.

The dynamite bounced off the pilot deck on the boat.

Milana kicked it, a perfect free-kick shot from her days playing high school soccer. It sailed off the boat and exploded a second later, close enough to knock her and Dante off their feet. A piece of red-hot shrapnel nicked her arm, while others whistled past her head, but they were otherwise all right.

For now, at least. "That was way too close," Milana said.

Dante nodded agreement, but he didn't know what else he could do. He had no other defense against the seaplane.

Where on earth was Charlie?

As the barge plowed past her, Charlie grabbed the side and struggled to pull herself aboard.

It was harder than she had expected. The swim had taken a lot out of her, and the current was trying to drag her under the boat. Her muscles screamed as she clambered up and flopped onto the deck of the barge, gasping for air. The deck was filthy and reeked of oil fumes, but every part of her exhausted body wanted to just lie there. Only, there was no time for that.

The seaplane was arcing around for another attack on the speedboat.

Charlie forced herself to her feet.

She was close to the rear of the barge. At the far end was a small pilot house, where the captain and two crewmen were. They were busy watching the seaplane and therefore didn't notice Charlie.

Behind the pilot house, two long tanker trucks were parked end to end. As was the case with much machinery in South America, they were older models than one would have seen on the roads in the United States. In fact, they had probably been used in the States for years, then shipped down here to be driven until they literally fell apart. The wear and tear on them was extreme. The tires were bald, the chassis were rusted, and the tanks were dented and dripping oil in spots where the seals had worn out.

Charlie ran to the rear of the first tanker and squeezed into the narrow gap between it and the front of the next truck. At the base of the cylindrical oil tank was a vertical opening the width of a large hose with a metal lid fitted over it, from which the oil would be pumped out at the next destination. Oil was dripping steadily here, too, indicating that the lid no longer fit as well as it should have.

The lid was secured with several latches.

Charlie quickly undid them.

The lid opened slightly, and oil spurted from the tank with such force that Charlie had to leap out of the way to avoid being doused. The oil quickly began flooding the barge, spreading out evenly across the flat surface beneath both tankers.

Charlie hated what she was about to do, as it would pollute the river, but she didn't see that she had any other option.

The seaplane was coming toward the speedboat again.

Even though her strength was fading and she had no way to defend herself, Charlie climbed up to the top of the second tanker, right out in the open, where Esmerelda and her brothers would have a clear shot at her.

Esmerelda was bearing down on the speedboat when Paolo yelled and pointed toward the girl.

Paolo was the one who had been shot by Milana. The bullet had caught the side of his arm, but it hadn't hit bone or an artery, so he would be fine. The original shock had stung badly enough to make Paolo drop his gun, but Paolo had the same genetic condition that his sister did—and Gianni, too, for that matter. While other people might still be reeling from the pain, he no longer felt it. He was making a tourniquet with a strip of his shirt to stanch the bleeding and would then be ready for action again.

The girl had somehow made it to a nearby barge, where she was trying to unlatch the lid of a large hatch on the top of it, probably trying to do something crazy like ignite the oil inside, but she didn't seem to be having any luck getting it open.

Esmerelda made a split-second decision and turned toward the barge.

The people on the speedboat had guns and the woman had already shown that she was surprisingly adept with hers. The girl was smart but unarmed. If Esmerelda got rid of her, maybe she wouldn't even need to get rid of the other two. They might be lost without her brains.

As Esmerelda approached the barge, Gianni took the remaining submachine gun, stepped out onto the pontoon, and prepared to shoot.

Charlie heard them coming. There was no way to hide the sound of the plane's propellers. She gave up on trying to open the hatch and ran along the top of the tanker, away from the pilot house and toward the rear of the barge. In her haste, she dropped something.

There was no time for her to even give it a second glance. She ran as fast as she could while the plane closed in on her.

Gianni opened fire. Bullets sparked off the metal skin of the oil tank.

Esmerelda bore down on Charlie, coming in low over the barge to give Gianni the best shot possible.

Charlie reached the end of the tanker and, without

missing a beat, dove off the end of it, intending to plunge into the safety of the river.

Gianni didn't mind. As long as Charlie was in the air, he had a shot at her. As the plane closed in, he had her in his sights.

And then the world erupted into flame.

SIXTEEN

The cigarette lighter that Charlie carried in her money belt had belonged to her grandfather. It was a piece of art, carved from jade with a beautiful dragon etched into it. The last time Charlie had seen Dante, she had been carrying it for years but had never replaced the lighter fluid in it, because she didn't smoke. She simply treasured the object, as it was a family heirloom.

But in the months she had been on the run, she had filled it with butane, because you never knew when you might need to start a fire.

Like when someone was trying to gun you down from an airplane, for instance.

Charlie hadn't really been trying to open the hatch at the top of the second tanker. She was only pretending to do so, waiting for the Castellos to notice her.

Meanwhile, she was giving the oil she had released from the tanker as much time as possible to pool on the deck of the barge.

That was happening quickly, and the deck was now sloshing like a saucer full of milk.

Charlie hated to lose the lighter. It was practically her only personal possession. But she had no choice.

It had been wrapped in a plastic baggie in her money belt, along with her passport, to keep them safe in case of emergency. Charlie hadn't expected to jump into the river quite so soon into her journey, but she had figured there was a decent chance of getting rained on, given that the Amazon basin was the world's biggest rain forest. (She hadn't taken the same care to protect the money, because money was waterproof and people usually didn't mind if it was wet.) So the lighter had stayed dry during her swim. Now she ignited it and dropped it as she ran along the top of the tanker, making sure it fell to the side of the truck so that Esmerelda and her brothers wouldn't see it.

Therefore they didn't see it land in the pool of oil that was spread out beneath the trucks and instantly set it on fire.

But they couldn't miss what happened next.

Charlie had no way to accurately assess exactly how big the resulting explosion would be, but it was much bigger than she had expected.

The tanker in front exploded first, which made sense, as that was the one that was still spilling oil. The flames raced into it, and the entire thing detonated.

Charlie had tried to time everything in order to lure the Castellos in as close as possible, so their plane was directly above the first tanker when it blew apart like an enormous firecracker. The blast tossed the plane like a toy, while a ball of fire and smoke enveloped it and a hundred bits of metal pierced its fuselage like buckshot.

Charlie was in midair when it happened, and the force of the explosion sent her cartwheeling into the river. She landed hard, but the water then protected her from the surge of heat and fire and the rain of metal that followed.

She was disoriented for a moment but quickly figured out which way was down and swam toward the bottom while pieces of the truck plopped into the water and sank, so hot from the blast that they sizzled.

Charlie held her breath as long as she could, then kicked for the surface again.

She emerged to find fire everywhere.

The barge was ablaze, flames surrounding the remaining oil tanker, which was making ominous popping noises as it heated up. The barge's pilot and crewmen had dived into the river for safety as well and were swimming for shore.

The seaplane was also on fire. As Charlie watched, it

landed, smoking, on the river in the distance, and then Esmerelda and her brothers leapt from it, their clothes on fire too. Just after they dove into the water, the plane blew up.

Even the river blazed. Slicks of oil were scattered on the surface, burning. The heat made the air shimmer, and with all the smoke, Charlie didn't see the speedboat until it was almost upon her. It emerged from the haze like a ghost ship.

Dante was still at the wheel. So it was Milana who reached over the side and extended an arm to Charlie. Charlie grabbed on, and Milana hauled her up into the boat, where Charlie sprawled on the deck, exhausted.

Dante glared at her angrily. "If you ever try another crazy stunt like that without my permission, I'll end this mission and haul you right back to the CIA."

"Awww," Charlie said. "You're hiding how worried you were for my safety behind a veil of fake anger. That's sweet."

"There's nothing fake about how angry I am," Dante growled. "You could have been killed out there!"

"Yes. Because the bad guys were trying to kill us. So I took a calculated risk. You're welcome for that, by the way."

Dante was so exasperated, he looked as though he

might burst into flames himself. "My plan would have worked just fine!"

"If we'd gone to shore, they would have dropped a stick of dynamite on our heads," Charlie replied. "Or they would have blown up our boat and stranded us, then gone on ahead and beaten us to Darwin's treasure. Now *they're* the ones who are stranded." She pointed up the river.

In the distance, through the smoke and fire, they could see Esmerelda and her brothers swimming for shore.

Dante seemed to recognize that Charlie was right, but he didn't admit it. Instead, he gunned the engine and started back upriver, toward the Castello family.

"What are you doing?" Charlie asked, alarmed. "We're going the wrong way."

"I can't just leave them there," Dante said.

"Yes you can!" Charlie exclaimed. "They're bad guys! This is the second time they tried to kill me *today!* If our positions were reversed, they wouldn't rescue us."

"I'm not like them."

"This is a mistake."

"That's not your call."

Charlie would have argued more, but at that moment, the second oil tanker exploded. The fire on the barge had heated it up like a popcorn kernel. The metal tank ruptured, and the entire vehicle was flung into the air and crashed back down into the river, starting a new blaze on the surface.

Milana watched the burning hulk sink into the Napo, then looked to Charlie. "Why is it that everywhere you go, chaos follows?"

Charlie sighed, feeling miserable about the destruction she had caused. "If there was any other way to save us, I would have done it," she said.

She sat sullenly on the bow, and they headed downstream to find the place where the river turned to blood.

SEVENTEEN

Any other family would have been in crippling pain.

Esmerelda and her brothers had all been badly burned by the fire that had engulfed their plane. Most of the burns were second-degree, blistered and red, although Gianni's arms and Paolo's back had third-degree burns where their clothes had caught fire. Esmerelda had a nasty second-degree burn, a streak of ruined skin crossing her left cheek and scarring her beautiful face.

She couldn't see what had been done while she was in the river, but she could feel it. It was far worse than the slight burn she had suffered back at the Basilica, when the climbing rope had struck her face. That would have healed; this would not. Charlie Thorne had made things even worse, and Esmerelda hated the girl for it.

As usual, the pain had passed quickly for the Castellos.

However, that didn't mean they were all right. Esmerelda and her brothers knew that while the quick passage of pain sometimes seemed like a blessing, it could also be a curse. Pain was important; it let you know when something was wrong with your body. A person who didn't know they had been badly injured could die. It had happened many times in the Castello family. So their mother had taught them to always err on the side of caution and seek medical help whenever they thought they might need it.

Thus they accepted the care that Dante and Milana gave them.

The CIA had fished them out of the river, bound their wrists and ankles with the lines from the boat, and then tended to their burns while Charlie drove the boat back upstream. Dante had asked them many questions, but the Castellos had responded to all of them by giving them baleful stares and pretending that they didn't understand English.

Dante and Milana were surprised by the family's unusual response to pain. Milana had read about it but had never encountered it, while it was entirely new to Dante.

Eventually, Dante gave up the interrogation and relieved Charlie at the helm.

The plan wasn't to return all the way to Coca; that would waste too much time. Instead, they were only heading to the refinery, which was close enough to see. They also stopped to pick up the crew from the barge so they could return them to the refinery as well.

During the brief time she had, Charlie went and sat next to Esmerelda. "Sorry about your face," she said.

Esmerelda glared hatefully at her in response.

"I get that you're angry," Charlie said. "But it *was* self-defense. You were trying to kill us. If you knew how to share, none of this would have happened."

Esmerelda spat at her.

Charlie leapt to her feet to avoid it. "I'm just saying, if you hadn't double-crossed me, we could have found this treasure together. But now that will never happen. That's on you, not me." She returned to the pilot deck.

Esmerelda couldn't control her rage anymore. She unleashed a torrent of insults and threats in Italian. Charlie wasn't fluent in the language, but she could understand enough of it. Esmerelda wanted her dead many times over. But it wasn't the words so much as the tone that unsettled Charlie. Esmerelda sounded as though she really wanted to kill her.

Dante docked at the refinery's rotted pier. Almost everyone who worked there had gathered, staring downriver, wondering what had happened to the barge and the oil tankers. They immediately crowded around the speed-boat, peppering the crew of the barge with questions.

In Spanish, Dante asked to speak to whoever was in charge of security at the refinery.

A heavyset middle-aged man stepped forward.

Dante flashed his CIA badge, along with Milana, and said that he was part of a joint task force working with the Ecuadorean government, and that the Castello family were ecoterrorists who had blown up the refinery's barge and tankers. He then claimed they were in search of more ecoterrorists and didn't have time to return to Coca, so they wanted the refinery's security to call the police in Coca and keep an eye on the Castellos until someone could come get them. The head of security didn't seem pleased about this until Dante slipped him a hundred-dollar bill, at which point his attitude changed dramatically.

He said he had a place to hold the prisoners and then went to call the police.

Dante stayed right beside him so he could eavesdrop on the call, listening to him make arrangements for the police to come at the end of the day. Then he had the head of security show him the area he intended to hold the Castellos. It was a full-on holding cell; the refinery occasionally had looters, or employees who got caught stealing. Dante watched as the Castellos were locked up inside, thanked the head of security for his time, and then returned to the boat with Milana and Charlie.

Charlie suggested there was only about a 50 percent chance that everything would work out as Dante hoped, but she didn't want to go all the way back to Coca to deliver the Castellos into custody, and neither did Dante and Milana. It would cost them the rest of the day.

Dante told Charlie she ought to have a little more faith in humanity and then steered the boat downriver again.

As it turned out, it was only an hour before someone showed up at the refinery to get the Castellos.

Only, it wasn't a member of the Coca police force.

It was Ivan Spetz.

EIGHTEEN

The Napo River
290 miles downriver from Coca
Peru

Since the rivers in the Amazon basin descended so slowly, there were no rapids and the water was invariably calm. This meant the speedboat could travel at its top speed.

Charlie could make a few educated assumptions about how fast Darwin might have traveled downriver in 1835. Given how flat the Amazon basin was, the current of the river was almost nonexistent. They might as well have been in a pond. That meant the only real method of locomotion would have been manpower. Darwin had probably traveled with other people, most likely in a raft or a canoe. More men meant more muscle, but also more goods to move and thus more weight. And given the thick vegetation along the riverbanks, it seemed that making camp would have been an ordeal, meaning they'd have to stop every day well before nightfall.

Therefore, thirty miles a day seemed like the maximum a team of men could do, and many days, they would have surely covered far less ground. Which meant that after four hours on the motorboat at top speed, they had probably gone as far as Darwin had in ten days. So Charlie was on the alert, watching the river and the forest, searching attentively for what Darwin had mentioned in his coded message:

Follow the Napo River east from Coca for ten days until the water turns to blood.

Then find the tree built like King's College Chapel.

That far downriver, the rain forest was much wilder. They still passed the occasional barge loaded with trucks or construction materials, but onshore, the signs of modern civilization had vanished. While Charlie enjoyed the feeling of the breeze on her skin as the boat raced downriver, she wished they had more time to take in their surroundings. The rain forest was only a blur as they sped by, and the roar of the motors was probably scaring off any wildlife.

At one point, she caught a glimpse of the pink dolphins that lived in the Amazon, leaping from the water in the distance, but Dante wouldn't even slow down for a few minutes to see them.

"We're running out of daylight," he had explained.

Which was true. The sun was sinking toward the

horizon, meaning that they would soon have to find a place to dock for the night.

Charlie began to grow concerned.

She had assumed she knew what Darwin's clue meant . . . but now she began to have doubts. The river wouldn't *really* turn to blood, of course; that was certainly just a metaphor. And yet she hadn't seen what she had expected. There were three reasons that might be true:

1) Darwin had traveled faster than she had calculated, so they had not reached the right spot yet.
2) She had misinterpreted what Darwin meant.
3) The river no longer turned to blood.

The third possibility concerned her the most. The physical world changed more than most people realized. Rivers shifted course, mountains grew, volcanoes created new land while earthquakes fractured the old. And the Amazon, with its seasonal flooding, probably changed more than most places on earth. Not to mention that humans had begun to affect the natural world in increasingly destructive ways. If the spot where the river turned to blood no longer existed, it would be virtually impossible to find the tree Darwin had indicated; there were certainly billions of trees in the Amazon basin.

Plus, the concern that Milana had voiced was also a possibility: Maybe the tree wasn't there anymore. Since Darwin's time, the tree could have died. Or, more likely, it had been chopped down.

However, even if the tree had been cut down, there might still be a stump indicating where it had been. Or perhaps some other remnant of it. But they would never find that without knowing where to look first, and to do that they had to find the place where—

"Look up there!" Milana exclaimed suddenly. She was seated on the bow of the speedboat, pointing downstream.

Charlie and Dante looked that way and instantly understood her excitement.

A short distance ahead of them, a large tributary flowed into the Napo River. Its water was dark red. Charlie presumed this was because it carried silt with a great deal of iron in it. It wasn't uncommon for rivers to run red; the Colorado River in the western United States got its name from the Spanish for "color red" for this very reason. As the red water of this tributary met the dark-brown water of the Napo, the currents didn't blend right away. Instead, the tributary created a great red patch that truly looked like the color of . . .

"Blood," Dante said. "The river's turned to blood." He cut the engines. Thanks to its inertia, the boat didn't stop right away, but continued moving down the river at a far faster rate than the current.

Without the noise of the motors, the river was startlingly quiet. It made Charlie realize, not for the first time, how loud the human world was. Now there was almost no sound at all, and what little there was carried a long way. Charlie could hear tree branches shaking as a troop of monkeys crashed through them on the distant bank, as well as the calls of a flock of parrots that looked to be a half mile away.

The speedboat drifted into the bloodred patch of water, cutting a swath through it.

Milana was carefully studying their surroundings as well. "This has to be the place Darwin meant in his message. But there must be ten thousand trees here. How are we supposed to find the right one?"

"I'll know it when I see it," Charlie said confidently.

"Why don't you just explain Darwin's clue to us?" Dante asked testily. "So *we'll* know it when *we* see it?"

Charlie shot him a look of disbelief. "You really haven't figured it out?"

"We can't all be geniuses like you. I have no idea how a tree is supposed to look like a church."

"Not a church. King's College Chapel."

"Which is a church . . . ," Dante began, getting annoyed at Charlie's smug attitude.

"Yes, but a very special one. It's located at Cambridge University, which is where Darwin got his education."

"What's so special about it?" Dante asked.

"The way it was built."

Milana sighed with exasperation. "Why couldn't Darwin have just said what type of tree we're looking for? So that someone who isn't an architect could find it?"

"He probably didn't know what type of tree it *was*," Charlie explained. "He wrote that message in 1835. Most of the Amazon basin hadn't been explored yet. Darwin might have been one of the first Europeans to visit this area—if not *the* first—and practically everything he saw would have been new to him. And even if he *did* know what type of tree it was, maybe the person he was leaving the clue for wouldn't. So he tried to describe it in terms he thought another British citizen would understand."

"Why British specifically?" Dante asked.

"He wrote his clues in English," Charlie replied. "So that rules out a lot of the world. And at the time, the British were the English speakers who were doing all the exploring. Every other country that spoke English had been colonized by them. And the Americans were busy exploring their own country, not poking around down here."

Dante nodded understanding. "So what, exactly, did King's College Chapel look like?"

"Like *that*," Charlie said, pointing to the riverbank.

Dante and Milana looked that way. They instantly knew exactly which tree Charlie meant—and understood why Darwin had described it that way.

The tree sat just south of the junction of the red-water tributary and the Napo River—and it was massive, towering another seventy feet above the rest of the canopy. Its upper branches formed a great canopy and had hundreds of other plants growing on them; they were bedecked with bromeliads and orchids and draped with vines. But it was the lower section of the tree that held their attention. It was as wide as a house—and its enormous roots flared out around it, forming wedges that were up to fifteen feet tall. It was obvious that their design provided stability to the tree, shoring up its great bulk, and thus they served the same purpose as—and looked exactly like—the flying buttresses on a cathedral.

"That must be our tree," Dante said.

Charlie nodded in response. She could see other large trees in the area, but they were much farther from the bank of the river, and this tree's resemblance to the design of King's College Chapel was inescapable. "It's called a kapok, I think."

To the west, the sun sank into the forest, casting them—and most of the river basin—into shadow. However, the kapok tree was so tall, it still remained in the sunlight, which illuminated thousands of pink flowers in its canopy.

It seemed to Charlie that a great shift came over the rain forest as twilight began, occurring so quickly, it was as though someone had flipped a switch. There was a sensation of a great stirring in the trees, of life awakening. Noises arose from the forest: the peeping of frogs, the calls of birds, the chirr of insects.

A splash in the river nearby drew Charlie's attention. Some pink dolphins were frolicking, performing aerobatic leaps into the air—but there was other movement too, like a dark tide sweeping down the water.

It took Charlie a moment to figure out what it was, and then a smile spread across her face.

"Hope you guys are okay with bats," she said.

"Bats?" Milana and Dante asked at once, although Milana was excited while Dante was unsettled. Which made sense; Milana had grown up in the wilderness, while Dante was a city boy. Charlie noticed him reflexively reach for his gun.

"Relax," she told him. "They're not going to mug you. They're just here for the insects."

Then the bats were upon them. They were huge, far bigger than any bats Charlie had ever seen before, with wingspans eighteen inches across. They came in low over the surface of the water, like fighter planes on a strafing run, gulping down the insects that were skimming about.

"Holy cow," Dante said, staring at them in shock. He hadn't relaxed at all. If anything, the size of the bats had made him even more nervous. "They're mutants."

"These are nothing," Charlie teased. "Wait until the fruit bats show up."

Even in the dim twilight, she could see Dante go pale at the thought.

Then Dante got ahold of himself, caring less about what Charlie thought of him than Milana, most likely, and started the engines again.

He didn't crank them all the way up, as the riverbank wasn't far away. Instead, he motored the boat slowly toward the kapok tree. The iron-rich water from the tributary no longer looked red in the darkening gloom, but instead an inky black.

The bats immediately adjusted to the boat's movement, sweeping around it with effortless grace.

As the boat pulled into the mouth of the tributary, Charlie was struck by how big it was. At first the tributary had seemed puny compared to the great, wide Napo River, which itself was only a tributary of the Amazon. But now Charlie recognized that the vastness of the Amazon basin was already skewing her sense of what was normal. In other places, like the western United States, this tributary would have been a major river, perhaps the lifeline for millions of people; but here it was merely one of thousands of branches of the Amazon, so insignificant it might not even have a name.

The bank of the tributary was thick with plant life, although there was a small gap hacked into the greenery where it appeared that someone might have moored a boat before. Milana hopped ashore with a bowline and cinched it around a tree trunk. Charlie and Dante then leapt to solid ground, and the three of them made their way to the kapok tree.

Even though night hadn't completely fallen yet, the rain forest was surprisingly dark. Charlie realized this was due to the cover of the trees. Above them, the sky was still blue and the upper reaches of the kapok remained in direct sunlight, but she could barely see that through the canopy of leaves. It was so thick, Charlie figured that the rain forest floor was probably dim even in the middle of the day; the sunlight simply couldn't get through. Now, due to the darkness, it was already getting hard to see where they were going—which was a concern given that they were on a hunt for a clue Darwin might have hidden.

However, Charlie, Milana, and Dante were the type of people who came prepared. Each had brought a flashlight. Dante and Milana had small handheld ones, while Charlie's was the type that strapped to her head with an elastic band, allowing her to keep her hands free. They all flipped them on. The beams barely made a dent in the darkness, but it was enough for them to at least find their way to the kapok without tripping over a root or falling into a hole.

It didn't take long to reach the tree, but the size of its base was immediately daunting. It was even bigger around than they had expected, with more than a dozen buttressing roots, each one of which was significantly taller than Dante.

"I hate to say this," Dante observed. "But we might have to wait until daylight to find this clue. I can barely see anything as it is . . . and we're about to get eaten alive out here."

Sure enough, the flashlights were attracting flying insects by the thousands, luring what appeared to be every mosquito in the Amazon. On their way down the river, Charlie had doused herself and her clothes in repellant, but the insects appeared to be either immune or impervious. Within seconds, she had suffered multiple bites.

And yet she wasn't ready to give up. "We can at least take a few minutes . . ."

"It'll take far more time than that to search this whole tree," Milana said, smacking mosquitoes off her arms. "And these little jerks have already siphoned a pint of blood out of me."

Despite the insects, Charlie still wasn't about to return to the boat. Not when they were so close. Instead, she began to circle the tree, aiming her light back and forth between the ground she was covering and the tree itself. "In theory, it shouldn't take that long to find the next clue. If this is the right tree, then Darwin probably wouldn't have hidden it."

"He hid the last one back in Quito," Dante countered.

"Because it was in the middle of a city and he didn't want random people stumbling across it. This one is way out in the wilderness. The only people who'd be poking around this tree are the ones Darwin sent to look for his clue. . . . Yikes!" As Charlie rounded one of the giant roots, something scuttled across her path and disappeared into the underbrush. It happened so fast, Charlie didn't even have time to tell what it was.

"Charlie!" Dante yelled, alarmed. There was already enough of the tree between them that he sounded sort of far away.

"I'm okay!" Charlie yelled back. "I just got spooked by something. It was either a medium-size reptile or a really big bug . . ." She trailed off as her flashlight illuminated something on the bark of the tree trunk.

"Charlie!" Dante yelled again, sounding more aggravated now.

Charlie ignored him. She was staring at the tree

trunk. There were more insects crawling across it, which wasn't surprising, as there were insects *everywhere*. Multiple trails of ants were filing up and down the tree while a centipede the size of a hot dog passed through them like a freight train. Several vines snaked across the trunk as well, because there were also vines almost everywhere you looked in the forest, spiraling around trees and dangling from the branches. But underneath all the foliage, there were *numbers*.

They had obviously been carved into the tree long before. They looked similar to the words that had been left on the tortoise shell, in that they had widened and split as the trunk had expanded, so what might have once been thin cuts in the bark were now an inch across. Despite the decades since they had been left there, they had remained at the exact same height above the ground, because trees grew from the top.

It was definitely Darwin's work. It was the same code that had appeared on the Devil's Stone: the numbers 1 through 5 in the same sort of patterns.

"I found it!" Charlie exclaimed. "The next part of Darwin's code! I *told* you guys it wouldn't take too long!"

"Charlie!" Dante yelled again, and this time Charlie realized that he wasn't yelling her name in exasperation, like he was annoyed at her. There was fear in his voice. And concern.

She reluctantly turned away from the numbers etched in the kapok tree and immediately discovered the reason Dante sounded so worried.

There were four men standing behind her. And they all had guns pointed her way.

NINETEEN

Chempro Refinery
The Napo River
25 miles south of Coca

Tell me what happened here today," Oz told his
foreman.

"I already have," Jose replied. "Twice."

"Then tell me again," Oz said. "I need to
understand."

Oswald Crutcher ran the oil refinery where Dante
and Milana had deposited the Castello family that
day, although he hadn't been on duty when that had
happened—or when the company's tanker trucks had
been blown to bits, for that matter. He had been upriver
at the time, in Coca, getting a much-needed break from
work. At the refinery, he worked five days straight, on call
twenty-four hours a day, and then got two days off, which
he tried to make the most of. There wasn't much to do in
Coca, but Oz always enjoyed his time there, because any
time away from the refinery was a joy. Life at the refinery

was awful. It was dull and exhausting and the refinery was brutally hot and always stank of petroleum fumes. But the job paid well, so Oz stuck with it.

Oz had come to the Amazon from about as far away as you could get. He had grown up in Point Barrow, Alaska, where his parents had both worked at refineries. The oil business was all Oz knew, so there had never been any doubt that he'd go into that line of work. But he had never liked the cold, so when the chance came to shift to the Amazon, he had jumped at it.

Oz was a big, strapping man, and well muscled from a lifetime of physical labor, although now that he was a manager, he didn't work quite as hard and thus he'd developed a sizable beer belly. He was only in his thirties; he had originally thought he'd been given the job running the Napo refinery because he knew the business well, but in truth, no one else wanted to work at that plant. In fact, Oz wasn't that smart, but he knew how a refinery worked and he was good at keeping the workers in line. Plus, he spoke Spanish, as many of the refinery workers in Point Barrow had been migrants. Oz simply ended up migrating in the opposite direction.

It was certainly warmer than Alaska down here. The coldest it ever got in the Amazon was a good twenty degrees warmer than it ever got in Point Barrow. And the surroundings were staggeringly different. Point Barrow was up above the arctic circle, farther north than most plants could grow. Trees had been rare up there; now Oz was surrounded by billions of them. But the jobs themselves had an eerie similarity. Refinery work was the same pretty much wherever you were.

Oz had been here fifteen months, and not much had happened, save for the grind of working day in and day out. As the only American, and the boss, he wasn't accepted into the social circle of his workers—and the refinery was too far from the closest town to visit except on his days off—so he spent most of his downtime alone, gaming on his computer. He often found himself calculating how many days it would be until he'd have enough money socked away to retire. At last count, it was more than seven thousand.

So when he had returned to the refinery and found everyone buzzing about the excitement of the day, he had been extremely intrigued. He had asked each of his employees to visit him in his office, one at a time, to explain what had happened.

Their stories had conflicted a great deal. Oz presumed that sometimes this was due to none of them knowing what had really happened, as when they tried to explain how his tanker trucks had blown up. And sometimes it was because they were lying to him, as when they explained what had occurred with the prisoners who had been brought there.

Oz didn't really care too much about the tanker trucks. Yes, losing them was a problem, but they were old and insured for much more than they'd been worth, so ultimately, Chempro would make money on their loss.

But the story of the prisoners was something else. He listened intently as Jose explained once again how two people claiming to be CIA agents accompanied by a teenager had brought two men and a woman to the refinery and then some police officers from Coca had come to get them.

"Which police officers?" Oz asked suspiciously. He knew all the officers in Coca, as many of his employees had a tendency to get into trouble on their days off.

"I forgot their names," Jose said evasively.

"So these officers showed up and you just handed the prisoners over to them?"

"Yes."

"So if I called the chief of police in Coca right now, the prisoners would be in his jail?"

Jose's eyes shifted away from Oz's. "Maybe not. Now that I think about it, maybe they weren't police. They might have been federal agents."

Oz drummed his fingers on his desk, letting Jose sweat for half a minute. Then he said, "Here's what I'm going to do, Jose. I'm going to pick up the phone and call the chief of police. And I'm going to tell him to come here and arrest you—unless you tell me the truth about who really picked up the prisoners."

Jose cracked: The man who had come for the prisoners wasn't local police or a federal agent. Jose had no idea who he worked for or where he was from. He had spoken perfect Spanish—although Jose was pretty sure the man wasn't local. And he'd had money. Plenty of money. He had bribed each and every one of the refinery employees to hand over the prisoners to him and then to keep their mouths shut.

When Jose finished his story, Oz didn't say anything for a while. He let Jose keep sweating while he thought things through.

The man who had come to collect the criminals might have been a criminal himself—but there was an equally good chance that he represented a big corporation. There were lots of corporations looking to make money in the Amazon, and they were always willing to spread money around—in the short term, at least. They'd come in, make the locals feel like they were all going to get rich, and then sucker them into deals they didn't understand and rob them blind.

That's what Chempro had done to get the oil leasing rights in this area. Other petroleum companies had done the same. There were also companies after logging rights or mining rights or making simple land grabs to raise cattle or grow palm oil. There were a lot of natural resources at stake in the Amazon basin, and people were doing anything they could to get them while they were still around.

Because they wouldn't last forever. Even though the rain forest seemed endless, it was disappearing fast. Sooner or later everything would be claimed, or the locals would wise up and stop letting corporations bully them, or the countries that owned the land would buckle under pressure to protect the environment from countries that probably hadn't protected theirs and now felt guilty about it.

So if someone was interested in cashing in on natural resources, this was the time to do it. The land rush was on. Oz had spent many hours wondering how to become a part of it and get rich himself.

That seemed like a far better option than spending another seven thousand days at this refinery.

Jose was now squirming in his seat, wondering if Oz was going to punish him or not.

Oz asked, "When these people left, did they go upriver, toward Coca?"

"No, sir. They went the other way."

Away from civilization, Oz thought. "In what type of boat?"

"An older cargo boat. Medium size."

"Did you by any chance take down the identification number?"

Jose looked at him curiously, wondering where this was going. "Yes."

"So you'd be able to recognize this boat again if you saw it?"

"Yes."

Oz smiled. "Then let's go find it."

TWENTY

Agua Rojo Eco-Lodge
Anaconda River

Sorry about the guns," Segundo said. "We thought you were thieves."

"What kind of thieves would be working all the way out here?" Milana asked.

"There is plenty worth stealing out here," Segundo replied. "People steal the animals for the illegal pet trade. Or hunt them for their skins. But more often than not, they're loggers after our trees. We've chased dozens away from that kapok this year alone." He shifted his gaze to Charlie. "I hope we didn't scare you too badly."

"It's cool," Charlie said.

She liked Segundo a lot. The moment he had realized she was only a girl, he had lowered his gun and then stepped in front of the others to protect her.

Now they were all at the eco-lodge that Segundo ran with the other members of his village. It was located a half mile up the tributary from where it met the Napo River. The tributary was known locally as the Anaconda River, in part because the snakes were plentiful along it, but also because it twisted and turned like an anaconda, so that half a mile along the river was only a five-minute walk across land.

The eco-lodge was a blend of traditional architecture and modern technology. All the buildings were simple and spare, with mud walls and thatch roofs, but the lodge also had electricity and Wi-Fi powered entirely by solar panels. In the very center was a great dining hall built around an even more enormous kapok tree than the one where Darwin had left his code. A viewing deck had been built in the upper canopy of the tree, so high up that it required seven flights of stairs to access. That was where Segundo and Charlie were sitting now, along with Dante, Milana, and the three other men who had found them at the tree. The adults were all drinking beer, while Charlie had a Coke. The drinks were refreshingly cold, thanks to a solar-powered refrigerator. (When Dante had expressed surprise that precious power was being used to cool beer, Segundo had replied, "Our lodge might be primitive, but we're not heathens.")

The lodge had been the idea of Segundo's parents, who had realized that eco-lodges were being built throughout the region, but they were all run by corporations and the local tribes got nothing. So they had decided their community should build their own lodge. Although they were still living in much the same way that they had for generations, they were well aware of the modern world and figured someone should venture out to learn the hotel business. Segundo had volunteered. He had done well at the small school in their village and spoke English fluently. He had been accepted into the School of Hotel Administration at Cornell, studied there for four years, then worked in the hotel business in New York City for another six. By the time he returned home, he had planned the eco-lodge down to the finest detail. It had taken four years to fund and build, and now it was turning a tidy profit for the community.

The view from the platform in the tree, even at night, was well worth the climb. It seemed to Charlie that she could see every star in the Milky Way.

Like most indigenous people of the Amazon, Segundo was of short stature, with a mop of black hair and dark-brown skin. He wore a button-down denim shirt and a baseball cap, both emblazoned with the Agua Rojo Eco-Lodge logo. He spoke English perfectly, although to Charlie's amusement, he had a slight New York accent after all his years in the city.

"Illegal logging has been a huge problem in this area," he explained. "So we make nightly patrols to check on all our big trees. However, we have always paid particular attention to the one where we found you. Since it's so close to the Napo River, it's an easy target for loggers. Plus, my community has been wondering about those markings for generations."

"How long has your community been here?" Dante asked.

"For as long as anyone can remember," Segundo replied. "Hundreds of years, at least."

They had passed the community on the way to the lodge. The homes there were simple one-room huts, some of which had been used for decades, although there had been some modernization over the years. The community now had a central bathroom with a rain collection system, which allowed for flush toilets and showers with hot water, a cultural center for guests from the lodge to visit, a schoolhouse, and a soccer field.

"Does your community have any theories about the markings on the tree?" Milana asked.

"There *is* a story," Segundo said. "But it is probably more myth than fact."

"What is it?" Charlie pressed.

Segundo took a sip of his beer and stared off in the direction of the great tree. "My great-grandfather says a man came in the time of *his* great-grandfather. A white explorer. Back then no one in the village had ever seen a white man before. At first they thought he might be a ghost. The young man was accompanied by some other white people, but he was very different from them. He was young and wild and fascinated by everything he saw, filling notebooks with drawings and strange words. He stayed here for five days and then continued up the river toward the Dark Lands."

"The Dark Lands?" Dante interrupted, sitting forward in his chair.

"Yes," Segundo said. "It is a region at the headwaters of the Anaconda River. My people have always stayed away from it."

"Why?" Milana asked.

"Our ancestors believed there was something dangerous there."

Charlie asked, "Do you know what it is?"

Segundo didn't answer right away. It seemed to Charlie that he was weighing how much to tell them. Finally, he said, "My ancestors' knowledge of this forest has always served us well. This forest is vast. If we have to avoid one small area of it, that's no big deal."

Charlie recognized that Segundo hadn't answered her question, but she didn't call him on it. Instead, she looked to Dante and Milana for their reactions.

Milana didn't appear very concerned by Segundo's fear of the Dark Lands—while Dante looked unusually ill at ease. But then, Dante's unsettled state might have also been due to the bats. He obviously had issues with bats, and now there were hundreds around them. Most were small ones, swarming around the viewing deck, snatching insects from the air, but there were also a dozen large fruit bats in the canopy of the kapok tree, eating the kapok's fruit. These bats were the size of small dogs, and even though they were harmless to humans, Charlie had to admit that the sounds of their gluttonous eating were a little disturbing.

"Anyhow," Segundo went on, "the story goes that the white explorer journeyed to the Dark Lands with ten other men—but only three of them returned. They carried a mysterious chest they had carved from a tree, although the explorer wouldn't reveal what was inside. This time, he and his men didn't stay in my community; they were in a great hurry to leave the forest. The young explorer stopped only long enough to carve those numbers into the tree—and then they headed back up the river and never returned."

Charlie had been focused on Segundo as he spoke, but now she shifted her attention to Milana and Dante again. Dante remained unsettled, but Milana's eyes were alive with excitement. Charlie guessed that Milana was thinking the same thing that she was: The white explorer sounded like Charles Darwin, which meant they were on the right track.

Segundo said, "My people have been waiting a very

long time for someone to come and explain the numbers to us. Now it appears that day has come. Do you know what they mean?"

"We know how to translate them," Charlie said.

Segundo's eyes lit up. He spoke to his friends in a language that Charlie didn't know, and they grew excited as well.

"I didn't get a chance to see all the numbers back in the forest," Charlie said. "Can we go back tonight?"

"There's no need for that," Segundo told her. He reached into a backpack and fished out a laptop computer. "I have what you need right here."

He set the computer on a table and began to search through his photos.

While they waited, Charlie asked, "Just out of interest, did you like New York City?"

"I did," Segundo replied. "I enjoyed my time there a great deal. But I couldn't have spent my whole life there. I missed this place."

Charlie asked, "Is there anything you miss about New York, now that you live here?"

"Pizza," said Segundo without hesitation. "Oh man, do I miss pizza. Ah. Here we are." He brought up a photo of Darwin's code that had been taken in broad daylight, so that the numbers were perfectly visible and easy to read. "What does it say?"

Charlie gave Segundo and his men a quick primer on how the code worked, sketching out the grid that Darwin had used on a cocktail napkin to help them understand. She had already memorized the system, so it wasn't hard to decode the words, but still, it helped to have the key to it all in front of her to verify that she wasn't making any mistakes.

Then she wrote out the translation:

> *Follow the red river upstream for a month until you reach a place that looks like the Thames.*
> *Then find the altar in the main temple in the city of stone.*

"The city of stone," Dante echoed, intrigued.

Charlie looked to him. Dante no longer appeared unsettled. Instead, he was now brimming with excitement. Milana was too.

But to their side, Segundo looked gravely concerned.

"What's wrong?" Charlie asked.

"This is telling you to head directly into the Dark Lands," he said. "If there really is a city of stone there, you would be wise to stay far away from it."

TWENTY-ONE

This city of stone," Dante said. "It's probably Paititi."

"What's Paititi?" Charlie asked.

Dante reacted with surprise. "You mean there's something you don't know?"

"I'm only twelve," Charlie said. "I haven't had time to learn *everything* yet. Like, I still haven't figured out why you haven't asked Milana out even though you're obviously crushing on her."

Dante choked on his beer. He looked to Milana, who was only a few feet away from them. He quickly decided it was best to act like Charlie's jab wasn't even worth a response. "Paititi is the lost city of the Incan Empire."

They were now in one of the guest suites. It was off-season, so there were several vacancies at the resort, and Dante had plenty of money to cover their lodging, thanks to the CIA. (Charlie had decided not to reveal how much cash was hidden in her money belt.) The suite wasn't fancy, but still far better than Charlie had expected to find deep in the Amazon; there were two connecting rooms, one with a bed for each of the women and a smaller room for Dante. The beds were surrounded by sheer white mosquito nets, which hung from the ceiling, making them look like personal tepees. There was no glass in the windows, only screens, on which thousands of insects were gathered, attracted by the lights in the rooms—as well as a dozen small lizards, which were hungrily gobbling up the insects. The door between the rooms was open. After dinner at the lodge, Segundo had shown them to their quarters and then advised them to get some sleep and think over any decision they made very carefully.

Dante and Charlie were in Dante's room, going over their equipment. Dante had brought another beer back to the room from the bar, while Charlie had brought a bottle of purified water.

Milana was sitting on the bed in her room, under the mosquito net, painting her fingernails. She said, "I thought Machu Picchu was the lost city of the Incan Empire."

Dante shook his head, looking relieved that he had managed to change the subject. "Machu Picchu is a relatively small site. Less than a thousand people lived there.

But there have always been rumors that the Incas had a much larger city located farther into the rain forest. A city where thousands of Incans lived, possibly even tens of thousands."

"You think there could have been a city that big all the way out here?" Charlie asked skeptically. "This area is awfully remote."

"It wasn't always," Dante told her. "Much of the world has this idea that the Amazon is pristine and unexplored. That most of it has barely been seen by humans, let alone settled by us. But the truth is, that's just based on limited observation. There has barely been any archaeological research in this part of the world—but there is a growing amount of evidence suggesting that there may have been a far more advanced civilization here than we realized."

"Then what happened to it?" Charlie asked.

"The same thing that happened to every indigenous civilization in the Americas," Milana said coldly. "They got decimated by the arrival of the Europeans."

Charlie looked at her curiously. "Pizarro conquered the Incas in the 1500s. But they never came this far inland."

Milana shook her head. "I didn't say they were *conquered* by the Europeans. I said they were *decimated* by the Europeans' arrival. Most likely by diseases that they had no immunity to. Do you know what the largest city in the United States was before 1880?"

"Actually, I do," Charlie said. "Cahokia."

Milana gave her a look of surprise, as if she wasn't used to people knowing this. "That's right."

"It was located close to what is now Saint Louis," Charlie went on. "And some people think there may have been as many as forty thousand indigenous people living there, which would have made it way bigger than Philadelphia or New York City."

"Right again," Milana said. "And Cahokia wasn't the only large city ever built in the Americas. But then the Europeans showed up and unwittingly transmitted their diseases—and entire native civilizations were decimated. Some were reduced to only a tenth of their original populations, which was devastating on every level: social, economic, psychological. And this happened throughout the Americas. The diseases traveled much faster than the Europeans did. So when explorers showed up in earnest, most of the civilizations they encountered had already been destroyed. Judging the civilizations of the Americas in that context would have been the same as judging European civilization after it had been obliterated by the plague in the 1300s."

"So then," Dante added, "it's very likely that the same thing happened to any Incan cities that had been built in the Amazon. Their populations were wiped out. And since the plant life here grows so quickly, it would swallow up any evidence of the cities within decades, if not sooner."

Charlie nodded agreement. She was well aware of many archaeological sites throughout the world that had been hidden by jungles for centuries. "Still, all we know is that Darwin found a city of stone. We don't know that it's Paititi."

"True," Dante admitted. "But it's evident that he found *something*. And the area we're heading to is the exact same region where Paititi is rumored to have been located: a remote section of the Peruvian rain forest. So at the very least, we're talking about an archaeological find of major significance."

Charlie gave him a distrustful look. "You sure know a lot about Paititi for someone who just happened to stumble upon its potential location."

"I happen to be fascinated by the legend," Dante replied defensively. "It's a coincidence."

"I don't believe in coincidence," Charlie said.

"That doesn't mean they don't occur," Dante replied. "As I recall, you happened to know plenty about Einstein when we recruited you to look for Pandora. No one thought that was suspicious."

"Yeah, but I'm a genius," Charlie said. "So it's not as surprising when I know something as when you do."

"I'll tell you what you don't know much about," Dante said heatedly. "Keeping your attitude in check."

"You knew I had an attitude when you blackmailed me into tracking down Pandora against my will. You didn't seem so concerned about it then." Charlie gave her brother a smug smile, letting him know she wasn't really angry at him; she was just trying to get under his skin.

Which only made Dante more annoyed at her. He was considering chewing her out when Milana spoke. "There's another issue about this site," she said, "beyond whether or not it's Paititi. It's located in an area that the locals consider dangerous. How seriously should we take that?"

"I don't think it's a concern," Dante told her. "It's probably just an old myth."

"A lot of myths have some basis in reality." Milana put the finishing touch of polish on the nails of her right hand. "Segundo's people have lived in this area for centuries. You've been here twelve hours. They certainly know more about this place than we do."

Dante shrugged dismissively. "I don't see how that area could be any more dangerous than any other section of the rain forest."

"I can think of plenty of reasons that might be the case," Milana said. "Maybe there's an extremely dangerous type of animal that lives up there. Or mosquitoes that carry some disease we've never heard about . . ."

"Or maybe there's an undiscovered tribe of humans up there," Charlie suggested.

Dante and Milana both looked to her.

"It's certainly a possibility," Charlie went on. "There's at least a hundred known tribes in the Amazon that haven't been contacted by us yet, either because they've chosen to avoid us or because we've chosen to let them be. So there could definitely be one up there that no one's discovered. And there's a chance they could be dangerous, like the tribe on North Sentinel Island."

Dante and Milana obviously understood what Charlie meant. North Sentinel Island was located in the Bay of Bengal, between India and Myanmar. It was a notoriously hard island to dock a ship at, and therefore the small indigenous tribe that lived there had little contact with humans throughout its history. They were known for being extremely hostile to outsiders—and so the rest of the world had let them be.

"I'd say that's an extremely plausible possibility," Milana said finally, then turned to Dante. "And it's a serious concern. Not only is it potentially dangerous for us to confront an uncontacted tribe—but it's generally not good for them, either. From a health or social perspective."

Dante nodded acceptance, but Charlie could tell he was frustrated; he seemed unhappy that Milana was casting doubts on the mission. He shifted his attention to Charlie. "Is that what you think too? Because this morning you seemed awfully gung ho about going after whatever Darwin found."

Milana said, "This morning Charlie didn't know how dangerous this trip might be."

"Oh, she knew," Dante said brusquely. "Charlie knows almost everything, remember?"

"You're right," Charlie confessed. "I knew there'd be risks. But now I figured that *you* should know about them too. This expedition isn't going to be easy."

Dante looked slightly offended, as though she had questioned his masculinity. "We can handle it," he said. "We've faced far bigger threats than some primitive tribesmen."

Milana gave him a hard look.

Dante withered under it, then added, "But . . . I promise I won't do anything that puts us—or *them*—at risk."

Milana held his gaze a long time, as though trying to decide whether he was being honest, then finally said, "All right. I'm in."

A smile spread across Dante's face. "Good."

Milana looked to Charlie. "It's late. You need to get some sleep."

Charlie considered protesting this on principle, but in truth, she was exhausted. It had been an extremely long day, during which she had barely survived two attempts on her life. She pried herself out of her chair and headed for her bed, pausing by Dante to whisper, "If you want to switch rooms, I'm happy to take this one to myself and let you and Milana share. . . ."

"Get to bed," Dante said gruffly, turning red with embarrassment.

Charlie went into the room she shared with Milana and shut the connecting door. Milana had now finished painting the nails of her left hand and was letting them dry. The polish was bright red.

"Not what I expected," Charlie said.

Milana looked at her curiously. "The color?"

"The polish, period. Especially here. We're gearing up to go into the wilderness. Every ounce of equipment counts. And you brought that?"

"It only weighs an ounce and I like how it looks. Plus, your fingernails can be a really effective weapon in a fight, and the polish makes them stronger." Milana held up a hand, displaying her nails. They weren't so long that they'd be a hindrance, but they were slightly raised above her fingertips, which would allow her to give someone a nasty scratch.

"Oh," Charlie said. "Makes sense."

"Have you ever painted your nails?"

"No."

"Would you like me to show you how?"

"Maybe later."

"Okay. Whenever you want. We'll have plenty of time together." Milana slipped out from underneath her mosquito net and went into the small bathroom to brush her teeth.

Charlie didn't get into bed right away. Instead, she went to the screened-in windows and stared out at the dark Amazonian night, thinking.

She had a lot on her mind.

She had lied when she said she didn't know about Paititi. She had come to learn that sometimes it was better to act uninformed to see what other people knew—or what they chose to share. And Dante had omitted something very important from their discussion. That bothered Charlie a great deal.

But something else was really weighing on her, something that appeared to have escaped Dante and Milana.

It was possible that Darwin's big discovery wasn't Paititi at all. Or any lost city. But something even more startling.

And Charlie had a very good idea what that was.

TWENTY-TWO

The confluence of the Napo and Anaconda Rivers

Two days later, another man arrived at Darwin's kapok tree. He arrived in a much slower boat and appeared to be working on his own—until Segundo and his men had surrounded him at the base of the tree.

"I'd lower those guns if I were you," Ivan Spetz said calmly.

"Why?" Segundo asked.

The answer was the click of a weapon being cocked behind him.

Segundo and his men turned around to find the Castellos all holding them at gunpoint.

Even if they hadn't been holding guns, the Castellos would have been a frightening sight. It was evident to Segundo that all three of them had been through a terrible tragedy recently—a fire, it seemed. Patches of their skin were badly blistered and burned. And yet none of them seemed to be affected by it, not physically, at least. Segundo would have expected people with burns like that to be reeling from the pain, but these people didn't seem to be hurting at all; they just seemed angry.

Segundo and his men all lowered their guns.

"That's better," Ivan Spetz said. Then he pointed at the place where, until the day before, Darwin's code had been etched in the tree. "Something used to be written here. I'd like to know what it said."

At the urging of Dante, Milana, and Charlie, Segundo had scraped Darwin's code off the kapok. It had taken him some time, although he knew how to do it in a way that wouldn't hurt the tree. He had scraped the bark off around the code and then singed the area with fire until it was charred black. It was still evident that *something* had been carved there, but no one could tell what.

"Others are going to come looking for this code," Milana had warned. "And there's a decent chance they won't be very good people. Since you now know what it says, there's no point in leaving it there for anyone else to find."

Segundo had agreed that made sense. He had come to believe that Dante, Milana, and Charlie were honorable and intelligent people, even if he couldn't talk them out of continuing on toward the Dark Lands. To that end, he had spent an entire day with them, teaching them everything he could about the rain forest so that they would be safer on their travels. He had taught them what fruits were ripe and how to find them, how to catch and cook a piranha, how to recognize and avoid toxic plants and bullet ants, and how to build a shelter at night that would protect them from the rain. (Charlie had turned out to be a startlingly good student, soaking up everything he told her almost instantly. So while Dante and Milana were still mastering the basics of survival, Segundo had taught Charlie a few more advanced skills, like how to patch a canoe with the sap from a brazil nut tree and how to catch a poison arrow frog and apply its toxin to an arrow.)

Charlie, Milana, and Dante had spent a second night at the lodge and started up the Anaconda River only that very morning, after which Segundo had gone to the kapok tree to remove Darwin's code.

Now, a mere twelve hours later, someone had come looking for it, exactly as Dante, Milana, and Charlie had feared.

It had taken Ivan and the Castellos much longer to arrive at that point than the CIA team for two reasons. First, their boat was significantly slower, a refurbished cargo ship built for hauling rather than for speed. Second, they hadn't been as sure as Charlie as to what Darwin's clues meant. Therefore, they had moved slowly along the Napo, making dozens of stops along the way to investigate what turned out to be dead ends, until they had finally reached the bloodred confluence with the Anaconda and realized that had to be the right place. After that, Esmerelda had quickly deduced which tree Darwin had meant, as she was familiar with King's College Chapel herself.

It had been Ivan's suggestion that he visit the tree first, as a search party, while the others served as backup. No matter where he went, Ivan was always preparing for trouble.

The scorch on the bark where the code had been still smelled like smoke and the tree oozed fresh sap, indicating that the wound was new. Even Ivan and the Castellos, who weren't nearly as familiar with the natural world as Segundo and his men, could tell that.

"It didn't say anything," Segundo told them now, lying as convincingly as he could. "It was only a series of marks made by illegal loggers. They send advance teams in to tag trees for harvest, and when we find such marks, we destroy them."

Ivan considered this answer for a few moments, then said, "I noticed there was a tourist lodge just up the river from here. I assume you have some connection to that?"

"Yes," Segundo said warily.

"Let's get something straight," Ivan told him. "The

way you're dealing with me right now, lying to me about what happened to this tree, means you're assuming that I'm a fool. Well, I'm not. I'm also not a very nice person. So here's how this is going to work. I'm going to ask you about the marks on this tree again. And if you lie to me, my colleagues and I are going to burn your resort to the ground. If you *still* lie to me after that, I'll start hurting people. And I won't stop until I get the truth. So it will cause all of us a lot less trouble if you'd just tell me what this said."

Segundo swallowed hard, aware that Ivan wasn't bluffing. And when he looked at the angry, blistered faces of the Castellos, he saw people who would be more than happy to make good on Ivan's threats.

So he told them what the code had said. Segundo was no fool, either. He didn't want to lose his lodge—and he certainly didn't want any of his family to be hurt.

Keeping the secret of the code wasn't worth all that. And to be honest, he wondered if sharing the information really mattered.

After all, there was a very good chance that if these people went up the river, they wouldn't come back alive.

TWENTY-THREE

Along the Anaconda River
Somewhere in the Amazon wilderness of Peru

It took eleven days before Charlie found what she was
looking for.

Up until then she had been the perfect member
of the team, foraging for food, cooking, and helping
navigate without ever complaining.

And there was plenty that she could have complained
about.

Traveling through the rain forest was the most difficult thing Charlie had ever done.

After five days on the Anaconda River, they had to
abandon their motorboat. The Anaconda had stopped
being much of a river at all and became what was known
as flooded forest, which composed a significant amount of
the Amazon basin. In it, the water level fluctuated greatly
throughout the year; sometimes there was dry land, but
just as often it could be more like a swamp. That was the

case now. The water was two feet deep, but there were trees everywhere in it, making it too narrow and shallow to get the boat through. Instead, they had to resort to a canoe, which Segundo had sold them and which they had been pulling behind the speedboat, aware this time would come.

The canoe was a lot more work than the speedboat, of course. They paddled until their arms ached and their hands blistered, and then they paddled more. Even though the canoe was a modern one, made in a factory and designed to be light and maneuverable and comfortable, navigating through the maze of flooded trees was extremely difficult. They often found themselves stuck in an impassable tangle of foliage, from which they would have to back out and try to find another route, or at a point where the water got too shallow to paddle through, forcing them to hoist the canoe and their gear up onto their shoulders and portage it through the ankle-deep muck. And despite the padded seats, Charlie still felt like someone had spent the last few days kicking her in the rear end.

Then there was the weather. It was either swelteringly hot and humid or raining in buckets. When the rains came, they got soaked, and due to the humidity, they never quite dried out, so everything they owned was starting to get slightly moldy and smell like cheese.

And finally, there were the insects. Everywhere. If you so much as leaned against a tree, you were likely to end up with ants crawling all over your body. If you lit a candle at night, flying insects would arrive by the thousand, throwing themselves into the flame like tiny kamikazes, in numbers so great that it was hard to keep the candle going. The insects worked their way into the gear and the food. And they were always swarming around you. In addition to the mosquitoes, there were sweat bees, which were attracted to your perspiration; scorpions, which would crawl into your boots if you took them off in a vain attempt to dry them out; and spiders, which Charlie knew weren't technically insects, but that didn't make them any less disgusting when you walked straight into a web and then found one the size of a walnut crawling through your hair.

Hundreds of times a day, if not thousands, Charlie thought about telling the others that coming this way had obviously been a bad idea and asking if they would mind turning back. Dante and Milana were putting on a good show of being tough, but Charlie sensed that both of them were miserable as well and would be happy to pack it in.

But neither of them suggested that they turn around, because neither of them ever gave up on a mission.

And Charlie never suggested turning around either, because she wanted answers.

She wanted to know if she was right in her suspicions about what Darwin had really found. And there was no way to do that except to keep following the clues to where they led.

The other questions she had were slightly easier to get answers to. That was where the quicksand came in.

In truth, what she was looking for wasn't technically quicksand. It was a feature of the Amazonian flooded forests that Segundo had referred to as "pechado," but it worked in a similar fashion and was even more dangerous. Essentially, it was a slurry of soil and water that looked stable—until you stepped into it.

Charlie and Dante were on a foraging expedition, looking for food, while Milana stayed with the canoe. (Segundo had warned them against ever leaving their supplies unattended. Even in the most remote stretches of the rain forest, there still might be other people who would make off with their things. And the monkeys had a tendency to steal as well.) Even though there were thousands of different plants in the Amazon basin, only a small percentage had fruits that were edible for humans, and they tended to be few and far between. The best way to find them was to follow the monkeys, which also ate them. It wasn't particularly hard to know when monkeys were around, as they were noisy, chattering constantly as they thrashed their way through the trees. However, spotting them was surprisingly difficult. The forest canopy was thick and had many layers, and the monkeys spent most of their time in the upper reaches. Following them required looking high above you at all times, keeping your neck craned back and your eyes alert for the slightest glimpse of fur flashing through the branches.

Unfortunately, keeping your gaze locked on what was above you meant that you couldn't watch what was on the forest floor, which was dangerous. The flooded forest was full of obstacles, like pools of water, slicks of mud, tree roots, vines, rocks, and the occasional pit, any of which you could stumble over or fall into. And then there were all the biological hazards: plants with sharp thorns or serrated leaves that cut like knives, venomous snakes, spiderwebs, hornets' nests, caimans, and maybe even jaguars. In addition, the forest floor was dark. Even in broad daylight, few of the sun's rays filtered down through the millions of leaves above; being on the ground of the forest meant living in permanent dusk—so you had to work even harder to observe the world around you.

So Charlie, Dante, and Milana had worked out a system: One of them would keep an eye on the monkeys, figuring out which way they needed to go, while the other kept an eye on the ground and worked out the path of least resistance.

At the time, Dante was doing the tracking, watching a

group of long-limbed spider monkeys crash through the canopy, while Charlie was navigating, as usual. Dante claimed that he had Charlie navigate most of the time because she was shorter and therefore better suited to seeing things close to the ground, but the truth was that Charlie had a better spatial memory. Finding the fruit was the easy part; finding your way back to camp again was much more difficult. A few days before, Dante and Milana had learned this the hard way. They had tracked down a moriche palm full of aguaje fruit within only a few minutes—and then spent another two hours trying to retrace their steps.

So now Charlie was keeping an eye on the ground ahead of them, while consistently looking behind them to remember the route back as well. Occasionally, she would pause to mark a tree to signal where the path was. Segundo had shown her the traditional way to do this, which was to hack a slash in the bark with a large knife; he had even given her one as a gift, which she was carrying right now. But Charlie had discovered something that worked even better: She used nail polish.

Milana had brought a few different colors. Charlie found that hot pink with sparkles worked the best, given that it was a color that didn't occur much in nature, even out here in the most biodiverse place on earth. A dab of it on the bark of a tree could be seen from a long distance away.

As for herself, Charlie was partial to the more muted

tones of polish. For the first time in her life, she was letting her nails grow, and Milana had helped her paint them olive green the night before. (Although the official name of the color was Verdant Lawn. Charlie wasn't crazy about calling it that, but she had to admit that she liked the look of it.)

She had just steered Dante around a thicket of particularly nasty saw-bladed grass when she spotted the pechado. It looked at first like an unusually nice, smooth patch of dirt overlaid with fallen leaves, but Charlie realized it was potentially hazardous.

Then she let Dante walk right into it.

He had gone only two steps when the ground seemed to give out beneath him. It didn't quite collapse, but almost seemed to come alive, sucking his feet down into it. This was accompanied by an eruption of air that sounded like an enormous belch. Within seconds, Dante found himself up to his ankles in muck, like a man who had suddenly had his feet locked into concrete. He tried to lift a leg out, but couldn't. Instead, the movement agitated the pechado and he sank a little deeper.

He swiveled around to Charlie. She could see that he was frightened but was trying his best to appear as though he wasn't. "Don't take another step!" he warned.

"I wasn't about to," Charlie replied calmly. "You look like you're in some trouble there."

Dante looked down at his feet, concerned, trying to

remember the survival lessons Segundo had given him. "This is pechado, right? It works kind of like quicksand."

"Exactly. The more you move, the more you sink."

"Segundo said the trick to escaping it is to distribute my weight more evenly. So if you could find a log or something to lay across it, I could use that to pull myself out."

Charlie nodded agreement, but she didn't make a move to help. Instead, she said, "How long have you known that Darwin discovered something out here?"

The look on Dante's face changed from concern to surprise—and then to annoyance. "I learned about Darwin's discovery from *you*. Now help get me out of here!"

"You knew about Darwin's discovery *before* I told you about it. I could see it in your eyes. Plus, you agreed to come out here and hunt for what he found way too easily. If the CIA was only interested in getting Pandora from me, they would have had you drag me onto the closest plane and haul me back to headquarters. They wouldn't have let you go poking around the rain forest for weeks for some other discovery—unless they were interested in getting their hands on that, too."

Now Dante looked like he was annoyed at himself, rather than Charlie; he had underestimated her again. Dante sank another inch and the thick slurry was oozing into his hiking boots. "You led me into this on purpose so you could interrogate me?"

"I didn't think I could trust you to tell me the truth if I just asked."

"I don't need your help to get out of here, you know. I can do it myself."

"Yes, but that involves lying down and trying to swim through this stuff, which is going to be kind of disgusting. Not only is it muddy, but it stinks. And we're more than a week from the closest shower, so I don't think Milana will want to get that close to you. . . ."

"I don't have any interest in Milana."

"Sure you don't. But if I were you, my *real* concern would be that bullet ant right there." Charlie pointed to a large black ant that was working its way across the pechado. Due to its minuscule weight, it didn't sink, but walked right over the surface toward Dante.

Dante's eyes went wide in fear. He looked warily at the ant as he sank slightly more. "That's not really a bullet ant, is it?"

Charlie made a show of scrutinizing it from the safety of the solid ground. "Sure looks like one to me. Without my help, you won't be able to get out of there before that guy reaches you."

"You have to be kidding. You're honestly blackmailing me right now?"

"I thought you were a fan of blackmail," Charlie said. "I mean, you blackmailed *me* into helping you find Pandora."

"That was different," Dante said angrily. "The safety of the world was at stake!"

"You still could have tried asking nicely." Charlie considered the bullet ant once again. "I've heard their sting feels like walking across a bed of nails that has been set on fire. Or skinny-dipping in a volcano . . ."

"All right!" Dante exploded. "Yes! I knew about Darwin's discovery before! Now get me out of here!"

Charlie stayed put. "How did you know about it?"

Dante huffed in exasperation.

Charlie sat down on a nearby tree stump, indicating that she had plenty of time. "I'd speak quickly if I were you. That ant's not very far away."

Dante considered his options—and gave in. "After you broke Einstein's code, the CIA figured that, maybe, he had left other messages behind that no one had noticed before. . . ."

"Or maybe clues to other equations he'd hidden?"

"Yes. That too. So teams of agents were sent to repositories of his work all over the world to comb through his papers. And a team in Princeton found something. Some notes he'd made to himself, using the same code, much later in his life. As you know, the way he wrote the code, it didn't look like words; it looked like a mathematical equation that didn't work, so no one had ever realized what it really was. And when they decoded it, it said that there had been other scientists before him who had discovered things like Pandora. . . ."

"That's exactly what it said?"

"I can't recall exactly what it said. I don't have a photographic memory like you. All I can give you is the gist: Einstein wasn't the first scientist to find something that humanity couldn't be trusted with. And the others had hidden their discoveries too."

Charlie got to her feet again and walked over to the remains of a tree that had fallen long before, a palm trunk that had been rotted by mold and gnawed by termites until it was only six feet long. "Did Einstein say how he knew this?"

"No. Only that he knew it. And Darwin was the only other scientist he mentioned."

Charlie gave him a skeptical look. "Really?"

"Well, he might have listed others, but the book that the note was found in had been damaged. So only Darwin's name could be made out."

Charlie studied Dante for a moment, assessing whether he was telling the truth or not, then grabbed one end of the palm trunk and dragged it toward the pechado. "Did Einstein say what Darwin had found?"

"No. Just that he had found something. We assumed that even Einstein didn't know what it was."

"But the CIA thinks it's Paititi? That's why you studied it before coming here?"

"The CIA has no idea what it is. Although they figure that Paititi is a distinct possibility."

"What business is it of the CIA's if Darwin found a lost city? If he did, it'd be the property of Peru or Ecuador or whatever country it's in. And any gold or artifacts there would be the property of that country as well."

"The CIA is merely interested in *what* Darwin found, that's all. Seeing as the last thing hidden by a genius was an equation that could destroy all life on earth, we figure it's in our best interests to get to these discoveries before anyone else does. As you've noticed, they tend to attract some pretty bad people."

Charlie reached the edge of the pechado, but stopped before dropping the tree trunk into it. "And you and Milana are now some kind of special team tasked with going out and finding these things?"

"Basically. Seeing as we had success finding Pandora."

Charlie frowned. "*I'm* the one who found Pandora."

"And it was my idea to recruit you."

"Which is why you had to come looking for me again. Because you guys can't do this on your own."

"It certainly helps to have you aboard," Dante admitted, glancing warily at the bullet ant, which was now only a foot away from him. "Now could you please get me out of here?"

"Okay." Charlie heaved the palm trunk into the pechado. One end landed with a wet *thwack* in front of Dante.

Dante had now sunk down to his knees. He bent forward, lying prone across the trunk, which allowed him to distribute his weight more evenly without flopping face-first into the pechado. However, he still couldn't keep entirely out of it. The palm trunk sank a bit, and it was too narrow for him to keep his entire body on it. His broad shoulders stuck out on both sides, and his arms dangled into the muck.

"Pull me out," he ordered Charlie.

"That's not physically possible," she replied. "You probably weigh twice what I do, not counting that tree trunk. And it's not like you're lying on a frictionless surface. You might as well be asking me to try to pull an elephant out of there."

Dante frowned, realizing she was right, and then fumbled his way out himself. He had to partially drag himself along the trunk and partially paddle through the pechado with his arms and legs, so he still ended up with foul-smelling gunk on him, although considerably less than if he had done it without the aid of the tree trunk. And he did it quickly enough to escape the bullet ant, leaving it behind on the surface of the pechado.

By the time he reached solid ground again, he was soiled, exhausted, and seething. He got to his feet, grabbed some dead leaves off the ground and attempted to wipe the mud off himself with them. "If you ever try anything like that again, I'll make you regret it."

"What are you gonna do?" Charlie asked. "Ground me? Am I not allowed to track down any more discoveries hidden by famous scientists for the next two weeks?"

"Don't push your luck, kiddo."

"Don't threaten me, Dante. You need me a heck of a lot more than I need you."

"I doubt that."

"You just said I was better at finding all these things than you."

"I was telling you what you wanted to hear so that you'd help me out of that muck." Dante gave Charlie a cocky smile. "Milana and I are perfectly capable of finding Paititi."

"Maybe so," Charlie replied. "But you'll still need me. Because Paititi wasn't Darwin's big discovery."

Dante's smile faded. "You're bluffing."

"I'm not. In fact, I know exactly what it was. And it's something far more important than a lost city."

Dante stared at Charlie. To his frustration, it seemed that she was being honest. "What is it?"

"I'll tell you in a bit." Charlie shifted her attention back to the pechado. "But first I need your help collecting something."

TWENTY-FOUR

Because she couldn't feel pain, Esmerelda had always been cautious where injuries were concerned. Any time she hurt herself, she went to the doctor to get checked out. She had been similarly protective of her brothers, always insisting that they look after their health, no matter how good they felt.

But now they weren't being cautious at all. Ivan Spetz hadn't allowed them to be.

She and her brothers had been badly injured in the fire Charlie Thorne had caused, but instead of going to a nice, sterile hospital for proper medical care, they had headed to one of the most dangerous places imaginable. There were probably a million ways their wounds could get infected out here in the Amazon basin, and if things took a bad turn for them, they were weeks from the closest doctor.

And yet this time Esmerelda probably would have been taking those same risks even if Ivan Spetz hadn't forced her into helping him.

Ivan had presented himself pleasantly enough when he had first arrived at the refinery, offering to be partners in their quest for Darwin's treasure. They each brought something to the table: Esmerelda and her brothers had knowledge, while Ivan had the funds. But Esmerelda didn't trust Ivan one bit, and she was quite sure that he didn't trust her or her brothers either. The man slept with a loaded gun holstered to his leg and a knife under his pillow. Plus, she had seen his true nature when he had intimidated the people at the kapok tree; that hadn't been an idle threat. He was willing to burn down their resort and start hurting people to get what he wanted.

But then, so was Esmerelda.

She had sacrificed so much for Darwin's treasure. So many years of her life. And now she had sacrificed her beauty as well. Her face was scarred forever, she was certain—thanks to Charlie Thorne. Not only was Esmerelda determined to find Darwin's treasure, but she was going to make Charlie pay for what she had done.

She just had to stay alive long enough to enjoy it.

She was well aware that any normal person who had suffered the injuries that she had would have still been in excruciating pain, even now, well over a week after it had happened. She knew that her body had been weakened by the accident, whether she felt it or not, and thus her resistance to disease and infection was lower than normal. So, as she worked her way up the Anaconda River with Ivan and her brothers, she took every precaution possible for her health. She sterilized and redressed her burned skin every day. She carefully tended to every insect bite and scratch. She had looted the small infirmary at the eco-lodge and she was taking medication every few hours to preemptively fight off any infection she might develop.

Still, the flooded forest was rife with dangers. Stinging insects swarmed. Piranhas abounded in the river. Venomous snakes lurked in the trees, while anacondas slithered through the shallow waters. The whole place was a death trap.

All that kept Esmerelda going was the lure of Darwin's treasure—and revenge.

It helped to have Charlie and the others leading the way. They had left a path, unaware that Esmerelda was following them. For starters, there had been their speedboat, moored at the point where the river became impassable for it. But now, in the flooded forest, there were more subtle markers: a few snapped tree branches to mark the best route through a thicket, the ashes of a fire to indicate a decent place to camp for the night. Esmerelda wasn't sure quite how far behind Charlie they were, but she felt they were making up time.

Ivan, who was an adept tracker, seemed to agree.

"This was made earlier today," Ivan said, studying a footprint in the mud. It was nine days after they had found the kapok tree where Darwin's code had been, and three since they had entered the flooded forest. The footprint was from a big, thick boot. The man's. "It's between six and eight hours old."

"We're closing in on them," Esmerelda observed.

"Yes, but not quickly enough." Ivan turned from the dry land on which he stood and considered both their canoes, which were moored in the shallow water and heavily laden with supplies. "We're dragging too much weight. If we dumped everything but the necessities, we could make much better time."

"Everything we have is potentially a necessity," Esmerelda argued. "We don't know what else we might encounter. And we could be out here for another few weeks."

"Weeks?" Ivan asked.

"We still might have a long way to go up this river. . . ."

Ivan shook his head. "No. The terrain is changing. It's subtle, but it's happening. We're getting near the end of the flooded forest. . . ."

"That doesn't mean our journey will be over."

"Darwin's clue said we should follow the red river

until we get to a place that looked like the Thames. That's the river through London. Therefore, this city of stone must be on the water."

"We have no idea *what* Darwin meant by that," Esmerelda cautioned. "We can't be cavalier here. It might be quite a bit longer until we reach this city of stone. And once we get there, we'll still have to get all the way back to civilization. That could take us twice as long."

"Twice as long?" Ivan repeated, curious.

Esmerelda realized she had made a mistake and said too much. She had been thinking that it would take longer to return to civilization because their canoes would be even more loaded down. If they found Darwin's treasure, they would be hauling plenty of it back with them. And, if all went according to her plan, there would only be three of them doing the work. Ivan Spetz would no longer be in the picture.

However, she hadn't let Ivan in on her theory that the city would be full of gold. And she certainly didn't want him to know she was thinking about abandoning him out in the jungle.

"It makes sense to err on the side of caution," Esmerelda said, to cover her mistake. "A thousand things could go wrong out here. Any one of which could cause us a delay in getting back up the river."

Ivan suddenly burst into laughter. It was the first time

Esmerelda had heard him laugh in all the days she had known him, and it was so sharp and loud that it startled her at first. "All this time, you've been thinking that we'll be going back the way we came?" he asked. "No. I have something much more efficient planned for our return."

"What?" Esmerelda asked.

"You'll see soon enough," Ivan replied. "Now help me dump some of these supplies. We need to pick up our pace."

TWENTY-FIVE

Charlie waited until she and Dante were back with Milana to explain her theory, so she wouldn't have to say everything twice.

It was nearing dusk. Milana had set up camp for the night, built a fire, and was already grilling two piranhas that she had caught. Each was the size, shape, and thickness of a small frisbee. She had run sharp sticks through their mouths, so they looked vaguely like piranha lollipops, and was roasting them over the flames.

Charlie and Dante had each brought an armload of aguaje fruit, which Dante was peeling with a Buck knife.

Charlie was holding a small plastic container in which she had placed the bullet ant she had caught earlier. There were three other bullet ants in there with it, which she had been carefully collecting throughout the journey. She had put some leaves inside for the ants and was watching the new one carefully to see if it would eat.

Insects were all around them, lured by the firelight. They were dying in the fire by the hundred, making tiny wet pops as they burned.

"Darwin might have found a lost city, but that's not what he would have been so excited about," Charlie said. "His carving on the tortoise shell in the Galápagos said he had discovered the greatest treasure in human history."

Dante said, "If Paititi has a lot of gold in it, that would make sense."

"Darwin was a scientist, not a treasure hunter," Charlie insisted. "Even if he found a thousand tons of gold, he wouldn't consider that the greatest treasure in human history. For him, a great treasure would be a scientific discovery. A huge one. One that would change the world."

Milana suddenly looked up from the fire, understanding what Charlie meant. "No," she said. "You don't think . . ."

"Yes," Charlie said. "I do."

"Hold on," Dante said. "I'm lost here. What are both of you talking about? What did Darwin find?"

"Evidence of evolution," Charlie said.

"He found evidence of evolution in the Galápagos," Dante said dismissively. "After he came here. That's what he based all his theories on. . . ."

"That's what he *claimed* he based all his theories on,"

Charlie corrected. "But it makes sense that he might have found something here first—*before* he got to the Galápagos—something concrete that convinced him evolution existed."

"Concrete?" Dante echoed. "Like what?"

"Like a missing link between apes and humans," Charlie said.

Dante and Milana both stared at her across the flames of the campfire, stunned by the very thought.

"That's not possible," Dante said finally. "Humans evolved in Africa. That's where all the fossil protohuman remains have been discovered. There's no way there could be a missing link all the way over here, on the other side of the world."

"First of all, protohuman remains have been found in plenty of places around the world," Charlie said. "Java man was discovered on a Pacific Island thousands of miles from Africa. Protohumans were extremely widespread."

"But they spread out *after* evolving from apes," Dante argued. "And all the evidence indicates that happened in Africa. It couldn't have happened more than once."

"Of course it could have," Charlie said. "Things like this happen all the time. It's called convergent evolution. Different species in different places evolve extremely similar traits in response to similar environments."

"Like what?" Dante asked.

Charlie waved to the sky above her, where bats were once again pinwheeling through the air in search of insects. "Bats evolved wings completely independently of birds. So did insects. And pterosaurs, for that matter. Bat wings and pterosaur wings evolved hundreds of millions of years apart, but they're extremely similar in design. Or, as another example, whales and dolphins evolved from terrestrial mammals, but they evolved fins very similar to those that evolved on fish hundreds of millions of years earlier."

"But that's just evolving similar traits," Dante argued. "You're claiming that *humans* developed in two different places. Which is very different."

Charlie shook her head. "No. I'm not saying that *humans* could have developed in two different places. That'd be impossible. I'm saying that something *similar to humans* could have evolved here. That evolution might have followed a similar track twice. And that is extremely possible. Like, there's a snake that lives around here, the emerald tree boa, which looks almost exactly the same as another snake that evolved in the South Pacific—the green tree python. It's nearly impossible to tell them apart unless you're a specialist. Both snakes are virtually the same color green and live in trees and have the same behaviors. Because they evolved separately to fill similar niches on opposite sides of the world."

"And you think that's what happened here?" Dante challenged. "That apes started evolving into men here as well as in Africa?"

"First of all, apes didn't evolve into men," Charlie said. "Humans and apes diverged from a common ancestor a couple of million years ago. But yes, I'm thinking that a divergence could have happened here as well, though from monkeys, seeing as apes didn't evolve in South America, as far as we know. It obviously didn't survive . . . but then, most protohuman lines died out. Like the Neanderthals. The only line that made it to the modern day was *us*."

Dante shifted his attention to Milana, who had been listening to all this intently while cooking the piranhas. "You agree that all this is possible?"

"Yes," she said, then asked Charlie, "So you're thinking that Darwin's big discovery was some fossils that looked like a link between monkeys and humans?"

"Right."

"But why didn't he just reveal them to the world back then?"

"Because the world wasn't ready for them," Charlie said.

TWENTY-SIX

Charlie explained. "Scientifically, the world was a very different place back when Darwin visited this area. For example, most of the world's greatest scientists didn't have the slightest idea how old the earth really was. They thought it might be only a few thousand years old, if that. And so did almost everyone else. The few people who suggested otherwise were considered lunatics, the same way Copernicus had been when he suggested that the earth revolved around the sun."

"And you think Darwin was worried about being considered a lunatic?" Dante asked.

"That's only part of it," Charlie replied. "The thing is, you have to know how incredibly old the earth is for evolution to make sense. Darwin couldn't have proposed that life evolved slowly over millions of years if everyone thought the earth was way younger than that. But science was changing dramatically at that time. Particularly geology. Humans were gaining the ability to cut through the earth to put in canals and roads, and every time they did, they exposed layers of rock. Geologists were starting to realize how those layers had formed and how long that might take. And eventually a Scottish geologist named Charles Lyell wrote a book called *Principles of Geology*, where he ended up proposing that the earth might actually be millions of years old. A lot of established scientists thought it was heretical. But Charles Darwin found it fascinating. He brought one of the first copies of it along on the *Beagle* and read it over and over.

"So, when Darwin was exploring South America, he kept seeing geological evidence that Lyell might be right about the age of the earth. In fact, early on during his voyage, he imagined that his big contribution to science would be a book on the geology of the continent. But his thoughts about how old the earth was started to affect his thoughts about biology. At the time, the general idea was that every species of animal had been around since the beginning of creation, and Darwin was starting to realize that theory didn't hold water. Like, it didn't explain dinosaur fossils. Plenty of those had already been found in Europe and no one had any idea how to explain them— and then Darwin found some fossils of giant extinct mammals in Patagonia. He also noticed plenty of examples of convergent evolution, like that there are giant birds called rheas in Argentina that fit the exact same ecological niche as ostriches in Africa. None of that really makes any sense in the old theory. Why would bones from giant animals that didn't exist anymore be scattered all over the planet? And why would there be one kind of giant bird on one continent and a whole different kind of giant bird on a different continent?"

"So he was already starting to think about evolution," Milana said.

"He was definitely searching for an explanation for everything he was seeing," Charlie replied. "And then he comes on an expedition to where we are right now and he finds exactly what he's looking for. Evidence that evolution exists—and that it isn't just animals that evolved over millions of years but humans, too. That's something he would consider an incredible discovery. The greatest treasure in human history. Literally.

"Unfortunately, the rest of the world was still struggling with the idea that the earth was way older than the Bible said. So imagine what it might have been like to present evidence that humans had *evolved*. There are plenty of people *today* who consider that idea to be blasphemous. Back then it would have been even worse."

Dante and Milana pondered that for a while. Dante gazed thoughtfully into the bonfire, listening to the pop and hiss of insects dying in the flames, while Milana pried the cooked piranhas off the skewers and removed the skin from them with a knife.

"I suppose that makes sense," Dante said finally. "But even so, I can't imagine that Darwin would leave such a great discovery behind."

"I doubt that he did." Charlie tucked the container with the bullet ants into her backpack. "I think he *tried* to bring back the fossils, and it didn't go well at all. I'm not sure what happened, though I assume Captain Fitz-Roy and the crew of the *Beagle* were horrified by what Darwin found. Which would explain why any record of the *Beagle* coming to Ecuador was removed from their journals."

"They covered up the discovery," Milana said.

"Exactly," Charlie agreed. "And they probably destroyed the fossils, too."

Dante asked, "You really think FitzRoy and the crew got that upset over some bones? None of them were scientists. How would they even know that they were the remains of a protohuman and not a monkey?"

Charlie said, "The skull of a protohuman doesn't look anything like the skull of a monkey. Or an ape. The crew would have recognized that it was something in between monkeys and humans—and it probably would have scared the pants off them. Darwin obviously feared that something might go wrong with the fossils since he left clues to return to the fossil site along his way back. But I'm betting the reaction was far worse than he had expected, because he never mentioned the fossils again. He almost didn't propose the theory of evolution at all."

Milana handed Charlie a plate full of piranha. "He didn't?"

"No. Darwin kept the theory to himself for nearly twenty years after he returned from his trip. And even then he might not have published his work if someone else hadn't come up with the exact same idea."

"Alfred Russel Wallace!" Dante said triumphantly. It seemed to Charlie that he'd been waiting to contribute something to the conversation, so that he could impress Milana. He looked to her as he elaborated, as if seeking her approval. "I've read about him. He was exploring in Indonesia and developed his own theory of evolution. And bizarrely, the very person he mailed his work to, to review it, was . . . Charles Darwin."

"Exactly. And Darwin kind of freaked out." Charlie shoveled a forkful of piranha into her mouth. The fish wasn't particularly flavorful, but she was famished after a long, grueling day of exploring. "I mean, Darwin had been sitting on top of this idea for two decades, wondering whether or not to share it, and then some other guy nearly stole his thunder. Even though Darwin was nervous about the reception his idea would get, he still didn't want to lose the credit for coming up with it. So Darwin went to the one man he could trust, Charles Lyell, and told him everything, and Lyell arranged to have both men's papers presented on the same day at a big scientific meeting in London. That way, both men shared the credit for the theory of evolution by natural selection. But Darwin obviously left out the part about the missing link. Instead, he claimed to have developed the idea the way we've always heard, by observing the differences in the animals of the Galápagos."

Charlie gulped down another mouthful of piranha, then continued. "Even then the papers sparked huge controversy and were called sacrilegious. Which probably convinced Darwin even more that he was right to keep whatever he really found down here a secret. For the rest of his life, he did his best to stay out of the public eye. He let other people defend his theories in London and remained at his home out in the countryside. In fact, Darwin was a very different man once he returned from his voyages around the world. The Darwin who visited South America was an avid explorer, always up for adventure. He spent weeks on horseback in Argentina, climbed mountains in Chile—and now we know he went on a major expedition into the Amazon, too. But after he got back, he lived a quiet life and rarely ventured far from home again."

Dante picked a piranha bone out of his teeth and studied Charlie carefully. "How long have you been working on this theory of yours?"

"Since I heard that Darwin had made a secret discovery down here."

"It makes sense," Dante said. "But it's all just speculation. You haven't offered any real proof that Darwin discovered a missing link at all."

Charlie said, "No offense, but I'm not slogging through the rain forest for days on end because it gives me quality time with you. If that's all I wanted, we could have just gone to Disneyland. I'm doing this because I want to see what he found for myself."

"Plus, anyone who finds proof of a missing link will become world-famous," Dante said. "It'd be like discovering electricity. Or DNA."

Charlie shrugged. "What's wrong with being famous for making a landmark scientific discovery? It's a lot better than being famous for assassinating someone. Or starting a war. Or being a corrupt politician." She scraped the last bits of piranha off her plate and wolfed them down. "Of course, that's assuming that we even find these fossils. Or that you guys don't force me to keep them a secret."

"Why do you think we'd do that?" Milana asked.

Charlie said, "Until we sat down for dinner, you guys

thought we were looking for a lost city of gold. Which means that's probably what the whole gang back at CIA headquarters thinks too. But now I've thrown you a curveball. Maybe our government would be just as afraid of sharing the news of a new missing link as Darwin was."

"As hard as it may be for you to believe, our government isn't always the bad guy," Dante said sharply. "The United States is a major supporter of science. The Smithsonian is the largest museum and research complex on earth. NASA is the world's preeminent space exploration agency. And the government gives out hundreds of millions in research grants to other scientific institutions as well. If we *do* find fossil evidence of a missing link—or a lost city—I can promise it will be well taken care of."

Charlie had to admit that was possible. And there wasn't much point to challenging Dante on the subject. So instead she said, "Good. I appreciate that."

Dante slapped a mosquito that was feeding on his hand, leaving a splotch of his own blood on his fingers. "The sooner we find this place, the better," he grumbled. "I'm tired of getting eaten alive out here." He looked to Charlie. "I don't suppose that genius brain of yours has any idea how much farther we have to go?"

Charlie was about to say no when, to her surprise—and Dante's—Milana spoke up instead.

"I think we're almost there," she said. "Today, while you were gone, I found evidence that there might be an ancient city close by."

Dante's eyes went wide. "Where?"

"You're sitting on it," Milana said.

TWENTY-SEVEN

Through the trees, Oz could see the campfire burning. It was so bright in the darkness of the rain forest, it might as well have been a spotlight.

Jose and the five other men he had brought with him saw it as well; they would have had to be blind to miss it. Without so much as a word or a signal from Oz, they all stopped paddling their canoes at once, letting them glide through the flooded forest.

Night in the Amazon basin was not quiet; the air was alive with the hum of insects, the chirp of bats, the call of frogs. But Oz could still hear the voices of the people in the camp carrying clearly across the water.

They spoke English, but their voices were all inflected with slight accents, as though it wasn't the mother tongue for any of them. It was the three people who had been arrested and brought to the refinery—the woman and the two men who had been badly burned—and the one who had bribed his men to pay for their release.

Oz had caught up to the first group of people he was following. He knew there was still yet another group ahead.

Oz and his men had found the boats of both groups moored at the same spot at the beginning of the flooded forest. His men had recognized the speedboat as the one that had belonged to the American law enforcement officials who had arrested the Italians; they had been somewhat surprised to find it there, as that indicated that the Americans were also looking for whatever was hidden up the river. Which made Oz wonder if the Americans were really law enforcement at all.

They had sunk both of the other groups' boats, blasting holes in them and letting the water drag them to the bottom of the Anaconda River. If there was a lot of money at stake, Oz didn't want to be racing anyone back to civilization.

The canoe Oz was in bumped up against dry land. Oz climbed out, taking great care to be as silent as possible. His men followed his lead. They quietly dragged their canoes onto land and began making camp.

All of the men Oz had brought with him had been born in this region. They knew the ways of the rain forest and had no need for a fire to make it through the night. In fact, they hardly needed any gear at all; during their journey, they had been subsisting on termites and local fruits and fish they had caught with a simple line, and they had been sleeping on the ground, under lean-tos fashioned out of palm leaves. It wasn't easy going, but for most of them, it was a pleasant change from the drudgery of the refinery. Oz had heard more than one of the men remark that this felt like a vacation.

Not that any of them had ever been on a real vacation before. The refinery barely paid them enough to support their families.

Oz would rather have been at a beach resort, but even he felt a degree of excitement. He was lugging along a bit more gear to make himself comfortable—a small camp stove, a bedroll, and plenty of bug repellant—although tonight, in the interest of not alerting the other travelers that they were close by, he would make do with less. He wasn't sure what they were heading toward, but this did feel like quite an adventure.

Oz stood in the dark forest, watching the campfire in the distance. Ivan and the Castellos had no idea he or his men were there, no clue that they were being followed. They spoke loudly, without any care that someone might overhear them. Oz couldn't make out everything they said, due to the distance and the great array of animal noises in the forest around him, but he could catch snippets of their conversation.

One word in particular grabbed his attention.

Treasure.

Oz tensed in excitement.

They were discussing a trove of Incan gold, talking about how much farther ahead it might be, how they would split it up, and what they would do with their riches when they had them.

A cruel smile played across Oz's face. A trove of Incan gold was far better than any mineral rights he might come across.

Jose and the others gathered around him. They were also listening to the other people in the distance, but Oz knew they didn't understand English well enough to follow.

"What are they talking about?" Jose whispered to him in Spanish.

"Nothing important," Oz replied. "They're complaining about the mosquitoes again." The more his men knew about any potential treasure, the less he could trust them. There was no loyalty among this bunch, himself included.

Jose nodded, then said, "We could ambush them tonight, while they're sleeping. Tie them up. Force them to tell us what they're looking for."

Oz had considered this already himself, but he had rejected the idea. Maybe they would get some answers— but then what were they supposed to do with their captives? Hold them prisoner in the rain forest? And what if their captives didn't give up the information? What was Oz supposed to do then? He and his men were refinery workers, not commandos.

"Let's just keep following them for now," he told Jose. "Until we find out what everyone is looking for here."

"And then what? Kill them?" Jose didn't say the words with menace. He seemed to be worried that this was Oz's plan.

"We won't have to do that," Oz replied. He was willing to do a lot to get rich, but killing someone in cold blood went a bit too far. Luckily, he had another plan that would work equally as well. "We'll just take their canoes and their gear and leave them out here."

Jose grinned, understanding.

Oz and his men wouldn't have to kill anyone at all. If they stranded the others out here, the rain forest would do it for them.

TWENTY-EIGHT

ante stared at the ground illuminated by the flames of the campfire. A thin layer of dirt stretched over gray limestone. "I don't see what's so important," he admitted. "It's just stone."

"That *is* what's important," Charlie said, understanding what Milana had meant. "We're sitting on stone!"

Dante appeared embarrassed that he wasn't grasping the idea. "And why is that exciting?"

"Because stone has been awfully rare out here," Charlie explained. "I just realized it myself: This whole ecosystem is built on soil. I guess it's kind of a giant river delta, a couple thousand miles wide. It's been dirt and mud and water, but not rock."

"Jeez," Dante said. He was even more embarrassed now, realizing his mistake. It was amazing what you took for granted, like rocks. He was used to the ground under his feet being a thin layer of soil over bedrock, but the Amazon basin was completely different.

"I dug around a bit while you were out foraging," Milana said. "The area with stones isn't very wide—only about six feet across—but it's *long*. It goes quite a distance through the forest in both directions from here."

"It's a road?" Charlie asked, excited.

"I think so," Milana replied. "I can't come up with any other explanation."

Charlie looked around her. Even knowing that they were sitting on an ancient road, she couldn't see any signs of it; the rain forest had reclaimed it, and the landscape around them was thick with trees. "Looks like it's been abandoned for a few hundred years."

"At least," Milana said. "From what I understand, the Incas built roads all through their empire. I'm guessing this connected to Paititi."

"Why didn't you say something earlier?" Dante asked.

"I was going to tell you when you got back. But both of you were eager to talk about what Charlie had come up with instead."

Charlie knelt beside the fire and swept away the dirt to fully expose the stone beneath it. It was limestone, pocked and pitted by centuries of rain and erosion. But it wasn't a smooth, continuous sheet. It was separate pieces of rock, some small, some quite large, fitted together like a giant mosaic. "This must have been a huge amount of work," she observed. "First they had to get all the rock here. And then they had to lay it down, for who knows how long a distance. This might have taken *years* to build."

"I've heard that the Incan road system rivaled the Romans'," Milana said. "But maybe it was even *more* advanced. This is an extremely difficult place to build a road. They would have had to cut down thousands of trees. And make sure the road didn't sink during floods. And then, in the mountains, they'd have a host of different problems. The Andes are a lot steeper than the Alps."

Charlie nodded agreement. Often, the civilizations of the Americas were looked upon as inferior to those of Europe or China. For example, the Incas were sometimes derided because they didn't domesticate many animals, but then, there hadn't been many animals that humans *could* domesticate in that area. Only llamas as pack animals and guinea pigs as a food source, while Europe had wild cattle and horses and pigs and goats and chickens and dogs. Without oxen or horses in the Incan empire, there was no point to having large carts to move goods around and thus no need to make the roads as wide, so they might have not seemed as impressive as the Roman roads at first. But they certainly were.

Charlie hadn't yet visited the great Incan archaeological sites like Machu Picchu, but she had heard that they were remarkable feats of engineering as well.

"Just because we're on a road doesn't mean we're close to Paititi yet," Dante cautioned. "The Incan road networks ran for hundreds of miles. This might be only the halfway point on some ancient highway."

"I thought of that," Milana said. "But I doubt that any road system around here would be extensive. The primary way to get from one place to another here is by river. No system of roads could improve upon that. So it wouldn't make sense to build roads over extremely long distances. But a large city would need cultivated areas close by to feed the residents, which might require a relatively small road network to transport the food."

Dante mulled that over, then admitted, "That makes sense."

"So," Milana concluded, "I'm betting we're less than twenty-four hours away."

Which turned out to be an accurate guess. Before noon the next day, they would be in the city of stone.

PART THREE

THE CITY OF STONE

The love for all living creatures is the most noble
attribute of man.

—CHARLES DARWIN

TWENTY-NINE

The smoking waters
Upper reaches of the Anaconda River
Peru

They knew they were close when they arrived at the point on the Anaconda River that looked like the Thames. Or rather, what the Thames had looked like in Darwin's time.

Once again, Darwin had been trying to describe something he didn't really have words for, other than to allude to a British landmark. And again, while the clue had seemed cryptic to Charlie, Dante, and Milana at first, once they got to the right place, they understood exactly what Darwin had meant.

London was built on the Thames River. In truth, London wouldn't have existed without the Thames; for centuries it was the lifeline of the city. Most of London's businesses were built close to its banks, as well as most of its great buildings: older edifices such as the Tower of London, the houses of Parliament, the Royal Observatory, and St Paul's Cathedral, or newer landmarks such as the London Eye, the Shard, or the Tate Modern museum. And yet, given how important the river was, the people of London had treated it terribly for most of the city's history. It was used as a garbage dump and a latrine. Factories flushed toxic chemicals into it, and it was common to find the carcasses of dead sheep, cattle—and even humans—floating in it. By Darwin's time, it was little more than a glorified sewer line and a breeding ground for disease. The river—and thus the entire city—became notorious for its noxious smell; at one point in the summer of 1858, it became so putrid that Parliament had to be suspended and nearly relocated from the city for good. Meanwhile, there were so many outbreaks of cholera and typhoid that life expectancy in London dropped to only thirty-seven years of age.

At the same time, London's air wasn't doing much better. In the Industrial Age, the main way to heat homes and power businesses was with coal, and tons of it was being burned every day. The result was a thick cloud of soot that hung over the city, which would then combine with London's notorious fogs to create an atmosphere so dark that it was often hard to see through even in the middle of the day. The soot turned London's buildings black and did far worse things to the Londoners themselves, filling their lungs with particles that impaired their ability to breathe. Bronchitis killed even more people than water-borne diseases. Between the foul air and the foul water, Londoners were so unhealthy that they could easily be discerned by their pale pallor, weak physiques, and the habit of breathing through their mouths because their nasal passages were so congested.

The new part of the Anaconda River that Charlie, Dante, and Milana encountered wasn't nearly as dangerous to their health as the Thames of the 1800s, but it looked eerily similar.

Around noon, they arrived at a break in the flooded forest. They saw it coming long before they reached it, because there was light ahead. For days they had been moving through the heavily shadowed permanent gloom of the rain forest floor, but suddenly there was brightness ahead, sunlight beaming down. It turned out to be a good-size lake, nearly a mile across. But while the surroundings were gorgeous—the lake was ringed with marsh grasses and pristine stands of forest—the water's surface was quite spooky. The water itself was so black, they couldn't see the ends of their paddle blades through it—probably due to a large amount of decaying plant life in it, Charlie figured—and smoke crept across it, even in the middle of the day.

Darwin's Thames would have also been coal black, with the smoke of ten thousand chimneys clinging to it.

Charlie, Dante, and Milana paused at the lake's edge, cautiously sniffing the air. Charlie detected a faint rotten egg smell. "Sulfur," she said.

"Yes," Milana agreed. "It's not smoke; it's steam. There must be a thermal spring nearby." The smell and sight made Milana feel strangely at home. She had grown up on the Blackfoot Indian Reservation in northern Montana, and her family had often taken trips to the southern reaches of the state, where there was a large amount of thermal activity. The most famous spot was Yellowstone National Park, which was located in the largest volcano caldera on earth, but there were many other, lesser-known areas close by with similar thermal activity. At these places, heat would vent up from the earth and turn to steam where it met the water. Milana had always loved those areas; the warm waters were wonderful to soak in, and she found them eerily beautiful as well.

She dipped her hand into the lake and found it to be quite cool, indicating that the steam vents were far away.

Charlie thought about Darwin's clue, as she had done thousands of times over the days since she had found it:

Follow the red river upstream for a month until you reach a place that looks like the Thames. Then find the altar in the main temple in the city of stone.

Dante must have been thinking the same thing,

because he said, "According to Darwin, the city of stone should be very close to here."

"Makes sense," Charlie said. "A big lake like this would be a good place to locate a city. Lots of fresh water, so probably plenty of fish to eat."

"But where is the city?" Dante asked, scrutinizing the forest along the lake.

"There." Charlie pointed to the farthest shore, where there was a bulge in the forest, like a small mountain of greenery. "Everywhere else in the Amazon basin has been flat as a pancake. I'm betting that any rise in elevation that big must be something man-made."

That made sense to the others, so they set off across the lake. After days on end of fighting their way through thick brush and portaging the canoe time and again, it was a relief to paddle across open water. The canoe glided easily across the smooth surface.

Compared with the forest, the lake also seemed to be far more full of life—or perhaps the life was simply easier to see out in the open. Although patches of steam occasionally obscured the shores of the lake, for the most part, they could see much farther than they had in the forest, and the bright sunlight helped as well. Hundreds of birds roosted in the trees by the lake's edge, including a dozen hoatzin, which were the size of turkeys but significantly prettier. Two families of howler monkeys foraged in trees on opposite sides of the lake, while a clan of giant river otters cavorted in the water. Charlie also spied several caimans lurking in the shallows, only their eyes and nostrils poking above the surface. She knew that the distance between eye and nostril was an indicator of how big each caiman was and deduced that some of them must be quite large, at least six feet long, if not more.

For the most part, however, they kept their eyes locked on the approaching shore, studying it for any sign of an abandoned city.

Dante was the first to notice something. "Look!" he exclaimed.

"Where?" Milana asked, scanning the shoreline.

"Not on land," Dante told her. "In the water. Below us."

Charlie and Milana both looked down into the lake and saw what Dante had.

Directly underneath them was a line of white stone blocks. The stones stood out despite the inky blackness of the water because they were only two inches below the surface and a dull white that reflected the sun. Charlie guessed they were limestone, like the stones that the road had been made of, and had probably been even lighter at some point, but now they were dulled from silt and plants growing on them. Still, they could see that the stones made a graceful arc on both sides of the canoe.

"Looks like a submerged wall," Milana observed.

"It's a fish pond!" Charlie exclaimed. "For a fish farm!"

"I think you're right," Dante agreed.

"Of course I'm right," Charlie told him. "I'm *me*."

The way she figured it, the large area created by the wall would have been perfect for raising fish. The wall would prevent big fish from escaping while also keeping predators out, while all the natural food and nutrients from the river could still flow into the pen.

A curtain of steam ahead of them drifted away, revealing that both ends of the curved wall extended to the shore where they believed the city was located. The shoreline was overgrown, so thick with reeds and grasses that they couldn't paddle the canoe through it—but the sunken wall provided a path to land.

Charlie, Dante, and Milana tied the canoe to the branches of a tree that had long ago fallen into the lake, then carefully stepped out onto the wall. They left most of their gear in the canoe, bringing only their small backpacks with them, loaded with the supplies they thought they would need, and headed for dry land.

Dante led the way, hacking through the reeds with a machete. The plants grew up to six feet out of the water, creating a wall of greenery on either side, so the route along the wall was narrow and claustrophobic. As Charlie edged along it, she was overcome by an unsettling feeling, like they weren't alone out there.

She turned back, staring across the lake toward the shore they had come from, but it was now obscured by the clouds of steam drifting over the surface.

A splash to Charlie's right startled her, and she wheeled around to see something as thick as a big tree limb slithering through the reeds.

"Anaconda," Milana said, sensing Charlie's unease and placing a hand on Charlie's arm to calm her.

Charlie was at once thankful for the small gesture and annoyed at herself for needing it.

She watched the snake vanish into the water, wondering if that was what had caused her ill ease. It was significantly bigger than any snake she had ever seen outside a zoo, but she knew they could get much larger.

"Hey!" Dante shouted from ahead. Not in alarm, but excitement.

Charlie realized he had made progress while she'd been watching the snake. She hurried along the sunken wall to shore, glad to be clear of the reeds, and found Dante staring into the forest.

"We found it!" he exclaimed triumphantly, smiling as broadly as she had ever seen.

Charlie stared into the forest too, letting her eyes adjust to the dark after being out in the bright sun. And then she saw what Dante had.

Charlie usually prided herself on being calm and

unflappable, but she couldn't manage that now. Her eyes went wide and she let out a gasp of surprise.

"Whoa," she said. "This is the coolest thing I've ever seen in my life."

THIRTY

J amilla Carter sat in her office, wondering where on earth Dante Garcia could be.

Technically, she knew he was in the Amazon basin. The last dead-drop message she had received from him indicated as much. But the Amazon basin was the same size as the United States. Knowing *where* in all that forest Dante was would have been nice.

According to Dante's last message, his mission was proceeding well. He had located Charlie Thorne, won back her trust, and co-opted her into tracking down whatever Darwin had discovered; Charlie even believed the decision had been her idea.

But it had been more than a week since then, and Carter had heard nothing else.

Carter knew that the rain forest was one of the last great stretches of wilderness on earth and therefore not easy to send a covert message from. She was also used to agents being in positions where they couldn't send messages; sometimes they went dark for weeks or months at a time.

However, that didn't make her feel any better.

There was so much that could go wrong on a mission like this. The Amazon basin was full of unpredictable factors: drug runners, guerilla factions, piranhas. But perhaps the most unpredictable factor in all this was Charlie Thorne herself.

Carter had never met Charlie. She had only read the girl's file. Her psychological profile was filled with terms that made Carter uneasy: headstrong, impetuous, distrustful of authority, too smart for her own good. The girl had already caused the CIA considerable trouble when they had gone looking for Pandora. Given, there had been plenty of other complications on that mission, but still, Charlie hadn't helped. Especially when she had decided to let everyone believe she was dead and then fled the country.

Carter logged into her private account on her computer, which required three separate passwords. Then she brought up the encrypted email that had kicked off this new mission.

The email contained photos of Einstein's coded message, the one that indicated there had been other scientists who had made discoveries before him, along with the translation of that message.

Jamilla Carter wanted to know what those discoveries were. In theory, they couldn't all be equations like Pandora, discoveries that had the potential to destroy millions of lives and thus give whoever controlled them great power. But who knew? Maybe there was something hidden out in the world that was even *more* powerful than Pandora. If so, Carter didn't want it falling into the wrong hands.

The same went for Pandora itself.

The game had changed. Charlie Thorne was no longer needed to search for Pandora. Charlie *was* Pandora. The only copy of Einstein's formula was inside her head, which complicated things even more. It made Charlie an asset for the United States—and a target for other countries. Carter had intel that the Russians were actively looking for the girl, which probably meant there were others who knew about Charlie too.

But she was also aware that Charlie wouldn't give up Pandora easily. In Dante Garcia's debriefing after the Pandora debacle, he had made it clear that Charlie didn't trust anyone else with Pandora, even the United States. Therefore, her confidence needed to be won again. Which was why Director Carter had sent Dante after her, rather than anyone else. Charlie might not have trusted

Dante very much, but that was still more than she trusted anyone else.

Although, at the end of the day, Carter wasn't 100 percent sure that *she* could trust Dante, either. The guy was Charlie's half brother. Which meant he might not be willing to do *everything* necessary to get Pandora from her.

Carter also wasn't sure she could fully trust Milana Moon. In a sense, Milana was tougher than Dante where Charlie was concerned, but Carter suspected that Milana might have developed a soft spot for the girl as well.

Therefore, she hadn't been completely honest with either of them. She had asked them to go easy on Charlie, to present themselves as friendly and kind to win her trust. She had told them that she truly believed that was the best way to get the kid to cough up Pandora.

But there were other ways to get information from someone. They weren't nice, and Carter didn't like the idea of using them on anyone, but the fate of humanity was at stake where Pandora was concerned. She simply couldn't trust a twelve-year-old girl with it.

Playing tough would only be a last resort, of course. Maybe the threat of that alone would be enough to make Charlie cooperate. But to make any of this work, she needed Dante to bring Charlie in.

That's what his orders were. Once they found Darwin's great discovery, he was to use any means necessary to get Charlie to CIA headquarters. And if Dante had second thoughts, then Milana would take over. Carter had made it very clear that any failure on either one of their parts to comply would result in the termination of their jobs.

Carter was certainly intrigued to learn what Darwin had found down in South America. She expected it would be important, possibly even revolutionary, and that controlling it might be of great value to the CIA.

But her main objective was recovering Pandora, once and for all, no matter what it took.

Charlie Thorne wasn't going to get away from her again.

THIRTY-ONE

The City of Stone
Upper Reaches of the Anaconda River
Peru

The lost city was surprisingly hard to see at first.

It was amazing how thoroughly the forest had reclaimed it. Charlie assumed that at one point everything around her would have been cleared of trees in order to build the city, but now it was as though the trees had fought back. Except for a few tiny glimpses of stone, everything that humans had built was hidden. Every single building, street, and wall had been consumed by plant life. If Charlie hadn't known to be looking for a city, she might have missed it completely.

But it was still there. Buried beneath tree roots and bushes and vines, there were the forms of buildings. And when Charlie looked closer, she could see a kind of symmetry to them; the city had been laid out with a distinct pattern. The lake formed the northern edge, with a road heading directly to the temple, which was probably the center of town. The road was no longer visible, of course, but its presence could be inferred. It was almost like the floor of a valley, flanked by small hills that were really ancient buildings bedecked by trees—and the biggest hill of all, by far, was the temple. It loomed at the far end of the road, one hundred feet tall, by Charlie's estimate. The buildings that surrounded the temple were arranged in what seemed to be concentric circles, although it was hard to tell for sure given how overgrown everything was.

"It's like the world's biggest Chia Pet," Charlie observed.

"It's incredible," Milana gasped. Her usual cool reserve had given way to the awe and excitement of discovery. "This could be one of the most important archaeological finds in history." She went to the nearest building and brushed aside a curtain of vines to reveal a rock wall underneath. "What do you think this might have been? A home? A store?"

"There'll be time to explore later," Dante said brusquely, heading down the road toward the temple. "Darwin said we need to find the altar in the city of stone. So let's find it."

Milana let the vines fall back into place with what Charlie interpreted as a look of disappointment, then followed Dante. But while Dante strode purposefully toward the temple, as if he were on a schedule, Milana and Charlie walked more slowly, trying to take everything in.

"Just think," Milana said reverently. "The last person to see this place might have been Charles Darwin. And before that . . . Who knows how long it's been since anyone walked these streets."

"Would you slowpokes move it?" Dante called impatiently, already far ahead of them.

"Relax!" Charlie called back. "It's not like the altar's going anywhere."

"Just move your butt, will you?" Dante yelled. "I want to find Darwin's next clue!" He stormed on ahead through a stand of trees—and screamed in fear as three large animals that had been hiding there suddenly burst out of their cover.

They were mammals the size of full-grown pigs, but with thicker hair, wider snouts, and more powerful legs. They fled down the road, racing between Charlie and Milana, then plunged into the lake and swam away.

Meanwhile, Dante's scream appeared to have startled a troop of monkeys somewhere in the city. Charlie could hear their shrieks and caught a distant glimpse of furry bodies crashing through the trees.

"What on earth were those things?" Dante asked, clutching his heart.

"Capybaras," Charlie told him. "The world's biggest rodents. They're harmless. So no need to soil yourself."

Dante grimaced. "I didn't soil myself. They just

startled me, is all. I had no idea a rat could get that big."
He continued toward the temple—although Charlie
noticed he now proceeded much more cautiously.

In the distance, the monkeys had calmed down. Their
shrieks had stopped and the trees were no longer shaking.
Charlie couldn't see them through the foliage, but she
had the eerie sense the monkeys were watching them.

She and Milana picked up their pace, catching Dante
as he reached the temple.

Even up close, it was so overgrown, it looked like
a natural formation, rather than a man-made one. The
stonework was buried beneath a riot of plant life. There
was a wide, flat area in front of it that had probably been a
central plaza at some point, but which was now reclaimed
by forest as well. The stone paving had eroded enough for
plants to get roots down through it. Given the great size
of some of the trees, Charlie estimated that it had been
several centuries since the city had been abandoned.

"Here!" Dante announced triumphantly. He was
standing at the center of the temple's base. "There's an
entrance!" He swept aside a curtain of vines to reveal a
dark passageway behind them.

Milana and Dante both fished their flashlights out of
their backpacks, flipped them on, and stepped inside.

Charlie took an extra moment to gather her nerve.
Although she was excited to explore the lost city and find

what Darwin had discovered, she was nervous about heading into the dark temple. The last time she had been inside a cramped underground space had been in Jerusalem, while searching for Pandora, and that had been quite unsettling.

Plus, Charlie couldn't shake her sense of unease. She had a feeling that she was missing something important, that something else was going on that she wasn't quite grasping.

Dante peered back out of the temple's entrance and gave her a cocky smile. "What's wrong? Are you scared to come in here?"

The taunt had the exact effect he had hoped it would, offending Charlie and spurring her to action. "Of course I'm not scared. I was just wondering how many bats might be in there."

Dante's smile faded.

"It might be man-made, but it's still a cave. There must be bats." Charlie savored the look of concern on Dante's face and then stepped past him into the temple.

There wasn't much to the interior. It was a single large rectangular room with a simple small stone altar in the center. The walls were unadorned with any sort of carvings or paintings, but this sparseness was deceptive; Charlie recognized that the walls themselves were incredible feats of engineering. Huge stone blocks had been somehow perfectly cut and stacked atop one another; there were no irregularities or gaps between them. Crafting stone with such precision even in modern times would have been extremely difficult; how the Incas had done it without machinery—or even metal tools—was a mystery.

The room was too big for the flashlights to fully illuminate, so the far reaches remained cloaked in shadow. It was dank and refreshingly cool compared to the humid forest outside, although it had a funky smell. Milana was examining the altar while Dante remained closer to the doorway, sniffing the air with disgust.

"What's that stink?" he asked.

"Guano," Charlie replied.

"Guano?" Dante repeated, confused.

"Bat poop." Charlie played her flashlight across the floor, which was covered with a layer of brown goo. "A couple centuries' worth, I'd guess."

Dante shivered with revulsion, then reluctantly edged farther into the temple.

In truth, there weren't quite as many bats inside as Charlie had expected, but there were still a few dozen. They were much smaller than the fruit bats, and they clung to the roof like fuzzy little stalactites. But even a few bats per night over hundreds of years had left a lot of residue. Charlie noted that the stones of the walls, which she had originally thought were brown, were actually covered in guano as well.

Which made her realize something else about the walls.

"There's nothing here," Milana said suddenly, sounding disappointed. She was playing the beam of her flashlight all around the altar.

Charlie and Dante joined her there, their feet slipping slightly on the guano-slickened floor. Charlie noticed Dante was grimacing in disgust with every step.

"Darwin's last clue said we needed to find the altar," Milana explained. "I figured he would have left another clue here, but it's blank."

Dante frowned in frustration. "Maybe this isn't the altar."

"It is," Charlie said, looking it over. It was only a spare stack of stone blocks, also coated with guano, but it was certainly the focal point of the room. There wasn't anything else.

"Then maybe there's another temple here," Dante suggested. "Or maybe we're in the wrong city of stone."

"How many lost cities do you think there are out here?" Charlie asked. "We're in the right place. There's a perfectly good reason why Darwin didn't leave any more clues: He didn't need to. This is exactly where he wanted us to be."

"But there's nothing here," Dante protested.

"There's plenty," Charlie said knowingly. "You just have to look closer."

Milana stared past the altar, toward the walls of the room, and made a gasp of understanding. She strode to the closest wall and ran a finger across it, wiping away a thin streak of guano.

Beneath it, the surface of the wall gleamed.

"Oh my," Milana said, so astonished that her voice was barely audible. "That's *gold*."

Dante's jaw dropped. He forgot all about being disgusted by the guano and ran his entire hand across another wall, creating an even larger swath. This too revealed gold underneath.

"This entire room is coated with it," he said, amazed. Then he wiped off another swath, and another, just to make sure. Each time, he revealed more gold.

Charlie wiped off some guano as well, finding yet more gold, then ran her fingers across it. It had been hammered into a sheet, which had then been fixed to the stone. The sheet was thin, but still, if the entire room was covered, Charlie calculated there was several million dollars' worth of gold around her—and this was only one room. There might have been more like it in the city.

Dante couldn't help but give Charlie a cocky smile.

"Looks like you were wrong. Darwin's treasure wasn't a fossil. It was actual *treasure*."

"Everyone's wrong now and then," Charlie conceded.

As she said this, her eyes fell upon the altar again. It was also covered with guano. Charlie went to the side of it that faced the entrance of the temple and wiped some bat poop off.

This time she didn't reveal gold. Instead, she found lines carved into the stone. *Darwin's next clue*, she thought. It was there after all.

Only this time, rather than making numbers or letters, the lines seemed to be part of a picture. Charlie had only exposed the very top of it so far.

"Guys!" Milana called to them. "Look at this!"

There was such urgency in her voice, Charlie forgot about uncovering the clue.

Milana had moved toward the corner of the room, into the area that had been hidden in the shadows. Now she shone her light on an alcove in the wall she had discovered there.

It was carved into the stone, two feet high and a foot across, with a graceful arch at the top. Since it was recessed, its walls had not been covered by guano dropping onto it from the ceiling, and so Charlie could see that they, too, were covered with gold.

But that wasn't what Milana was looking at.

Nestled on a small pedestal inside the alcove was a skull.

It wasn't complete, and it was broken into several pieces. But even from what remained, they could tell it was humanoid. It was brown from age, as though it had been there for a very long time.

"Then again," Charlie said, "maybe I was right about the fossils after all."

THIRTY-TWO

They all gathered around the alcove to inspect the skull better.

Since it was broken apart, it was sort of like a three-dimensional jigsaw puzzle, only considerably harder in that they didn't know exactly what they were assembling, they were doing it in the darkness, and they certainly had pieces missing. The first order of business was to find every fragment of bone that they could. There were a few more shards of skull at the base of the alcove, along with a few stray teeth, and then they found several more pieces of bone scattered on the floor below the alcove. These were from bigger bones, arms, and legs, although they had also been broken. They appeared to have been lying on the ground for quite some time, as they were buried under a good amount of guano.

"We should take this outside," Milana said. "It'll be easier to assemble in the sunlight." Without waiting for the others to agree, she swept everything she could up into her arms and headed for the door.

Charlie and Dante grabbed the remaining pieces of bone and followed her. Once again, Charlie was overcome with a feeling of unease, although this had to do with desecrating the dead. In their excitement over the skull, it was easy to forget that it had once been part of a living being. And yet she certainly wanted to examine it better herself.

As she neared the doorway, one of the busted leg bones she was carrying slipped from her arms and tumbled to the floor. Charlie knelt to pick it up—and noticed something else in the beam of her flashlight. Something she had missed on the way into the temple. She and the others had been so busy looking at the walls of the room, no one had bothered to look at the floor.

Meanwhile, outside the temple, Milana and Dante had found a spot on the ground that was relatively free of plants and leaf litter. They knelt there and began to lay out the fragments of bone.

Now that they had them out of the dark room and in the sunlight, they began to notice things that concerned them as well.

"The fractures in this skull don't look like they're due to it falling apart from age," Milana observed. "This looks more like an injury."

"Blunt-force trauma," Dante said, by way of agreement. Sadly, as a field agent, he had seen the results of plenty of human brutality. "Someone else bashed this guy's head in."

Back in the temple, Charlie was examining what she had found on the floor. It was a footprint, left in the layer of guano. A human footprint. From a bare foot. Although whoever had left it had walked somewhat strangely. The toes and ball of the foot were pressed much deeper in the guano than the heel.

She found a few more prints close by, obviously left by the same person, moving through the temple. And some different markings in the guano that struck her as odd, four small depressions, each two inches long, lined up beside one another.

There were other odd things about the footprints as well.

Outside, Dante picked one of the teeth off the ground. It looked like a human molar, only there was a dark patch in it. Dante examined it closely. "This looks like metal," he said. "Like a filling."

Milana leaned in toward the fossil to examine it too.

The filling wasn't nearly as well done as what she could have gotten at a modern dentist, but the concept was the same. A metal alloy of some sort had been placed into a hole in the tooth.

At the CIA, they also learned quite a bit about forensic dentistry. Often, the only way to recognize a dead body was via its teeth.

"Fillings weren't developed until the early 1800s," Milana said, growing concerned. "This isn't a fossil. It's a murder victim."

At the same time, inside the temple, Charlie was still staring at the footprints. The toes, in particular, were unusual. They were farther from the rest of the foot than they should have been, and arced, almost like thumbs.

Charlie knew what she was looking at, but she was having trouble believing it. It seemed impossible. But there was no other explanation she could think of.

Her eyes fell on the altar again. In all the excitement over the bones, she had neglected to uncover Darwin's final clue.

She went to it now and made a few great swipes through the guano with her hands, uncovering what was hidden beneath.

The drawing that Darwin had etched there immediately confirmed Charlie's fears. As did the three words that were etched beneath it. They weren't coded this time, but were in simple English. Anyone who made it this far deserved to know the truth.

There was also no time to waste.

She raced outside, to where the others were crouched over the bones, and announced, "I've made a really big mistake. We have to get out of here *now*."

THIRTY-THREE

Explain yourself!" Dante yelled to Charlie. He and Milana were racing after her through the ancient city. Charlie was running full-tilt back toward the lake.

"I'll explain in the canoe!" Charlie yelled back. "Once we're far away from here!"

Dante stopped running. "That's not how things work around here," he said. "I'm in charge of this mission, not you. So tell us what's going on."

Milana followed Dante's lead and stopped chasing Charlie as well.

Charlie had no choice but to stop herself. She couldn't leave both of them here. Not with what was living in the forest. She turned back and told them, "Darwin's treasure wasn't fossils of the missing link. He found actual pre-hominids. They're still alive!"

The footprints she had found in the temple had been made by something that wasn't quite monkey and wasn't quite human, either. The prints indicated a creature that wasn't walking upright yet; the heels weren't being placed on the ground, only the ball of the foot and the toes, while the four depressions were the fingers of the hands, clenched into fists. The creatures were knuckle-walking, like chimpanzees did.

Scientists estimated it had taken humans approximately four million years of evolution to shift from walking on all fours to walking upright. These creatures were still in the process.

Darwin's final clue had confirmed her thoughts. The drawing he had etched was crude, but obviously a pre-hominid. And beneath it, he had inscribed three words:

They live here.

Charlie was upset at herself for not considering the possibility of a living fossil earlier. Evolution was a constant process; all animals, including humans, were always evolving. So if a primate in the rain forest had begun to evolve into something like a human, why wouldn't that process still be going on?

Dante and Milana remained standing in the forest, unsure whether to believe Charlie. After all, they hadn't seen the footprints. "That's not possible," Dante said, then added, "Is it?"

"It's not just possible," Charlie said. "It's *true*. You asked the question yourself last night: Why would Fitz-Roy and the crew have been so upset by mere fossils? The answer is that Darwin *didn't* bring fossils back to the *Beagle*. He brought an actual prehominid. Something between monkey and man. To FitzRoy and the others, it would have been blasphemy."

Milana asked, "You really think that Darwin dragged a living prehominid all the way back to the coast from here?"

"No, probably not a living one," Charlie answered. "Darwin never kept a specimen alive unless he planned to eat it. But who knows? Maybe he *tried* to bring back a living creature and it died along the way. The point is, he brought *something* back that was undeniable proof that men had evolved from something else."

Charlie could imagine the scene, back in 1835: Darwin returning to the *Beagle* with the body of a dead missing link, FitzRoy and the crew seeing it and being horrified by what it meant, then plotting to get rid of it. Most likely, they threw it overboard, then swore everyone to secrecy and forced Darwin to rewrite his diaries and hide all evidence of what he had found. Which would have made Darwin bitter and angry and hesitant to ever speak of his discovery—or even the idea of evolution at all—for decades to come.

Charlie warily glanced at the forest around her, the

truth growing clearer and clearer. The prehominids wouldn't have been advanced enough to have a civilization; this city had been built by Incas who had abandoned it for some reason or another. The prehominids couldn't even maintain this city, which explained why it had become overgrown once again. At most, they would have had simple tools, stones they used for hammering— or attacking the unfortunate member of Darwin's team whose skull Milana had found.

Charlie had no doubt that the prehominids could be dangerous. Chimpanzees were known to go to war against one another—and humans did it all the time—so a creature somewhere between them on the evolutionary line would likely be menacing as well. Now that Charlie understood the real story of the prehominids, she also understood why she had been feeling uneasy since arriving in the city. Something *had* been watching her from the forest. The prehominids. It was likely that they were even watching her *now*.

But, in fact, she wasn't really worried about herself. She was worried about what would happen to the prehominids if their existence was revealed.

"Please," she told the others. "We need to go."

Only, to her dismay, Dante and Milana didn't seem to share her concern. Now that they grasped the truth, they grew extremely excited.

"Go?" Dante echoed. "When there are living prehominids here? We need to find them! Darwin was right; this *is* the greatest treasure ever known to man! This would be the greatest scientific find of all time!"

"No," Charlie warned. "We can't let the world know about them. It would be a disaster."

Milana looked at her curiously. "Charlie, if these things exist, we can't keep it a secret. It's too important."

"Important for *us* maybe," Charlie argued. "But not *them*. Look, if we were just talking about some ancient bones here, I'd be fine with bringing them back and telling the entire world. But these are living creatures. Most likely, really intelligent ones. And if the world finds out they exist, they'll end up as science experiments and tourist attractions."

Thunder rumbled surprisingly close by. A slight breeze stirred the trees. Charlie realized she had been so focused on the prehominids that she hadn't been paying attention to the weather. It was changing quickly. Above her, the sky was darkening. A big storm was moving in.

Dante was giving Charlie his usual look of frustration. "So now you want to do the same thing with these creatures that you did with Pandora? Just keep them to yourself? You don't get to decide what the world gets and doesn't get, Charlie!"

"Sometimes things need to be protected," Charlie

argued. "Sometimes humans can't be trusted to do the right thing. . . ."

"Where on earth did you get this idea that humanity is so terrible?" Dante demanded angrily.

"I think it was around the time that people started trying to kill me on a regular basis," Charlie snapped. "I *know* there are good people out there, Dante. And I know that you and Milana are two of them. But I also know that you don't have the power to protect these creatures. Or Pandora. The only way to keep them safe is to keep them hidden. Einstein and Darwin both recognized that. . . ."

"Then why did you even come out here?" Dante demanded.

"Because I didn't know they'd be alive!" Charlie shouted back. "I thought we'd be finding fossils!"

"Living creatures are even more exciting than fossils. . . ."

"They're also far more dangerous. Why do you think Segundo's people avoid this place? What do you think happened to that person whose remains we just found? You think his skull just collapsed on itself? These creatures killed him. And we need to get out of here before they kill *us*."

"If they cause trouble, we can handle them," Dante said confidently.

"That's exactly what I'm worried about," Charlie

replied. "I don't want to go to war with these creatures. I just want to leave them alone." She turned around and started for the canoe again.

Dante held his ground. "You can't leave by yourself! And I'm not going anywhere!"

Charlie didn't stop, though. She was done arguing.

The wind was picking up ahead of the storm, pushing the clouds of steam off the lake. They now began to drift through the lost city like fog, quickly obscuring her from Dante's sight.

A great gust of air violently shook the trees throughout the surrounding forest, provoking a new round of primate shrieks in the distance.

Charlie froze, paying more attention to them than she had before. This time the noise sent a chill up her spine. She spun back around and yelled to Dante through the fog. "Those aren't monkeys! It's *them*! We need to go!"

Dante was about to yell back to her, when Milana clutched his arm.

She was listening intently to the shrieks as well, warily studying the forest around them. "Charlie's right. It's not safe here."

Dante gave her a look of betrayal, but it quickly shifted to concern. He trusted Milana's instincts better than Charlie's—and realized with frustration that he probably needed to start trusting Charlie's more as well.

However, that didn't make him any less angry at Charlie and her attitude. He started back toward the lake, muttering under his breath, "I *hate* that kid being right all the time."

"Wasn't that why you wanted to recruit her in the first place?" Milana said.

Ahead of them, Charlie had realized they were coming and paused by a stone building to wait. She dropped in beside them as they passed. "I'm glad one of you has some sense," she said.

Dante glared at her. "Our exercising caution here does not mean that we're done with this discussion. The world still deserves to know about these creatures."

"The world will be just fine without knowing about them," Charlie said.

"What's your plan, then?" Dante asked angrily. "You think you can just take your knowledge of them and run off and hide from the world again, the same way you did with Pandora?"

"I'm trying to keep humanity from destroying itself!" Charlie exploded. "You think I *like* being stuck with Pandora? You think I *want* this responsibility? I was happy before you showed up and dragged me into all of this! Now I have the key to the destruction of all life on earth locked in my brain and I'm saddled with keeping it safe. You're not the only one who wants it. There's plenty of other jerks out there. That's not exactly a recipe for a carefree life."

They had reached the shore of the lake. But before they could return to their canoe, Ivan and the Castellos emerged from the fog around them, guns pointed their way.

"Where's the treasure?" Esmerelda demanded.

Charlie turned to Dante. "See what I mean?" she asked.

THIRTY-FOUR

here is no treasure," Dante told the others. "We looked everywhere. If there was ever anything here, it's long gone."

Ivan and the Castellos were forcing them back into the lost city at gunpoint, moving them away from the safety of the lake. The fog was everywhere now, cloaking the forest in a curtain of gray.

Although Charlie, Dante, and Milana hadn't been able to speak to one another, they were all of the same mind: It would be a mistake to allow Ivan and the Castellos to know about any of the treasures in the city, particularly the prehominids. They would certainly exploit whatever they discovered.

"Don't lie to us," Esmerelda snapped. "We heard you arguing. We know you found *something* here. What is it?"

"Maybe you haven't noticed," Charlie said. "But you're

smack in the middle of a lost Incan city. Most people would think that was pretty awesome." She turned to Ivan, who stood the closest to her. "We haven't met yet. . . ."

"No, but I know exactly who you are, Charlie Thorne." Although Ivan's tone seemed friendly, it frightened Charlie. He was obviously telling her the truth, and in that single statement, he confirmed exactly what she had feared for so long: that despite all her efforts to hide from the world, there were people who knew all about her and Pandora.

Still, she did her best to act like she wasn't scared. "So who are you?"

"His name's Ivan Spetz," Dante said. "He works for the Russians."

If Ivan was surprised that Dante knew his identity, he didn't show it. "That's true," he admitted, never taking his eyes off Charlie. "My people are hoping that you will work for them too. They will see to it that you are extremely well compensated."

"And if I say no?" Charlie asked.

Ivan shook his head and made a *tsk-tsk-tsk* with his tongue. "That would be a very bad career move."

Charlie noticed Esmerelda give Ivan a look of sudden understanding. Charlie figured Ivan hadn't been honest about why he wanted Charlie, and Esmerelda was now realizing that she had been used as a pawn.

Meanwhile, Gianni and Paolo didn't seem to be concerned by any of this. They were still focused on the treasure. Gianni said, "Darwin's clue told us to find the altar in the temple. So where's the temple?"

Milana started to answer, but before she could, Esmerelda interrupted. "And, just so we're clear, if you lie to me, I'll shoot the kid."

Milana recognized that Esmerelda wasn't bluffing. So she told the truth. "It's another fifty yards ahead."

She continued leading them back into the city.

Charlie had noticed Ivan stiffen slightly when Esmerelda threatened her, like he was worried. *He needs me alive,* Charlie thought. Which made sense. There was no recovering Pandora if she was dead.

However, that didn't make her feel much safer. Once they reached the temple, it probably wouldn't take long for the Castellos to realize how much gold there was inside—and once they did, there would no longer be any point in letting Dante and Milana live. Charlie had already learned that the Castellos didn't like to share.

She figured that Dante and Milana knew this too, but there was little they could do at the moment.

And if that weren't bad enough, she could hear the faint sounds of the hominids coming closer. Every so often, there was a soft call from the trees. The rain forest didn't sound much different from usual, like maybe there was a troop of monkeys in the near distance, but Charlie now knew they were something else entirely. Once again, she had a feeling that she was being watched, although it was hard to see *anything* around her.

The fog of steam had grown thicker, obscuring much of the city, while dark clouds were amassing above, casting the forest in a dark shadow. It was as though night had fallen in the middle of the day. Even the enormous temple had vanished in the gloom.

But Charlie knew it was close. And she knew that she needed to act before she got there. Once they were inside the temple, Dante and Milana were as good as dead. There was only one way in or out of the temple, and Ivan and the Castellos would certainly keep it blocked off, meaning the others would be trapped inside.

Luckily, Charlie had a plan. Although it involved getting into her backpack.

They passed through the last ring of stone buildings into what had been the plaza in front of the temple.

Charlie shrugged her backpack off her shoulders, trying to make it look casual.

In an instant, all three of the Castellos were aiming their guns at her.

"What are you doing?" Esmerelda demanded.

"Getting a drink of water," Charlie lied. "I'm thirsty."

"I don't care," Esmerelda said, then narrowed her

eyes in suspicion. "In fact, give me your pack."

Charlie tried to hide her disappointment, but she didn't do it quickly enough, which only convinced Esmerelda that she was up to something. Esmerelda had learned the hard way to never let her guard down around Charlie.

She raised her gun slightly, so it was now pointed at Charlie's head. "The pack. Now."

"Okay." Charlie stopped walking, extending the pack to Esmerelda.

Which meant everyone else stopped walking for a moment as well.

Charlie was suddenly aware of a change in the air. It felt as though every molecule around her had been charged.

"Catch," Charlie said suddenly, and made like she was going to throw her pack to Esmerelda.

But she didn't do it. She only faked it, starting the motion of throwing it while still keeping her hand clasped tightly around the straps, drawing the attention of everyone with the guns.

A split second later, lightning struck. Just as Charlie had expected, given the charge in the atmosphere around her.

It happened so close by that the thunderclap came simultaneously. It was as though a bomb had gone off, with a blinding flash of light and an intense concussion of sound.

In that moment, Dante and Milana sprang into action.

Both had extensive combat training and were waiting for the right opportunity to strike—and Charlie had given it to them.

They targeted the Castellos first. Gianni and Paolo were amateurs. They were obviously strong, but sometimes that was a weakness in itself. Strong men often thought they didn't need to learn how to fight; they figured they could simply overpower anyone.

Dante and Milana made quick work of them.

While pain didn't linger in the Castellos' bodies, they still felt the initial shock of it. It took only seconds for Dante and Milana to drop them and wrest their guns away.

Ivan and Esmerelda both spun toward them, running and opening fire at once while Dante and Milana shot back.

"Charlie, run!" Milana shouted.

Charlie did what she was told. In this situation, she knew not to question the CIA agents. She raced back through the rain forest, toward the lake, leaving the others to handle the battle.

The storm arrived in force. It was as though the clouds had been torn open. Sheets of rain poured through the canopy. It was the heaviest rain Charlie had ever experienced, coming down so hard that it nearly knocked her off her feet and so fast that she was drenched within seconds. The forest floor quickly turned to mud, making it difficult to run.

Still, Charlie did her best. Between the fog, the darkness, and the rain, she could see only a few feet ahead of her, making it a struggle to even know what direction to run in. Behind her, she heard the pop of gunshots, muffled by the roar of the storm.

Water coursed along the forest floor, forming puddles and streams. Charlie splashed through it, fumbling through her backpack as she ran, hoping the canoe wouldn't be swamped and sunk by the time she reached it. Or that the Castellos hadn't sunk it already out of spite. She staggered through the outermost ring of stone buildings, indicating that she was nearing the lake.

She almost didn't see the other men with guns. Not until she was only a few feet away from them. There were six of them, standing in a line between her and the lake, listening to the others fight, letting them waste their ammunition and their energy.

Charlie tried to stop. Her feet went out from under her in the mud and she landed on her rear in a puddle.

The men all laughed.

Oz stood slightly in front of the other men, obviously

their leader. "Hey there, girlie," he said, giving her a cruel smile over the barrel of his gun. "Put your hands up where we can see them."

Charlie had no choice but to raise her hands in surrender. She was out in the open, with no cover.

However, the new men who had arrived on the scene with guns weren't her biggest concern at the moment.

It was that, only five feet away from her, a living prehominid had emerged from the rain.

THIRTY-FIVE

Genetically, humans and other primates are far more closely related than most people realize. Humans and chimpanzees are estimated to share almost 99 percent of their DNA, meaning that in an evolutionary sense, humans are more closely related to chimps than chimps are to gorillas.

The gap between humans and monkeys was greater, but both species were still closely related enough to be placed on the same branch of the evolutionary tree: the primates. The first monkeys had arrived in South America approximately forty million years earlier, one hundred million years after that continent had split off from Africa. No one knew exactly how this had happened—scientists theorized that perhaps monkeys had accidentally floated across the Atlantic on rafts of vegetation—but the monkeys had certainly thrived in their new home, evolving into more than one hundred known new species. . . .

As well as the one higher species that had never been documented.

It must have been *seen*, Charlie figured, as she stared at the creature standing in the rain by her. The inhabitants of the ancient city must have known of them—and perhaps Segundo's ancestors had as well, but then tried to keep people away by warning that the area was dangerous and calling it the Dark Lands. Certainly, this was what Darwin had encountered: He had etched a drawing of one of them into the altar. It definitely appeared to be a link between men and monkeys, undeniable proof of evolution.

It wasn't a direct link; it couldn't have been, as humans were proven to have evolved in Africa. But as Charlie had suspected, convergent evolution had taken place. The creature still had much in common with monkeys, such as hair all over its body and large canine teeth—but it had developed some attributes in common with humans.

It had begun the shift to walking upright, moving with the knuckle-walk of chimps and gorillas rather than the four-legged scurry of monkeys; its hands were dexterous; its tail was gone; and most significantly, its head was large for its body, indicating that it had a sizable brain. The prehominid was much smaller than an adult human, only about the size of a kindergartener, which made sense, as the monkeys it had evolved from weren't that big. (Most previously discovered prehominid species had been considerably smaller than modern humans as well.) For a moment Charlie thought it might have been a youngster, only five or six years old. But then it looked directly at her and she saw the intelligence in its eyes. Which made her realize it was an adult.

The creature had its guard up. The hair on the nape of its neck was raised and it was in a defensive crouch, the same way that a monkey or a dog would display agitation. It was also making a low, guttural growl, and its teeth were bared. But when Charlie met its eyes, she saw it regard her with curiosity, as though it wanted to understand what she was.

Charlie was fascinated. Amazed. Astonished.

And worried. Not because she felt threatened by the creature. But because of how Oz and his men were looking at it.

They regarded it with horror and disgust. And fear. In the way that humans had so often regarded something they didn't understand.

The creature shifted its attention from Charlie to Oz.

And Oz responded by turning his gun on it.

"No!" Charlie screamed.

But Oz opened fire anyway.

The creature was on the alert for trouble—and

Charlie's scream had startled it into action. It leapt away at the last moment, so Oz's shot only grazed its hip. The creature shrieked in pain and tumbled across the wet ground, then rolled back to its feet and scampered away into the cover of the rain, eluding a few more shots from Oz.

Once it was safe again, the noise it was making changed. It became a howl. There was anger in it, but Charlie recognized something else.

It sounded to her like communication.

And then the other creatures, which had been hiding in the shadows, attacked.

To Charlie, the way the creatures struck was further evidence of their intelligence.

To begin with, they had arranged themselves in a semicircle around Oz and his men, which showed forethought. And they hadn't blindly attacked, but had waited to see if the humans were a threat. Now that Oz had foolishly proven that he *was* dangerous, he and his men found themselves in a very bad position: with their backs to the lake and no escape route.

Then the creatures' assault was quick and well coordinated. And while their weapons were rudimentary, only rocks and sticks, they wielded them with terrifying skill.

They moved so fast, Charlie wasn't even sure how many there were. It might have been ten, but maybe it was as few as six. They were merely blurs in the rain.

To Charlie's surprise, they didn't attack her, even though they could have. Maybe they had perceived that she meant them no harm. Or maybe they had recognized that she was young and therefore didn't consider her a threat. Whatever the case, they focused their attack on Oz and his men.

The creatures were ruthless and efficient. Two of Oz's men went down before they even knew what was coming.

Because Oz already had his gun ready, with his finger on the trigger, he was in a better position to defend himself. He opened fire as he ran toward the prehominids. He hit one as it lunged for him, and it crumpled into the mud, whimpering in pain. Having created a hole in the creatures' line, Oz raced through it and fled into the city.

Jose fell in behind him, laying down a spray of cover fire to keep the prehominids at bay.

Some of the creatures went after them, while others took care of Oz's two remaining men.

While all that was happening, Charlie ran.

Although the prehominids hadn't attacked her, she was still frightened of them. They obviously now recognized that humans were dangerous, so it was possible that they still might come for her.

The only place Charlie could imagine she might be safe was the canoe. Most monkeys and apes couldn't swim; maybe these creatures couldn't either. So she headed for the lake.

Only, with the fog and the darkness and the pouring rain, she could barely see anything. All the landmarks around her had vanished, and she had become disoriented while escaping. She found water running along the ground and presumed it was running toward the lake, so she followed it.

Charlie wasn't used to being wrong, but this time she was. She was heading in the wrong direction.

Dante and Milana raced through the rain, heading for the lake.

Dante was trusting Milana. She had an innate sense of direction unlike any he had ever encountered, so whatever way she chose had a far better chance of being right than his choice.

They knew Ivan and the Castellos were still out there somewhere. All the Castellos. Even though they had taken down the brothers in ways that would have laid out normal people, the Castellos weren't normal. The pain would have already passed for them, which meant they were probably back on their feet and ready for another fight.

But what really frightened Dante were the opponents who weren't human. He had heard the sounds of their attack, the shrieks and howls. And since he didn't know about Oz and his men, the only one he could imagine they had attacked was Charlie.

So even though they should have been silent, lying low from their enemies, he and Milana were calling Charlie's name, trying to figure out where she was, or if she was even still alive. The storm was so loud, with the water rattling the trees and pounding the ground and the wind roaring and the thunder rumbling, that their voices were swallowed up. They could barely even hear themselves, but still, they kept yelling, desperately hoping for a response from Charlie but staying alert for the likely possibility that someone else would attack them first.

Which was exactly what happened.

THIRTY-SIX

Oz fled through the city, feeling as though he had been plunged into a nightmare.

Only minutes before, everything had been going better than he could have ever imagined. First, the thermal activity around the lake indicated a wealth of natural resources that could be exploited. Probably natural gas, but there was a chance of oil pockets in the area too. Sure, it was remote, but at the rate the Amazon was disappearing, nothing was going to stay remote for long. He could stake a claim to the land rights and sell them for a fortune down the road.

And then they had come upon the remains of the city. A freaking lost city, hidden in the rain forest. He and his men had barely seen any of it, but they could already tell it was big. Bigger than Machu Picchu for sure.

A lost Incan city was a gold mine. Maybe even a literal one. The place looked as though no one had ever found it—which meant no one had looted it yet. There was bound to be some gold around, as well as plenty of other priceless artifacts. He could rob the place dry. . . .

Or perhaps he could simply announce to the world that he'd found it. It had been decades since anyone had discovered a lost city anywhere on earth. The news would catapult him to fame. He'd end up with a huge book deal, do the talk show circuit, rake in money from speaking fees. That wouldn't be a bad life. . . .

But now it had all gone sideways. *What on earth are those creatures?* Oz wondered. In all his time in the Amazon, he had never heard of anything like them. They were so frightening-looking, so vicious, and . . . There was something eerily *human* about them, he thought, and the idea alone sent a chill through him.

Now he was running as fast as he could, knowing it was a bad idea, knowing he was going the wrong way from his canoe and supplies and backup ammunition, plunging farther into the lost city where these *things* lived. There could be hundreds more of them here. Thousands maybe. But he didn't have any other options. He had to get away from the ones that were chasing him and pray that there weren't others ahead.

There was a scream from close behind him. Jose.

"Jose!" Oz yelled, unable to keep the fear out of his voice. "Are you all right?"

There was no response, only the sound of the storm.

Oz chanced a look back, but he didn't stop. He couldn't see anything but rain.

He slipped in the mud, almost went down, but managed to steady himself at the last instant. That had been close. If he fell, the creatures would be on him in a second. He couldn't risk another look back. So he kept on running, alone now. Jose was gone.

Something large suddenly loomed to his right. A mountain, it seemed . . . only, there were no mountains in the Amazon. Which meant it was another human construction of some sort. He ran closer to it, spotted a gap at the base, and ducked through it.

Which brought him into the temple. Only, he didn't know what it was, because now it was too dark to see and he didn't want to alert the creatures by turning on a light. For now it simply seemed safe. At the very least, it was a place where he could keep his gun pointed at the door and make a stand against anything that tried to come in.

His heart was pounding a mile a minute and he could barely breathe from his exertion. He hadn't run like that in years. He leaned against the wall to steady himself and discovered that it was coated with something disgustingly slimy . . . but he also felt something surprisingly hard and smooth underneath. Not like rock exactly.

Despite his fear of the creatures, he couldn't help but give in to his curiosity. He wiped the slimy stuff away, revealing what lay beneath it.

A bolt of lightning flashed outside, followed by the accompanying crack of thunder, and the light flickered through the room, illuminating the wall for a sliver of a second. But that was enough. Oz had seen the color of the metal.

Gold. The room was lined with gold.

If he could get out of here alive, he'd be rich beyond his wildest dreams.

Oz allowed himself only a moment to imagine the wealth, the yacht and the private jet, and all the mansions he could buy, then focused on the situation at hand. He had to escape from this horrible place.

But he had a plan now. The creatures were just a bunch of stupid animals, armed with rocks and sticks. He was a human being with a gun and plenty of ammunition. He quickly slapped a new clip into his weapon, keeping an eye on the entrance to the temple.

Outside, it seemed that the heart of the storm had passed. It was still raining, but the rain was no longer coming down in sheets, and the roar of it was no longer deafening.

In fact, Oz could hear something just outside the

entrance of the temple. The sounds of the creatures sniffing around and chattering softly to one another.

Stupid animals, Oz thought to himself. They had given their position away. Now he knew they were there. He raised his gun, ready to blast them the moment they came through the door.

Suddenly, there was a clatter from inside the room itself, to his side. He swung that way, fearing one of the creatures had found another entrance, and unleashed a burst of gunfire.

Another flash of lightning illuminated the room.

It was empty. There was no creature where Oz had been shooting. Only a rock the size of a grapefruit, tumbling across the floor.

Oz realized that one of the creatures must have thrown it into the room to make noise and distract him. They weren't as stupid as he'd thought. In fact, they weren't stupid at all.

Oz wheeled back toward the entrance to the room, but it was too late. The distraction had worked perfectly. The creatures were already through the door, the sound of their attack covered by the boom of thunder.

Before Oz could shoot, they were upon him.

Charlie had been running for too long before she realized her mistake. The flowing water she was following didn't lead to the lake at all, but instead to a creek that was now so swollen, it was several feet deep. In theory, the creek would lead to the lake, but it passed into underbrush too thick to follow through. She would have to retrace her steps.

Charlie cursed herself for being so stupid. Of all the times to make a mistake, this was the worst. There were enemies with guns all about, not to mention the creatures. She had almost nothing to defend herself with and was soaked to the bone.

So this time, she didn't act in haste. Rather than just turning around and running back the way she had come, she took a moment to analyze the situation.

Her eyes fell upon a shrub in the creek. Normally it would have been on dry land but was now partly submerged by the rising waters. It had oval leaves and bright-red berries, and she recognized it from her time with Segundo, learning about the rain forest. It was a plant that could come in handy. She stepped to the edge of the creek, snapped off a small branch, then reached out over the water for another. . . .

And heard a call of alarm behind her.

It wasn't human.

Charlie spun around and saw the creature that had made the noise. It wasn't trying to hide. Instead, it was out in the open behind her, looking at her with what Charlie took to be concern.

She realized it was the creature that had first confronted the men with the guns. And it had been wounded worse than she'd realized. It was bleeding from its leg where Oz's bullet had struck it and was obviously in pain.

This Charlie could handle. She had a small emergency kit in her backpack, along with a few other things.

But the creature had to let her do it.

The rain was starting to let up, and the sky was lightening slightly. Charlie held up her hands, palms out, showing she was unarmed, and spoke in as soothing a voice as she could muster. "Hi," she said. "I'm Charlie. And I'm not going to hurt you."

She took a step toward the creature, which tensed.

"You don't have to fear me," Charlie said. "I can help you."

The creature stayed where it was, keeping its eyes locked on her. It no longer looked as threatening as it had when first confronting the men with the guns; instead, it looked small and meek and bedraggled.

Charlie realized it was a female.

"You're a girl," she said, not so much because it was a brilliant observation, but because it seemed her voice was calming the creature. "Cool. We girls need to stick together. How about if I call you Eve?" She took off her backpack, slipped the piece of the plant she had collected inside, and dug out the emergency kit. "I can stop your bleeding, Eve. I wish I could do more, but hopefully that's all you need."

Eve kept her eyes locked on Charlie as Charlie approached. The creature was obviously tense and wary, looking like she might bolt at any moment, but she stayed put.

Charlie removed some medical supplies from the emergency kit, then tore off a tiny strip of gauze and held it out to Eve. "I'm going to put some of this around your leg. But it won't hurt you. See?"

Eve tentatively reached out and touched the gauze, then plucked it from Charlie's hand. She looked at it curiously—and then ate it.

Charlie winced. "That is *not* what you're supposed to do with gauze." She looked up from Eve, taking in the forest around her, wondering how far she had run in the wrong direction and thus how far she was from everyone else. Including the other creatures.

The forest was no longer deafening from the pounding rain, but the storm was still quite loud, with water coming down through the trees and thunder rumbling. Charlie couldn't hear anyone else, but she knew they were all out there.

She knew she should be trying to regroup with Dante and Milana, but she was worried about Eve. If she didn't do something to stop the bleeding, the poor creature might die.

Charlie tore open the package of sterile padding and unwound a longer strip of gauze. "This isn't food, Eve. I have to put it on you to make you better. Which means I need to touch you. Is that okay?"

Eve cocked her head curiously at Charlie, but let her approach. Charlie reached out and placed the sterile padding on the wound on Eve's leg.

Eve flinched but didn't run.

Charlie wondered how long it had been since a human had been this close to this species. Generations, perhaps.

Eve had a musty smell, like a wet dog, which made sense given that she was soaked. The hair on her leg was short and wiry, like that of a chimpanzee. She watched Charlie with fascination, although Charlie had the sense that Eve was focused on everything else around her as well.

Thankfully, the wound in Eve's leg wasn't deep. It looked to Charlie as though the creature's thigh muscle had been grazed, but if the bleeding was stopped, she would be all right.

Charlie quickly wrapped the gauze around Eve's leg to hold the padding in place. Eve made a whimper of pain but remained still. The padding slowly saturated, turning red, but the flow of blood appeared to stop.

"There you go," Charlie said cheerfully. "Not exactly good as new, but I think you're going to be all right."

Eve suddenly leapt up, so quickly Charlie thought the creature might be attacking her, but then she turned toward a stand of trees, on the defensive, her hair raised and teeth bared.

A second later, Paolo and Gianni Castello emerged from the forest.

THIRTY-SEVEN

Dante and Milana were almost back at the lake when a creature bounded into their path.

It was an unsettling sight for both of them, not only because the creature looked so much like a link between primates and humans, but because it had obviously been in a fight recently. There was blood on its teeth and matted in its fur.

Dante raised the gun he had taken from Paolo Castello. The creature appeared dangerous and primed to attack, and his first instinct was to shoot it before it could do that.

But then Charlie's words came back to him. When he'd said that he could handle the creatures if they caused trouble, Charlie had replied, "That's what I'm worried about." And then said that she didn't want to start a war with them. She only wanted to leave them alone.

So Dante ignored his instinct and didn't shoot. Instead, he held up his hands, the gun in one of them, trying to show that he wasn't threatening.

Beside him, Milana followed his lead, doing the same thing with the gun she had taken from Gianni.

The creature relaxed slightly. It was still on guard, but it stopped baring its teeth and the hair on its neck lowered. Then it made a short, high-pitched yip.

It was only now that Dante noticed the other creatures surrounding them. They had been lurking in the forest, having gathered so quietly that Dante and Milana hadn't even noticed them. At least two dozen were visible, which meant there were probably even more close by. Dante realized that if the creatures had attacked, he and Milana would have been easily overwhelmed.

But they didn't attack. They just watched Dante and Milana closely. The first one made some more noise, a bit of communication that the others seemed to completely comprehend. All of the creatures backed away, then quickly vanished into the trees.

Dante and Milana stared after them, at once amazed by what they had seen—and relieved by what they had avoided.

And then something bit Dante in the neck.

Or that was what it felt like. The bite of a very large insect, like an enormous mosquito. He reached up to swat the bug away and realized he hadn't been bitten all.

There was a tiny dart sticking out of his neck.

"Milana!" he yelled. "Run!"

But it was too late. A dart hit her in the neck too.

Dante turned to see who had shot him, but his vision was already going blurry. His mind was clouding. His strength was ebbing.

His knees buckled under him and he collapsed in the mud.

Esmerelda understood everything now.

She had seen the creatures from a distance as they surrounded Dante and Milana, then watched them disappear into the forest.

She had spent enough time studying Darwin and his writings to recognize what they were. "*They're* the treasure," she told Ivan as they hurried through the lost city. "They're proof of evolution!"

"So there's no actual treasure here?" Ivan asked gruffly. He still had the dart gun he had shot Dante and Milana with at the ready. His intent had been to use it on Charlie, whom he needed alive, but it had been useful against her CIA handlers as well. "I thought you said there'd be gold."

"Those things are worth *more* than gold!" Esmerelda exclaimed. "If we could get one back to civilization and show it to the world, we'd make a fortune. We'd go down in history just like Darwin did."

Ivan gave her a sideways glance. "I'd rather have the gold."

"This is better. We found a missing link *and* a lost city. That's guaranteed fame and fortune."

Ivan thought that over. He had no interest in fame, and he wasn't sure she was right about the fortune. But he had another way to cash in. A guaranteed way. The girl was somewhere close by, and when he delivered her to his superiors, they would be pleased. *Very* pleased. It would be a great coup, finding Pandora, and he knew he would be well rewarded for it. A sizable chunk of money would be placed in an untraceable foreign bank account for him. Maybe it wouldn't be millions, but it would be enough for him to give up the spy game once and for all, get a nice place on the beach somewhere in Central America, and live out his days in ease.

Plus, the girl was the target of the mission. She was what Russia wanted, and he remained loyal to his country.

And yet . . .

Esmerelda was right about how significant it would be to reveal what they had found. Perhaps he couldn't take the credit for finding the missing link or the city . . . but *Russia* could. Back during the space race in the 1960s, Russia had been at the forefront of science. Now that was no longer the case. So it would be quite a triumph for Russia to reveal not one, but two major scientific discoveries.

"All right," he agreed. "You can try to catch one of those things if you want. But my priority is the girl. Once I've got her, I'm not going to wait around."

"You won't have to." Esmerelda looked to the dart gun in Ivan's hands. "You might want something more powerful than that. These creatures look dangerous."

Ivan shook his head. "I need the girl alive. And if you're really interested in making history, a living missing link would be much more of a sensation than a dead one."

Esmerelda realized he was right. She had already been imagining the fame she would receive if she brought the body of one of the creatures back to civilization. . . . But a *live* one would make headlines all over the world. She would become as well known as any great scientist before her—and all her father's hard work and struggle would finally be vindicated.

"I don't suppose you have another one of those dart guns?" she asked.

THIRTY-EIGHT

Meanwhile, Charlie was facing down Esmerelda's brothers with the swollen creek at her back. Paolo and Gianni no longer had guns—Dante and Milana had taken theirs—but they did have brute strength. Charlie knew some basics of self-defense, but not enough to defeat both men at once.

Plus, she had Eve to protect.

Eve obviously recognized the men as a threat. She was facing them in a defensive posture, signaling she was ready to protect herself, but Charlie suspected it was just a front; the wounded creature didn't have much fight left in her.

Even worse, the behavior seemed to be producing the wrong response from the Castellos. Both men regarded Eve fearfully, but instead of backing off, they armed themselves, grabbing large pieces of wood to use as clubs.

"You're gonna pay for what you did to us," Gianni warned Charlie menacingly, then told his brother in Italian, "If that thing comes near us, bash its head in."

"I'll bash it even if it doesn't come near us," Paolo replied.

Charlie understood Italian. She placed a hand on Eve, who flinched at her touch, but then looked to her with questioning eyes.

The Castello brothers came toward them, brandishing their clubs menacingly.

Charlie turned and ran. Eve understood they were opting for flight over fight and came with her.

Rather than try to swim across the flooded creek, Eve scampered up a tree that arched over the water. Despite her wounded leg, she climbed with the grace and agility of an animal equally comfortable in a tree as on the ground. She paused halfway up to look back at Charlie expectantly, as if wanting her to follow.

Charlie didn't hesitate. It certainly would have been easier to simply swim across the creek, as she wasn't designed for climbing like Eve, but she remembered the howl of warning Eve had given when she had gotten too close to the water before. So she clambered up the tree. She probably didn't look good doing it, as the bark was slick from the rain, but she was still spry and nimble and got up all right.

The Castellos charged, racing toward the tree, although Charlie scrambled high enough to be out of their reach.

Eve skillfully used the tree as a bridge over the creek, but when she dropped down to the opposite bank, her wounded leg crumpled beneath her and she let out a wail of pain.

"Eve!" Charlie yelled. She was moving much more slowly across the tree, exercising caution to make sure she didn't slip off and plunge into the water.

The Castellos now shifted their focus to Eve, who was limping along, dragging her wounded leg. The men were too big and clumsy to climb the tree, so they simply waded into the creek, intending to ford it and grab Eve.

The anaconda attacked when they were halfway across.

It had been lurking in the water only a few feet from where Charlie had been before. Since much of the snake was hidden by the murky water, Charlie couldn't tell how long it was, but its body was over a foot wide. It moved with startling speed for such a big creature, first sinking its teeth into Gianni's torso and then coiling around him.

Gianni was quickly overwhelmed. While the man didn't feel residual pain, he was certainly hurting now—and he was terrified. Anacondas didn't kill by crushing their victims, but by suffocating them, squeezing them so tightly that they couldn't breathe. Plus, the snake was big enough to overpower Gianni and drag him underwater.

Paolo raced to his brother's aid. He whacked the anaconda with his club as hard as he could, but to no effect. The wood splintered apart on the snake's leathery hide, after which Paolo resorted to using his bare hands, desperately trying to pry the snake off his brother. The snake responded by wrapping its tail end around Paolo as well.

From her perch in the tree above, Charlie watched what was happening with horror, although she knew there was nothing she could do. If the snake could overwhelm two men as big and powerful as the Castellos at once, she would have no power to stop it. To save them, she had to find someone with a weapon. Knowing the men were quickly running out of time, she made it the rest of the way across the branch, dropped to the far bank, scooped Eve up in her arms, and ran off to look for help.

Milana felt like she had been hit by a truck. She opened her eyes and found herself lying in the mud. Her muscles were numb and her mind was so sluggish, it took her a few moments to recall what had happened.

Someone had shot her with a tranquilizer dart. She had seen Dante get hit right before her, so she had reacted quickly when she had been struck, knocking the dart away before its full dose could be injected into her, but still, some had gotten into her system. Enough to knock her out for a bit and go to work on her muscles. Every movement was now a struggle for her.

She rolled her head to the side and saw Dante splayed on the ground a few feet away. For a moment she feared he was dead, but then she saw his chest rise slightly as he breathed in.

However, there was no sign of Charlie or any of the others.

The storm had passed, but so much water was dripping from the canopy above, it was as though she were still caught in a light rain. She could hear thunder rumbling in the distance. . . .

And something else. A whirring noise, quite far away, but getting louder.

Milana recognized the sound.

Oh no, she thought.

She willed herself to get up, mustering every ounce of strength she had, but the best she could do was prop herself up on her arms. Her legs were completely useless.

Which meant *she* was completely useless.

Wherever Charlie was, she was on her own.

Esmerelda was horrified.

She and Ivan had split up to search the lost city for Charlie Thorne. Esmerelda had come across Charlie's footsteps and followed them to the creek . . . where she found what had become of her brothers. She had arrived too late to save them. The anaconda had already killed them both. Gianni's body was floating facedown in the creek, while the giant snake was actually consuming Paolo. It had unhinged its jaw and begun the long process of swallowing her brother headfirst. Esmerelda was so shaken by the sight of it that she couldn't even move. She could only stare in shock.

And then that shock turned to rage. Rage at Charlie Thorne.

Because none of this would have happened if it weren't for Charlie. Esmerelda's brothers would still be alive. Her beautiful face wouldn't be ruined. Darwin's treasure would have been hers to claim with ease.

Ivan Spetz had told her he wanted Charlie alive. And so Esmerelda would leave her alive for now, for long enough to let Ivan get her out of this cursed place. But after that she would have her revenge.

Charlie Thorne would pay.

It took Charlie a few minutes to find a place to cross back over the swollen creek and reenter the lost city. She didn't want to risk running into any more anacondas—or caimans or piranhas, for that matter—and she was still carrying Eve. If big men like the Castellos could fall prey to something in the rain forest, a small, wounded creature like Eve would be in great peril. Charlie knew she had to return Eve to her family.

As she passed through the ruins again, she heard the whirring sound and recognized what it was.

A helicopter.

It came in low, buzzing right over the top of the canopy, the wind from its rotors shaking the trees so hard that all the water gathered in their leaves fell off and rained down again. It was large and dark green, like a military troop transport, rather than a smaller tourist chopper, and its landing skids were fitted with air-filled pontoons, which made sense, as there was no place to land a helicopter in the dense rain forest except for on the water. Sure enough, the helicopter swung around over the lake and began to lower onto it.

Eve made a sudden squawk in Charlie's arms, indicating she had been spooked by something, but before Charlie could react, she felt the sting of a dart in her thigh. She whirled around to see Ivan Spetz behind her with the dart gun in his hand and a satisfied grin on his face, like he was having fun.

Charlie tried to run, but the sedative was already acting on her. All she could do was cradle Eve in her arms to protect her as she fell.

And that was the last thing she remembered.

THIRTY-NINE

Somewhere over the Peruvian Amazon

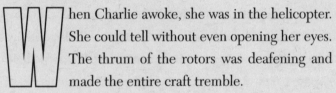hen Charlie awoke, she was in the helicopter. She could tell without even opening her eyes. The thrum of the rotors was deafening and made the entire craft tremble.

She kept her eyes shut, not wanting to give away that she was awake yet. In truth, she didn't feel that she *was* awake yet. Thanks to the sedative, she was still in the hazy place between consciousness and sleep, which wasn't optimal. So she tried to deduce what she could about her surroundings, hoping that solving those problems would help sharpen her wits.

She was lying on the floor, which was metal and thus cool against her cheek. Her wrists were bound with plastic zip ties, but in front of her body, rather than behind her back, which gave her at least a little use of her hands. Something warm and wet was resting against her. Her slightly addled mind immediately thought of a pet dog, but then she realized it was Eve. The creature was snuggled up against her so closely that Charlie could feel her heartbeat; it was relatively slow, indicating that Eve was asleep.

Charlie could also hear voices. The rotors were too loud for her to discern what anyone was saying, but that indicated everyone was a good distance away from her, which made her feel it was safe to open her eyes.

She did, and discovered she was right about everything she had deduced so far. The helicopter was definitely designed for military use; it was big and empty to allow for carrying as many people as possible, and a row of jump seats ran along both walls. Each side also had a large sliding door, which was currently locked. Everything was lit by a single dim fixture at the top of the cabin. The interior was painted dark green, with occasional words stenciled on the sides in both Russian and Spanish: instructions to the passengers to remain seated while in flight and to not deploy parachutes inside. The Spanish lettering was much sloppier, indicating to Charlie that the helicopter had originally been used for the Russian military and then sold to Peru.

Apparently, the SVR was still allowed the use of it when needed. Charlie assumed Ivan Spetz had called for it upon arriving at the lost city, probably with some sort of advanced satellite phone. (Whatever he had used, it was much better than the phones Dante and Milana had carried, which hadn't found a signal in over a week.) The cockpit was open to the body of the helicopter, unlike that of an airplane, and Ivan was seated in the copilot's seat. Charlie couldn't make out anything about the pilot from her position.

The sky out the windows in front of them was dark, although there was still a sliver of light along the horizon. Sunset. Charlie had been unconscious for more than an hour. Given the location of the sun, they were heading south.

Esmerelda sat in the closest jump seat to the cockpit, discussing something with Ivan. Both had radio headsets on, in part to shut out the din of the rotors and in part to make conversation easier over the noise.

Charlie was feeling better, more awake. To make sure she had all her wits about her, she performed a few complex mathematical equations in her mind.

Next Charlie tested her muscles to see if she had regained control over them. She could move all her fingers and toes, which was a good sign.

Esmerelda was still focused on Ivan, unaware that Charlie was awake.

Charlie shifted her head slightly, looking for what she needed most: her backpack.

She spotted it hanging on a row of hooks on the wall, along with everyone else's packs. It was ten feet away, much closer to Esmerelda than it was to Charlie, which was a problem. Charlie would be lucky to get to it before Esmerelda noticed her and would have only seconds after that at best.

Therefore, she would have to think everything through very carefully. Dante and Milana were no longer with her. It was up to her to protect Eve—and Eve's entire species.

Charlie closed her eyes again, giving the impression she was asleep, and ran through what she needed to do over and over, until she had everything worked out. Then she took a few deep breaths to steady her nerves.

In the cockpit, she thought she heard Ivan say they would reach the airport in Cuzco in fifteen minutes. Which meant Charlie had to act fast.

She slowly shifted herself away from Eve, trying not to wake her up. The creature was probably heavily sedated, but Charlie didn't want to take any chances. Eve's chest kept rising and falling slowly, indicating she was still asleep. Charlie cradled Eve's head as she slipped away and carefully laid it on the metal floor. Eve remained unconscious.

Then, as quickly as she could, Charlie leapt to her feet and went for her backpack. There was no point in trying to be slow and stealthy; that would only increase the amount of time in which the others might notice her. As it was, the roar of the rotors covered any noise she made.

Unfortunately, her legs weren't as steady as she'd hoped. Between the sedative and the shimmy of the helicopter, she was off-balance. She nearly fell once, then threw herself forward with too much force, slamming into the wall beside the backpack, making a dull thud.

Esmerelda heard it and turned. The moment she spotted Charlie, hatred flashed in her eyes. She leapt from her seat, on the attack. "She's up!" she yelled, getting Ivan's attention too.

Charlie grabbed the backpack and tumbled backward to the floor. Her hands were working far better than her legs, so she managed to open the pack and reach inside. The piece of the plant she had found by the swollen creek was on top. She pulled it out of the way, reaching deeper into the pack for what she needed. . . .

And then Esmerelda was on top of her, roughly yanking her to her feet and slamming her into one of the jump seats. She wrenched the backpack away from Charlie and dug into it herself, coming up with the large hunting knife that had been tucked inside, the gift from Segundo. "Is this what you were looking for?" Esmerelda challenged mockingly. "What did you think you were going to do, fight your way out of here? We're five thousand feet in the air."

Charlie didn't answer that. Instead, she said, "I don't care what you do with me. But you need to let Eve go."

"Eve?" Esmerelda glanced at the creature still sleeping on the floor of the helicopter. "You named her? Like a pet?"

"Like a *human*," Charlie replied defiantly. "You can't take her back to civilization. Please."

Esmerelda brandished Charlie's own knife at her menacingly. "You're in no position to make demands."

Ivan came to Esmerelda's side and, with one deft move, snatched the knife from her hands. Then he looked to Charlie curiously. "We're not going to do Eve any harm," he said reassuringly. "We're only going to reveal her existence to the world."

"But that *will* harm her," Charlie argued. "What happens to her *after* the world knows about her? She won't be returned to the wild to be with her family. She'll probably be kept in a lab for the rest of her life. And then scientists will come for the rest of them, too. The life they know will be over."

"Scientists study plenty of animals in the wild," Ivan countered. "Intelligent animals. Jane Goodall didn't ruin the lives of the chimpanzees she studied."

"No," Charlie admitted. "But chimps were still probably better off before humans knew they existed. All creatures were. And these creatures are *different*. They're smarter than anything else we've encountered before. . . ."

"They're *brutal*," Esmerelda spat. "I saw what they did to those idiots from the refinery."

"Because those men tried to hurt them," Charlie insisted. "*They* attacked the creatures first. They shot Eve. Look at her." Charlie pointed to the sleeping creature.

Esmerelda and Ivan did.

"They would have killed her," Charlie said. "That's how it goes with every species. For every person who wants to study them, there's someone else who wants to kill them. For food. Or for hunting trophies . . ."

"No one would hunt *these*," Ivan said. "They're too close to being human."

"That might be exactly why someone would want to kill them," Charlie said. "Because their similarity to us scares people. What do you think happened when Darwin found them? Why do you think *he* didn't bring one back to England? It would have been irrefutable proof of evolution, that humans evolved from other species. But the world wasn't ready for them."

"That was a long time ago," Ivan said. "The world has changed."

"Not enough," Charlie replied. "There are still plenty of places in the world, even in America, where evolution isn't accepted, where talk of it is regarded as blasphemy.

Those people claim that all the fossils we've found aren't really evidence for evolution—or are hoaxes—but what could they possibly say about Eve? I know she's not evolving into a human, but she's definitely evolving into something *like* us. And that's going to be a problem."

Ivan considered Eve again, as though intrigued by Charlie's arguments. "We could still protect the others of her species . . . ," he began.

"The only way to *really* protect them is to keep their existence a secret," Charlie said assuredly.

"Don't be a fool," Esmerelda told her. "It's not like that will work forever. Sooner or later, someone else will find them. In fact, at the rate the Amazon is being destroyed, those creatures will be lucky to have a home for another fifty years."

"Then they'll at least have fifty more years," Charlie said. "I know they won't be able to be protected forever. But *I* don't want to be responsible for ending everything. I'd rather be the one who gives them more time."

Esmerelda laughed sharply, like Charlie was an idiot, but Ivan stared at her thoughtfully.

"What's it worth to you to protect them?" he asked.

Charlie held his gaze. "I'll give you Pandora."

Ivan grinned. "Deal."

Esmerelda whirled on him, furious. "You can't agree to that! What about me? I have rights to that creature too!"

"The only reason you're even here right now and not back in the jungle is because of me," Ivan told her. "I'm in charge here."

"Do you know what that creature cost me?" Esmerelda raged. "Both my brothers! And my face! You can't just give her up like that!"

"The price was right," said Ivan. Then he gave Charlie a friendly smile. "Let's figure out how to make this work."

"No!" Esmerelda yelled. "That treasure is mine as much as yours!"

Despite the amiable demeanor Ivan was presenting, he had no intention of letting Eve go. He merely wanted to manipulate Charlie into coughing up Pandora.

Charlie had suspected as much. She had no intention of giving Pandora to Ivan. She was simply trying to distract him and Esmerelda. In truth, she hadn't been trying to get the knife out of her backpack. She had only wanted Esmerelda to think that. She had really been trying to get something else, a small plastic container she had palmed. When she had asked Esmerelda and Ivan to look at Eve, she had popped it open, and now that Ivan and Esmerelda were arguing, she used what was inside of it.

Bullet ants.

She had been collecting them throughout the trip, keeping them alive but safely tucked away in case she ran into trouble.

Like being kidnapped by the SVR, for example.

Now, in one quick motion, she flicked the container, flinging the ants onto Esmerelda and Ivan. The ants were so light, neither of the others felt them . . . until the agitated insects attacked.

Ivan felt the sting first. He had been subjected to plenty of pain in his life. At the SVR, he had even been trained in how to withstand it. But he had never experienced anything like this. It felt as though every nerve ending in his body had suddenly caught fire. It was so intense that it leveled him.

Esmerelda went down next. Her immunity to pain didn't apply to the initial shock of it. She sank to the floor as well, gripped by convulsions.

Charlie pried the knife from Ivan's hands, returned it to her backpack, and ran to the cockpit. The pilot was looking back toward the others with concern, trying to figure out what had happened. Out the windshield, she could see the dark forms of the Andes Mountains rising into the sky. The glow of Cuzco's lights was still a few miles ahead; for now they were on the fringe of civilization.

To Ivan's surprise, the pain wasn't receding, but getting worse. He was reeling from it.

But for Esmerelda, the worst had already passed. Her body's unusual chemistry could even overwhelm the venom of the bullet ant. She staggered back to her feet and lunged for Charlie, seething with hatred.

Charlie intercepted her attack, catching Esmerelda's arms in her hands. She used her fingernails as a weapon, like Milana had told her, digging them deep into Esmerelda's skin, but Esmerelda didn't even flinch.

"You little fool," she snarled at Charlie. "I thought you understood my condition. It'll take more than a bullet ant to incapacitate me."

"Oh, I didn't want you incapacitated," Charlie said. "I need you to land the helicopter."

Esmerelda faltered in her attack, wondering what Charlie had done.

And then the pilot screamed and succumbed to the pain from the bullet ant that Charlie had dropped on him. He collapsed in his seat, throwing the helicopter into a dive.

FORTY

Five thousand feet above the Andes, Peru

Charlie had known her plan was risky, but desperate times called for desperate measures.

After all, it was extremely difficult to beat anyone in a fight when they were ultimately immune to pain.

She was aware that flying a plane and a helicopter were different skills, but she figured that knowing how to do one would aid in doing the other. At the very least, given the circumstances, Esmerelda would have to give flying the helicopter a shot.

Which was exactly what happened. While Charlie dragged the pain-racked pilot out of the cockpit, Esmerelda slipped into his seat and took the controls. She was able to pull them out of the dive, although the helicopter still wheeled dangerously in the sky.

"You little lunatic!" Esmerelda yelled at Charlie. "I don't know how to control this thing!"

"Then just bring it down," Charlie replied.

"Where?" Between the residual effects of the ant bite and the shock of taking the controls, Esmerelda was on the edge of panic. "There's nothing but mountains around us!"

Charlie raced back to the cockpit and looked through the window. Esmerelda had a point. They needed a flat place to land, and the Andes were a jumble of jagged peaks; flat land was in short supply.

But there was one patch below them to the left. "There!" Charlie exclaimed, pointing.

Esmerelda had no choice but to aim for it, although her first instinct was to push too hard on the stick. The helicopter veered downward too quickly until she realized her mistake and pulled back.

Charlie fought aside a wave of nausea, keeping her eyes locked on the place she had chosen to land. It sat atop a butte surrounded by the horseshoe bend of a river, along which there was a small town. As they came closer, Charlie realized the flat spot was actually a series of man-made terraces, with a steep pinnacle of rock at one end.

"Oh my." She gasped. "I think we're about to crash-land in Machu Picchu."

• • •

The most famous icon of Incan civilization, Machu Picchu was used for only about a century. Although often mistaken for a city, it was really an estate built for the emperor Pachacuti in the mid-1400s, and abandoned around the time the Spanish conquistadores arrived. While explorer Hiram Bingham had received international fame for his "discovery" of it in 1911, locals had known of its existence all along and had even shown it to other explorers. What Bingham had really done was make it famous.

It was understandable why the site had captured the attention of the world; it was an astounding display of Incan architecture in a gorgeous and somewhat improbable setting. Since Bingham's arrival, Machu Picchu had become the most popular tourist site in Peru, attracting more than 1.5 million visitors a year, despite its somewhat remote location in the mountains. It had also been declared one of the New Seven Wonders of the World and a UNESCO World Heritage Site.

To protect the site, visitors were not allowed there at night. The great terraces had been crawling with tourists only an hour before, but were now thankfully clear as the helicopter came down.

The flattest area, in the center, was still a difficult target, as it was surrounded by the remnants of ancient stone buildings as well as a few steep, stony peaks, most notably Huayna Picchu, an eight-hundred-and-fifty-foot-tall pillar of rock with the ruins of temples atop it, where Incan priests were rumored to have lived.

In the darkness, Huayna Picchu was nearly invisible, and Esmerelda almost crashed right into it. Instead, she veered away at the last instant, coming so close that the helicopter's rotors nicked the stone walls, sparking off the rocks and kicking the chopper into a spin.

Charlie was flung backward from the cockpit, tumbling across the floor over both the pilot and Ivan Spetz. Eve skittered into the wall and gave a yelp, indicating that she had regained consciousness. Charlie looked to her and saw her eyes, open wide and round in fear, no doubt wondering what could possibly be happening to her.

The helicopter came down hard on a terrace by the edge of Machu Picchu, landing so roughly that the pontoons blew out and one of the skids collapsed. The craft slid through a protective fence and came to a stop balanced precariously on the edge of the gorge, fifteen hundred feet above the Urubamba River.

Although Eve was awake again, she was groggy from the sedative. While Esmerelda was still in the pilot's seat, Charlie picked Eve up and flung open the helicopter door, intending to flee into the ruins.

But Ivan Spetz wasn't out of the game yet. Even though he was sprawled on the floor of the helicopter, racked with pain, he grabbed Charlie's ankle with surprising strength, tripping her as she tried to escape. She went down hard, banging her shoulder and head as she tried to protect Eve with her own body.

The helicopter shifted ominously, sliding a bit farther on the edge of the gorge.

Charlie kicked Ivan in the arm as hard as she could, causing him even more pain and getting him to release her, but by the time she got back to her feet with Eve in her arms, Esmerelda was blocking the doorway, holding the knife. Her face was a mask of rage—but there was something else in her eyes. A slight disorientation.

"First you're going to give me that creature," she said. "And then you're going to die."

Charlie said, "If you kill me, you'll die too."

The tone of her voice was so steady, Esmerelda realized she wasn't bluffing. "What do you mean?"

"You might not feel the pain, but you realize that something's wrong with you, yes? Your muscles are weakening and you're starting to have trouble breathing."

Esmerelda's face filled with concern, then anger again. "What did you do to me?"

"I poisoned you. With *these*." Charlie held up her hand, displaying her fingernails.

Esmerelda looked to her arm, where Charlie had dug her nails into her skin a few minutes before. There were red slashes where blood had come to the surface. "Curare," she gasped.

"Oh," Charlie said. "You've heard of it."

The plant she had found back where the anaconda had been lurking had a poisonous resin that Segundo had taught her about. Amazon natives had been poisoning the tips of their arrows with it for centuries, although it could also be delivered to the bloodstream via a good scratch.

"You little rat," Esmerelda seethed—although despite her anger, her strength was fading. She had to steady herself against the wall.

The helicopter shifted again, sliding a bit more over the edge of the gorge.

"We need to get out of here *now*," Charlie said. "The choice is simple. None of us has to die. The curare acts fast—but you still have time left. If you let me go, I can run to town and get a doctor. But if you kill me . . . then we're both dead. I think both of us can agree that's the worst option."

To Charlie's surprise, Esmerelda didn't back down. Instead, she raised the knife in her trembling hand. "I don't have *any* options here. You'll never get help for me."

Charlie swallowed hard, worried. It had never occurred to her that Esmerelda might think she was so evil. "Of course I'll get help. I'm not a jerk. I don't want you to die."

"Right," Esmerelda said sarcastically. "Since I'm gonna end up dead either way, I might as well take you with me. . . ." She suddenly lunged for Charlie with the knife.

Eve screeched in anger and flung herself out of Charlie's arms. For a small creature that had been recently sedated, she was surprisingly powerful. She slammed into Esmerelda, sending her reeling backward into the cockpit. The motion jostled the entire helicopter, which began to slide over the lip of the gorge.

Charlie wanted to grab Eve, but there was no time. She dove for the open doorway of the helicopter.

Luckily, Eve was smart enough to realize what was happening. She sprang away from Esmerelda and bounded out the door as well.

Charlie and the little creature tumbled across the rocky ground as the helicopter tipped over the edge.

Inside, Esmerelda wasn't quick enough to follow. And Ivan was too crippled with pain. They could only scream as they realized what was happening.

The helicopter plummeted into the gorge, crashed into the river fifteen hundred feet below, and exploded in a ball of fire.

Charlie lay on the rocky lip, battered and bruised. In the glow of the fire, she saw that Eve was all right. In fact, the little creature was surprisingly resilient, looking as though she was almost back to normal, despite every-thing that had happened.

Voices echoed through the night. Charlie sat up and saw flashlight beams cutting through the ruins in the distance.

Probably security guards, she thought, alerted by the crash.

She turned back to Eve, thinking that she was going to have to run off and hide in the ruins with the creature to keep her hidden.

But Eve was already on the move, loping away as fast as she could, her wounded leg holding up well now that Charlie had bandaged it.

"Eve!" Charlie shouted.

Eve stopped and looked back. Charlie wasn't sure, but it seemed that the little creature gave her a slight smile.

Then she scampered off, disappearing into the shadows.

Charlie got to her feet. She knew she wouldn't be able to catch up to Eve, but despite all her bruises and bumps, she was still in good enough shape to move.

So she slipped away into the ruins before anyone could find her and start asking questions.

FORTY-ONE

Agua Rojo Eco-Lodge

t took Dante and Milana a week to get back through the flooded forest to the resort. Although Oz and his men had sunk their canoe, and Ivan's as well, the canoe that Oz had come in was still moored there.

The trip was difficult and exhausting, made worse by the fact that both of them were plagued by feelings of doubt, failure—and concern about Charlie. Neither of them had any idea what had happened to her, and they couldn't help but assume the worst.

So even though they were desperate for food and hot showers and sleep when they arrived, the first thing Dante did was use the resort's computer and Wi-Fi to check his email accounts, hoping there was some word of what had happened.

To his relief, there was.

Buried in hundreds of emails from work, friends, and his superiors, there was a brief message.

> Hey, Dante—
> I'm safe. But . . . if you tell *anyone* about the creatures or the lost city, then I will never, *ever* give you Pandora.
> —Charlie
> P.S. Have you kissed Milana yet?

Dante was overcome with relief and joy, knowing that Charlie was all right. And then that turned to shock and surprise.

He hurried into the restaurant, where he found Milana wolfing down a lunch that Segundo had made for her. She was also halfway through her second beer. There was another plate for Dante, but Dante ignored it.

"She's alive and well," he said.

Milana grinned with relief. "Thank goodness. She emailed you?"

"Yes. From my own secure CIA account."

Milana set down her beer, stunned. "How? That has six layers of encryption. And she shouldn't even know it exists."

"She's *Charlie*," Dante said. "She knows *everything*." He sat at the table across from Milana. "If she has access to that email account, then she can hack the CIA's system. Which means she's probably read *all* of my emails."

"Oh," Milana said, with concern.

"Exactly. All the information about Einstein's other coded message was on there. Including the entire translation of it. Like the part about Darwin having discovered something too."

Milana smiled, despite herself. She couldn't help but respect the kid. "She knew all along? So it wasn't a coincidence that she was in Galápagos when all this started."

Dante shook his head. "Like she kept telling us, there's no such thing as coincidence. She didn't go there only to be far away from anyone who might want Pandora. She was looking for the first clue to Darwin's treasure."

"And if she's read the entire message, then she knows there are others who hid their discoveries too."

"Right."

Milana started laughing.

"What's so funny?" Dante asked.

"She played us perfectly. Here we were, thinking that we were manipulating her into joining this search for us, when she was manipulating *us* into it."

Dante nodded, and then he found himself laughing too. "That kid is such a pain in my butt," he said.

"True," Milana said. "But I'm glad she's on our side. I think."

"Yeah," Dante agreed. And then, while he was sitting there, laughing and enjoying the moment, he figured maybe he ought to stop being so annoyed at Charlie for being right all the time and just listen to her advice.

So he kissed Milana Moon.

EPILOGUE

Iguazu Falls
The border of Argentina and Brazil

harlie Thorne stood at the edge of the largest waterfall system on earth, thinking.

Before her, the Iguazu River spilled over a dozen separate cataracts into the gorge known as the Devil's Throat. (The South Americans apparently liked to name things after the devil.) The mist it created swirled and eddied around her, cool on her skin.

It had taken her three weeks to get here from Cuzco. Originally, she had intended only to go as far as La Paz, the capital of Bolivia, and catch a plane out of South America, but on the train there from Cuzco, she had met some backpackers who raved about Iguazu, so she figured she ought to check it out.

They had been right. It was incredible.

Charlie hadn't been able to find Eve at Machu Picchu. She assumed the creature was trying to return home to her family, but by Charlie's calculations, that was a journey of hundreds of miles through the Amazon basin. It would have been arduous, if not impossible, for a human on her own, but she hoped Eve was hardy enough to make it.

Then Charlie had fled the area before anyone noticed her.

There were thousands of backpackers making their way around that part of Peru, and since Charlie looked and acted older than her age, it wasn't hard for her to blend in. She was still wearing her money belt, which had enough cash to get her to La Paz, and once there, she had made a call to her bank to arrange an untraceable delivery of more funds. With those, she had purchased a fake Bolivian passport. In most countries, it wasn't hard to get false documents if you had the funds.

The question was where to go now.

Charlie had learned it was pointless to lie low on the fringes of civilization and hope that no one found her. Ivan Spetz had tracked her down, and there would certainly be more people like Ivan. So it made sense to keep moving, to never stay in the same place for long. That wasn't necessarily an easy life, but it was certainly less boring than spending the rest of her years in the boonies. The earth was a big planet, and there were plenty of amazing places to see.

Plus, thanks to the CIA, she knew there were other geniuses from throughout history who had hidden their discoveries.

As long as she was on the run, she might as well track those down. It wasn't as if she could end up in *more* danger. And those discoveries, whatever they might be, were probably better off in her hands than anyone else's.

Dante had told Charlie a lie about Einstein's message, thinking she didn't know the truth. He had said Darwin was the only name that Einstein mentioned. In fact, Einstein had provided a long list of fellow geniuses and detailed where to start looking for what each of them had found. Of course, Charlie had memorized it all.

Now she ran through it in her mind, wondering whose discovery would be the most interesting to pursue next.

There were many fascinating, incredible people on the list, but at the moment, one name stood out to her over the others.

Cleopatra.

It would be fun to find out what another brilliant woman had discovered.

Charlie took a final look at the falls, then went to book a flight to Egypt.

AUTHOR'S NOTE

After *Charlie Thorne and the Last Equation* came out, I got a lot of mail from people wondering how much of what I said about Albert Einstein was true and how much I had made up. I expect that the same might happen after the publication of this book, so I figure, maybe I should include a note in this book to that effect.

However, after having written an entire book positing something exciting about what *might* have happened, it feels a little weird to now add a note saying that it *didn't* happen. Obviously you're aware that the book you just read is a work of fiction, but still, part of the fun to me is making you wonder if it could have really been possible. That said, I do want you to know what an absolutely amazing person Darwin was and want you to have some serious respect for his science. He really changed the world with his ideas. So here are the facts:

As far as we know, Darwin did not go to Ecuador, or venture into the interior of the Amazon from the west. But he *did* explore the Amazon from the east, as well as much of Patagonia in South America. The *Beagle* really did spend four years exploring South America, which was far longer than intended. Although Darwin was really asked aboard to provide companionship and intellectual stimulation for Captain FitzRoy, he proved to be a rugged adventurer and spent far more days on land than he did on the ship. He collected many fossils and natural specimens and did so much geological work, he originally believed his great contribution to science after the trip would be in the field of geology.

Darwin did *not* find an undiscovered group of prehominids. The convergent evolution that I describe in the book for many species is well documented, but the chance of prehominids developing in two places is unlikely. Instead, Darwin needed no such obvious signs of evolution to develop his famous theory, which makes him even more impressive, really.

So, Darwin did not disappear from the *Beagle* for a year on a mysterious journey. Nor did he leave a series of clues behind to track down a tribe of prehominids. But everything else I wrote about him in this book is true: His fascination with Charles Lyell's geologic discoveries, his skill with a rifle, his falling out with FitzRoy, his concern about revealing his theory of evolution to the world until Alfred Russell Wallace hit upon exactly the same idea and sent it to him. His journal really is missing fifty pages (no one knows why) and he really did ride on a Galápagos tortoise and fling a marine iguana into the ocean over and over again. (Science was a little different back then.) Charles Darwin was a great thinker, a great researcher, and a great adventurer.

And here's one other cool fact about him that I couldn't figure out how to work into the story: He was born on the exact same day as another incredibly influential, brilliant man: Abraham Lincoln. February 12, 1809. Although there are many notable cases of famous people dying on the same day, there is no other example of two such incredible people sharing a birthday in history.

ACKNOWLEDGMENTS

I had been toying with the idea of a story of Darwin discovering a group of prehominids since long before I ever thought of Charlie Thorne. However, I could never have written this book without visiting the areas it takes place. So first and foremost, I ought to thank my traveling companions: my children, Dashiell and Violet; my in-laws, Barry and Carole Patmore—and, of course, my wife Suzanne. Sadly, this was the last great trip that my wife went on, as she passed away tragically shortly afterward. She had originally expressed some reservations about visiting the Amazon and the Galápagos, but she knew that I really wanted to go there, and so she agreed. Thankfully, she had a great time there—as did we all.

So I also owe thanks to everyone at the Napo Conservation Center in the Ecuadorean Amazon—and to the entire crew of the *Anahi* in the Galápagos—for all you did to make our trip so wonderful, and for answering the thousands of questions I asked.

This book is also somewhat based on the first trip I took to the Amazon, many years ago, and to Machu

Picchu, with my good friend Jeff Peachin, who has always been an excellent travel companion. On that trip, we stayed at the wonderful Explorama Lodge, which also had fantastic guides.

Even with these inspirational visits, I still needed plenty of extra research for this book. So huge thanks to my outstanding interns, Kelly Heinzerling and Caroline Harris, and all the invaluable work you did for me. And thanks to Mingo Reynolds, R.J. Bernocco, and everyone at the Kelly Writer's House at the University of Pennsylvania for finding me such great interns every year.

And now for the usual round of thanks to everyone who helps to make my life easier and advises me on how to do my job better:

First, there's my incredible team at Simon & Schuster: Krista Vitola, Justin Chanda, Lucy Cummins, Kendra Levin, Dainese Santos, Anne Zafian, Milena Giunco, Audrey Gibbons, Lisa Moraleda, Jenica Nasworthy, Penina Lopez, Chrissy Noh, Anna Jarzab, Brian Murray, Devin MacDonald, Christina Pecorale, Victor Iannone, Emily Hutton, Caitlin Nalven, and Theresa Pang. Also, thanks to Liz Kossnar, who was my editor when I began this book, but who has sadly moved on to a new job. And massive thanks to my incredible agent, Jennifer Joel, for making all this possible.

Thanks to my amazing fellow writers (and support

group) James Ponti, Sarah Mlynowski, Julie Buxbaum, Christina Soontornvat, Karina Yan Glaser, Max Brallier, Gordon Korman, Julia Devillers, Leslie Margolis, and Rose Brock.

Thanks to all the school librarians and parent associations who have arranged for me to visit, all the bookstore owners and employees who have shilled my books, and all the amazingly tireless festival organizers and volunteers who have invited me to participate.

Thanks to the home team: Ronald and Jane Gibbs; Suz, Darragh, and Ciara Howard; Andrea Lee Gomez and Georgia Simon.

Dash and Violet, one last shout-out. You're the best kids in the universe. I love you more than words can say.

READING GROUP GUIDE
for *Charlie Thorne and the Lost City*
by Stuart Gibbs

About the Book

Charlie Thorne is a genius. Charlie Thorne is a fugitive. Charlie Thorne isn't even thirteen. After saving the world, Charlie is ready to take it easy in the Galápagos Islands. That is, until she's approached by the mysterious Esmeralda Castle, who has a code she knows only Charlie can decipher. In 1835, Charles Darwin diverted his ship's journey so he could spend ten months in South America on a secret solo expedition. When he returned, he carried a treasure that inspired both awe and terror in his crew. Afterward, it vanished, but Darwin left a trail of clues behind for those brave and clever enough to search for it. In a daring adventure that takes her across South America, Charlie must crack Darwin's two-hundred-year-old clues to track down his mysterious discovery. However, when an ancient hidden treasure is at stake, people will do anything to find it first. Is Charlie smart enough to know who she can trust?

Discussion Questions

The following questions may be utilized throughout the study of *Charlie Thorne and the Lost City* as reflective writing prompts, or alternatively, they can be used as targeted questions for group discussion and reflection.

1. In the book's prologue, readers learn that Robert Fitz-Roy, the captain of the HMS *Beagle*, is ready to abandon Darwin; Darwin has repeatedly delayed the ship's departure from Ecuador without providing an appropriate rationale for doing so. Darwin finally tells Fitz-Roy, "'I saw many incredible things on my journey . . . they all paled compared to this. Everything I have ever encountered in my life pales compared to this.'" In what ways does the opening scene set the stage for the events to follow? Explain your answer using examples from the book.

2. Given his behavior in the prologue, why does Darwin go to such great lengths to keep the lost city and the missing link from being discovered? How do you feel about Darwin's decisions? Explain your answers.

3. As a large hammerhead shark swims under her surfboard, Charlie is filled with excitement rather than fear.

What can you infer about Charlie based on her reaction? Describe other scenes throughout the book that support your conclusion.

4. Part one, "The Edge of the Earth," opens with the following Darwin quote: "Nothing can be more improving to a young naturalist than a journey in distant countries." What do you think Darwin means by this? In what ways can this be seen as a call to action? Explain your answers.

5. Though she works hard to remain inconspicuous in Puerto Villamil, Charlie had "already become legendary among the few who lived there. Even surfers with decades of experience mistimed a wave on occasion, but Charlie never did. Somehow, she was always exactly where she needed to be." Why does Charlie's ability ultimately cause her to be in danger?

6. Charlie speaks "over a dozen languages and could understand many more." In what ways does Charlie's affinity for languages work in her favor? Do you know any words in any of the languages she speaks?

7. Puerto Villamil, on the southern fringe of Isla Isabela in the Galápagos Islands, is about as far from civilization as one can get. Why do you think feeling that she's on "the

very edge of the earth" appeals to Charlie? In what ways does isolation offer her a sense of security?

8. Charlie was "always on the lookout for things that were out of the ordinary. When you lived your life on the run, you had to stay attuned to your surroundings at all times." What are some of the challenges and benefits to Charlie's lifestyle? Do you think she enjoys living the way she does? Explain your answers.

9. CIA Director Jamilla Carter realized that "finding Charlie Thorne was of paramount importance to the CIA. And they needed to find her before anyone else did." Consider the CIA's motivations: Do you believe they have Charlie's best interests at heart? Based on what you've learned about her, what makes Charlie a great asset to the CIA? Explain your answers using examples from the book.

10. Darwin's carvings on the tortoise suggest he has knowledge of "the greatest treasure in human history." How do you interpret his statement? Share your ideas of what the word "treasure" means to you.

11. After Charlie deciphers Darwin's code, Esmerelda tells her, "'Apparently, I came to the right person. You fig-

ured that out immediately when an entire team of scientists couldn't do it in two days!'" Why is Esmerelda so surprised that Charlie has been able to accomplish this? Do you think her reaction is typical or atypical to the responses Charlie usually receives for her work?

12. How does Charlie misjudge Esmerelda? What does this reveal about Charlie?

13. Describe Charlie based on what you've learned about her in *Charlie Thorne and the Lost City*. Are there any new traits you've learned about her character that surprise you?

14. As they begin to travel down the Amazon, Charlie asks Milana, "'What have you been up to since betraying my trust a few months ago?'" What can you infer from their exchange?

15. Charlie believes that what they have uncovered in the Amazon needs to remain secret. Do you agree or disagree with her evaluation? What do you predict the outcome would be if the knowledge did get out?

16. Ivan Spetz, the Russian agent after Charlie, is a formidable foe in many ways. What makes him so dangerous?

Are there any ways in which he and Charlie are actually alike? Explain your answers using examples from the book.

17. Readers learn more about ecotourism efforts in the Amazon as well as the Galápagos Islands. In what ways do such opportunities support these destinations? Are there any drawbacks you can think of?

18. As they're being attacked by a seaplane, Charlie devises a plan, telling Dante, "'I don't have time to explain everything!'" He retorts by saying, "'It's too dangerous.'" Why is he so confident that he knows what's best for Charlie? Do you agree or disagree with this belief? Based on their interactions in *Charlie Thorne and the Lost City*, what can you glean about Charlie's relationship with her brother? How does it continue to change?

19. What do you think about Milana Moon, given all you've learned about her in *Charlie Thorne and the Lost City*? Are there ways in which Charlie's relationship with Milana is changing as they spend more time together? Explain your answers using examples from the book.

20. Charlie's participation in this mission takes her around the world; besides the new places she sees, what do you

think are the most important things she discovers along the way?

21. In the epilogue, readers learn that "Charlie had learned it was pointless to lie low on the fringes of civilization and hope that no one found her. Ivan Spetz had tracked her down, and there would certainly be more people like Ivan. So it made sense to keep moving, to never stay in the same place for long. That wasn't necessarily an easy life, but it was certainly less boring than spending the rest of her years in the boonies. The earth was a big planet, and there were plenty of amazing places to see." Reflect on Charlie's outlook for her future: What do you think of her attitude and approach? What would you do if you were in her position?

22. Considering the book's conclusion, what do you predict Charlie's next adventure will be?

Extension Activities

1. In *Charlie Thorne and the Lost City*, maintaining secrecy around the discovery of Darwin's missing link is a major fictional plot point. Read "What is the missing link?" at LiveScience (https://www.livescience.com/32530 -what-is-the-missing-link.html) to better gain a better

understanding of the term. Next, utilize your library's resources to further research this evolutionary theory. Taking what you've learned, engage in a group discussion where you share what you've found to be most interesting about your new knowledge. What other information about Darwin or evolution would you like to know?

2. Early in the book, readers learn about a tortoise whose shell is carved with a message from Darwin; this makes the creature likely two hundred years old. Learn more about how the ages of animals are regularly determined by reading this guide to aging animals from National Geographic: https://www.nationalgeographic.com/animals /article/130730-aging-animals-fish-cats-science-primate -oldest-animal-clam. After reading, talk as a small group about what've you learned. Did anyone have questions that were left unanswered? Come up with a plan to work together to discover the answers to any outstanding questions.

3. In the book's prologue, readers observe Darwin returning to the HMS *Beagle* in Ecuador after forcing the crew to wait for him as he engages in a mysterious mission. Research to discover more about Darwin's time on the HMS *Beagle*, being sure to learn more about the following:

- When did Darwin's HMS *Beagle* journey take place, and where did it take him and the crew?
- Who were the other important figures on board besides Darwin?
- How was the voyage documented?
- What were some of the voyage's primary accomplishments?
- What were the journey's greatest challenges or obstacles?

After examining what you've learned, engage in a classroom discussion about Darwin's actions and analyze the outcomes.

4. Charles Darwin is often considered to be the most influential scientist and naturalist of the nineteenth century. Using resources from the library and the internet, investigate his life and work, being sure to look closely at the following:

- When and where did Darwin live?
- What was his educational background?
- What were his most important scientific contributions?
- What were his goals as a naturalist?
- How did his contributions reshape the world?
- What other facts did you find most interesting?

After conducting your research, create and share a digital artifact that synthesizes the highlights of your findings.

5. Charlie's mission to uncover Darwin's secrets takes her on a number of grand adventures. Working in a small group, create a map of Charlie's whereabouts that includes all the locations she visits. Calculate the distances she travels from point to point, as well as an estimated length of time the journey takes her. If you could take a similar trip, would you? Upon completion, pair up with another group and compare and contrast your findings. Then engage in a discussion about embarking on a similar adventure. What do you think you'd learn about yourselves?

6. Charlie's quest for answers lands her in the Amazon, where readers are introduced to the Amazon River, the second longest river in the world. Use the library or the internet to learn more about the great Amazon, being sure to consider the following:

- Where is the Amazon River located?
- How long is it?
- What animals live near or in the Amazon River?
- What makes navigating the river particularly challenging or dangerous?

- What are some of the reasons the Amazon River is famous?
- Why is the Amazon and the land surrounding it in need of protection?
- What are some simple conservation efforts you can make to help care for it?

After completing your research, share your new knowledge with your group. Then brainstorm how best to share information about protection and conservation with the rest of your school or community.

7. At the beginning of the novel, readers discover that Charlie has been hiding in the Galápagos to protect herself. Research more about the Galápagos Islands, being sure to focus on the following:

- Where are the islands located?
- Why are they considered so important?
- What is Darwin's connection to this area?
- What are the unique types of wildlife found there?
- What are the most important conservation efforts happening there?
- What makes those efforts challenging?

After discovering answers to these questions, discuss your findings with your group. Next, talk about your own town or state. Are there wildlife areas in your community that need to be protected? Are there conservation efforts taking place? How might you help?

This guide was created by Dr. Rose Brock, an assistant professor at Sam Houston State University. Dr. Brock holds a Ph.D. in Library Science, specializing in children's and young adult literature.

This guide has been provided by Simon & Schuster for classroom, library, and reading group use. It may be reproduced in its entirety or excerpted for these purposes. For more Simon & Schuster guides, please visit simonandschuster.net or simonandschuster.net/thebookpantry.

Turn the page for a sneak peek at

CHARLIE THORNE

AND THE
CURSE OF CLEOPATRA

Giza, Egypt
Present Day

On the evening of her thirteenth birthday, Charlie Thorne committed a crime.

As crimes went, it was a minor one, merely illegal entry. Charlie had no intention to steal anything or hurt anyone—although she knew from experience that even the most carefully thought-out plans often went wrong.

Which was exactly what happened that night.

The location was the penthouse condominium of Ahmet Shah, the oldest son of an extremely wealthy Egyptian shipping magnate. Charlie had been plotting the crime for two weeks, surveying the building, doing research, learning everything she could about Ahmet and his home.

Charlie was exceptionally smart. She had an extremely high IQ and a gift for languages; since arriving in the country, she had taught herself Egyptian Arabic. She could have hacked Ahmet's computer to get the information she wanted—although that hadn't been necessary. Ahmet loved the spotlight and was extremely active on social media, and so he had unwittingly posted everything Charlie needed to know online.

Ahmet was a vice president at his father's company, but he didn't appear to work very much—if at all. Instead, his main profession seemed to be spending money. He had vacation homes in Aspen and Malibu and an eight-bedroom yacht that was currently anchored in Ibiza. He belonged to seventeen different country clubs around the world, three of which he had never even visited. He had just returned to Giza after spending two weeks in a $10,000-a-night hotel room in Bali.

And now he was throwing a massive party to celebrate his return.

Charlie had briefly considered breaking into Ahmet's condo while he was in Bali, but the security system was elaborate and state-of-the-art, and the building was patrolled by armed guards. Charlie had many talents, but breaking and entering wasn't one of them. Besides, there were far easier ways to get into someone's home, no matter how well protected it was.

Under the right circumstances, you could just walk through the door.

Ahmet Shah loved entertaining. It hadn't taken Charlie long to learn that about him; her first Google image search for the young man turned up hundreds of party photos taken at his penthouse. Large, crowded, glamorous parties, the kind that certain types of people were desperate to score invitations to.

The condo had also been featured in several architectural and design magazines, which allowed Charlie to easily memorize the layout of the rooms and catalog most of the artifacts on display.

Including one artifact in particular. The one Charlie had been trying to locate for the past two months. In a magazine photo, it was in the background behind Ahmet as he showed off another piece of art that wasn't anywhere nearly as important.

An artifact so powerful and significant should never have been in a private collection. Ahmet Shah would have been wise to keep its location a secret. But then, Ahmet did not appear to be a very wise person. From Charlie's research, he appeared to be a wealthy brat who wanted to be famous—and he didn't even know what he possessed.

Charlie took it as a good sign that the party happened to be on her birthday. She felt like celebrating, but unfortunately, she was no longer in touch with any of her friends. Four months earlier, circumstances beyond her control had forced her to cut ties with all of them and vanish from their lives. None of them had heard from her since then. None had the slightest idea what had happened to her.

And as for celebrating with family, well . . . Charlie had some very unusual family issues. Her half brother Dante was a CIA agent who had blackmailed her into working for the government. He was the reason she was now on the run, pursued by intelligence agencies and criminals around the globe.

Although, Charlie had to admit, thanks to Dante, her life had become quite exciting. If it wasn't for him, she wouldn't have even known about the artifact in Ahmet Shah's penthouse.

To access the party, all Charlie had to do was pretend to be a member of the catering staff, which was easy. The party was going to be a big one, with more than sixty servers. And caterers all over the world wore virtually the same uniform: white shirt and black pants. The clothes were cheap and readily available—not that Charlie had to worry about money.

Charlie was tall for her age and behaved with a maturity that made her come across as someone who was several years older. In addition, she was extremely racially diverse—partially Latina, Black, Asian, Middle Eastern, and Caucasian—and multilingual; with her caterer's uniform and her newfound mastery of Egyptian Arabic, she easily blended in with the other hired help.

While the building where the party was taking place was imposing and opulent in the front, it was basic and industrial in the back. There was a rear entrance for nights like this, so that the catering supplies and staff wouldn't have to come through the main lobby and tie up the elevators. As Charlie had expected, the scene at the rear entrance in the hour before the party was chaotic; the catering staff was scrambling to unload truckloads of food, glassware, serving dishes, utensils, and linens and get them up to the penthouse. Charlie simply grabbed a tray of canapés and fell in line. The single security guard stationed there was distracted, trying to get the phone number of an attractive young caterer, and Charlie walked right past him and into the service elevator without any trouble at all.

The penthouse was even more spectacular than she had expected. The magazine photos hadn't done it justice. It was extremely modern in design, which served as a stark juxtaposition to the ancient treasures in Ahmet Shah's art collection: papyrus scrolls and sandstone sculptures that were thousands of years old. But for most visitors, the most amazing aspect was the view of the pyramids.

The western walls of the penthouse were floor-to-ceiling glass, fronting an outdoor deck with an infinity pool. All of it faced the famous Giza pyramid complex. Although the ancient tombs were still surrounded by the sands of the northern Sahara, the modern city came surprisingly close to them, creating a jarring clash of the old and the new. The edge of the pyramid complex was lined with other luxury condominium towers, high-end housing developments, ghettos, shopping centers, school campuses, and even a golf course, whose irrigated green fairways looked bizarrely out of place beside the desert sands. At night, the great pyramids were lit with flood-lights, so they practically gleamed against the dark sky.

However, as impressive as the view of the pyramids was, Charlie was far more interested in something inside the penthouse.

And yet she couldn't go see it right away. There were security cameras in every room and plenty of guards patrolling the condo. So Charlie bided her time, wait-ing for the right moment. For a few hours, she worked dutifully as a caterer, first by helping set up for the party, arranging banquet tables and prepping food, and then, once the guests began to arrive, by carrying around trays of hors d'oeuvres and collecting empty glasses. When the party finally reached its peak, and the rooms were jammed with guests, Charlie decided it was time to make her move.

She ducked into a bathroom and took off her cater-ing clothes, revealing the party dress she'd been wear-ing underneath them all along. Ahmet Shah's guests were rich, and so, to blend in, Charlie had splurged on a designer outfit. It was sleek and stylish—although not so stylish that it would grab attention. Attention was the last thing Charlie wanted. She quickly put up her hair, did her makeup, and crammed the caterer's uniform into a cabinet under the sink. Then she stepped out and joined the party.

Charlie had little concern about the other caterers recognizing her; the lights were dim and the condo was packed. She even managed to pluck a few sliders and a soda off the trays of passing servers without being noticed. She worked her way through the crowds, ignoring two separate attempts by young male guests—unaware of her age—to flirt with her, and finally reached what she had gone through so much trouble to find.

It was in Ahmet's office at the more private end of the penthouse, where the bedrooms were. The door had a simple lock that Charlie picked with a hairpin in twenty seconds. Then she stepped inside and locked it again behind her.

The walls of the room were thick and soundproofed, immediately reducing the raucous noise of the party to a distant murmur. A security camera was mounted at the far-upper corner of the room, facing the door; Charlie couldn't do much about it except keep her head down so that there wouldn't be a clear view of her face, work quickly—and hope that if anyone was monitoring the system, they were too distracted by the rest of the party to notice her.

The office was designed in traditional Western fashion, with a large oaken desk and built-in bookshelves. There was nothing on the desk, save for an unused notepad and a desk calendar that still showed April, even though it was June, indicating that Ahmet didn't do much work in there. And there were very few books on the shelves, two of which were upside down, indicating that Ahmet didn't read much either. Instead, the shelves were mostly lined with pieces of art: sculptures and bits of pottery, some of which were tacky junk, and some of which were incredibly valuable.

The wall opposite the desk was dominated by a large, garish piece of modern art. The tablet Charlie was looking for was mounted to the side of the artwork, toward the corner, as though it wasn't important.

Still, it took Charlie's breath away.

Because Charlie, unlike Ahmet, knew what it was.

In Ahmet's defense, the tablet didn't look very impressive. It was a pale slab of sandstone into which words had been crudely etched in Latin, and so old that the surface had been worn down, leaving much of the inscription only faintly visible. Furthermore, it was broken; a thin crack split it from top to bottom, and its edges had crumbled away, leaving the sentences—and many of the words—incomplete. As a result, even though Charlie knew Latin, she still couldn't fully translate the text.

MEA CÆSARION CARISSIMA

PIS PHARAONIS SVNT TALIA VT VRBA
T ECCILAM OMNEM POTESTATVM HOS
NONNE BELLVM NOSTRARVM AN I
VIR QVÆSITVM AD FONTEM IVVE E
S A REGNO AMBVLABVNT ET PVNGNAB
GISTRVM FIENT ET ORIGINEM MONSTR
ER ES ROGANT QVID INVENIAS ET ALIQ
VENE VOS QVIDEM GLORIAM LAVDVE
ET NOSCE TE IPSVM ET QVARE PARERE
GC EX SVNT ET VNDE QVINQVAGINTA R
ORATORES ILLZA PVLCHRÆ NAVES MINAS
D DEVM FACVT MVLTA VESTI ATRÆ HABE
LVS HOSTES AD FEMINÆ PROFECTÆ CONS
HOC SERVI REGINÆ IN DOMO SVNT ETS
T FO CONSILIO REFVGIEBANT ET CIVES
E RB I ES MEMENTO STATVS QVO ET CLA
A EST ET VINCIET OMNIA VNVM VERIT
MAGNÆ OBORTÆ VNDÆ VELVM PELLVN
COR ET ANIMA VIRAGINIS ATRVM SVNT
EM DIVVS MAGNVS ME REDIIT PHAR

The tablet was mounted to the wall with steel brackets. As Charlie had noted in the magazine photos, Ahmet hadn't even bothered to put it in a protective case.

Which was good, because Charlie needed to touch it.

She snapped a few photographs with her phone first, but assumed those wouldn't tell her everything she needed to know. The photos could barely capture the faint words, let alone the texture of the stone.

To do that, Charlie removed a roll of thin, almost translucent paper from her dress, as well as a stick of red graphite. Then she set to work creating a rubbing. She unfurled the paper, pressed it firmly against the tablet, and then dragged the graphite back and forth across it. Wherever the paper touched the stone, the graphite left a coating of red, while the places that were sunken, like the etched words, remained white. In this way, Charlie was able to duplicate the tablet on the paper. The technique was simple but effective; even the faintest words on the tablet were easily readable on the rubbing. Although Charlie feared getting caught, she didn't rush, making sure her rubbing was as accurate as possible; any mistakes she made in haste could alter the message left in the stone.

She was almost finished when she heard the office door rattle. Someone was putting a key in the lock.

There was no place for Charlie to hide. All she could do was back away from the tablet and drop the rubbing and the graphite in a wastebasket beside the desk.

The office door opened, and Ahmet Shah entered. He froze in surprise upon seeing Charlie in his private office. And then his surprise turned to suspicion.

"What are you doing in here?" he demanded in Arabic.

Although she was worried, Charlie smiled at him brightly. "It's a funny story . . . ," she began.

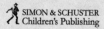

CAN AN UNDERCOVER NERD BECOME A SUPERSTAR AGENT? FIND OUT IN STUART GIBBS'S *NEW YORK TIMES* BESTSELLING SPY SCHOOL SERIES!

CRACK THE CASE WITH *NEW YORK TIMES*-BESTSELLING AUTHOR STUART GIBBS IN THESE WILD MYSTERIES!

LIVING ON A MOON BASE SHOULD BE EXCITING—BUT NOT *THIS* EXCITING.

The City Spies are on the case!
From bestselling author
JAMES PONTI
comes another must-read,
action-packed mystery series
that is sure to thrill.